Makin'
Miracles

Center Point
Large Print

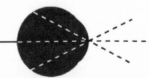

**This Large Print Book carries the
Seal of Approval of N.A.V.H.**

Makin' Miracles

A SMOKY MOUNTAIN NOVEL

Lin Stepp

CENTER POINT LARGE PRINT
THORNDIKE, MAINE

This Center Point Large Print edition is published
in the year 2015 by arrangement with
Kensington Publishing Corp.

The text of this Large Print edition is unabridged.
In other aspects, this book may vary
from the original edition.
Printed in the United States of America
on permanent paper.
Set in 16-point Times New Roman type.

ISBN: 978-1-62899-482-7

Library of Congress Cataloging-in-Publication Data

Stepp, Lin.
Makin' miracles : a Smoky Mountain novel / Lin Stepp. —
    Center Point Large Print edition.
    pages cm
    Summary: "Zola Devin is proud of her Tahitian heritage and reflects it
in her gift shop in Gatlinburg. Photographer Spencer Jackson owns the
gallery next door to Zola's shop, and they find themselves at odds at
times. As their lives become unavoidably intertwined, they will discover
the beauty of truth and the joy of the unexpected"—Provided by
publisher.
    ISBN 978-1-62899-482-7 (library binding : alk. paper)
    1. Great Smoky Mountains (N.C. and Tenn.)—Fiction.
    2. Large type books. I. Title. II. Title: Making miracles.
PS3619.T47695M35 2015
813'.6—dc23
                                                        2014046991

This book is dedicated to all my fans
who love my work and read every book I write.
Thank you so much. If you keep reading,
I'll keep writing!

Acknowledgments

No one who achieves success does so without acknowledging the help of others.
—A. N. Whitehead

Thank you to all who have helped, supported, and believed in me.

Loving thanks to my husband and partner, J. L. Stepp, who travels the road tirelessly with me and helps with my marketing and publicity. Thanks, also, to my talented daughter Katherine Stepp, who assists with my author's Web site and social media.

Heartfelt thanks to my wonderful editor and encourager, Audrey LaFehr. And additional thanks to all the staff at Kensington Publishing who help make my books the best they can be and bring them into my readers' hands . . . Associate Editor Martin Biro; Publicist Jane Nutter; Production Editor Paula Reedy; Copy Editor Brittany Dowdle; Book Cover Art Director Kristine Mills; Book Cover Illustrator Judy York; Inventory Manager Guy Chapman; and many more. You're the best.

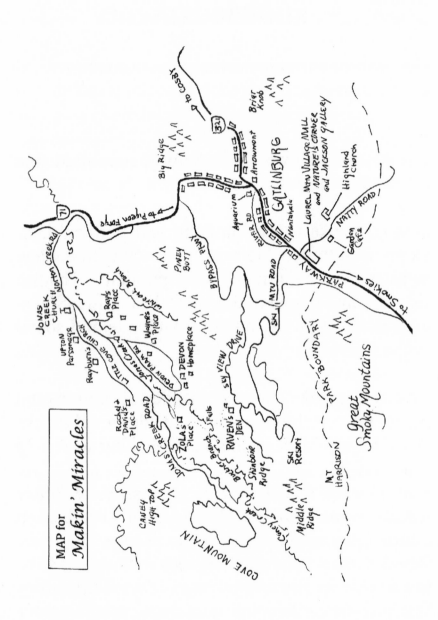

Chapter 1

Zola heard the bell on the door chime and looked up to see a young couple head into the store. They talked as they began wandering around the aisles, so she didn't make eye contact and offer the greeting she usually gave to her customers. She would later.

For the moment, she turned her attention back to her current customer at the counter. It was a busy day at Nature's Corner. The warm weekend in late February had drawn an unexpected rush of tourists to Gatlinburg—all eager to get out after a rash of cold, snowy weeks in Tennessee.

The plump, older woman at the counter smiled at Zola. "I am so tickled to find this new book by Vera Leeds." She tapped the colorfully illustrated children's book stacked with her other purchases. "I read that Vera Leeds started writing children's fairy books. I'm sure my little Karen will be thrilled to get this fairy story by her for a birthday gift. My granddaughters all love Vera Leeds's *Foster Girls* books and the television series, too."

Zola thought about telling her that Vera Leeds, aka Vivian Jamison, lived nearby in Wears Valley. Instead, she said, "I'm sure your granddaughter will be pleased with the book, Mrs. Springer—and with the fairy wings, garland, and wand you bought her, too." Zola tucked the items into a gift box, tore off a sheet of fanciful paper, and began to wrap the present. Nature's Corner provided gift-wrapping, for a fee, in three paper choices.

Mrs. Springer tucked her credit card back in her paisley purse. "I do thank you for helping me pick out these things for Karen. Birthdays are so special for little ones." She looked at Zola speculatively. "Do you have children, dear?"

"No. I'm not married yet, Mrs. Springer. I've been busy finishing school, learning the retail business, and establishing my own store." Zola deftly wrapped green ribbon around the box covered in butterfly paper, added a ribbon loop to the top, and taped on the Nature's Corner gold sticker in the center.

Mrs. Springer wagged a finger at Zola. "Well, I'm sure the right man will come along for a pretty girl like you."

A voice slipped into Zola's consciousness before she could reply. *She's left her lights on.*

Zola paused. "Are you planning on doing other shopping today, Mrs. Springer?"

The woman nodded, smoothing down a pink pullover sweater over her ample figure. "Oh, yes. Raymond and I just got here. He's over in the woodcraft shop. We're going to spend the whole day in Gatlinburg enjoying the sunshine."

Zola laid a hand over hers. "Promise me you'll put this gift in your car before you shop anymore, Mrs. Springer. There's been a rash of people leaving their lights on lately after they park, and I'd like you to check your car. On a busy day like this, it's hard to get help in Gatlinburg if you experience car trouble."

Mrs. Springer pursed her lips and leaned forward. "That's a nice suggestion, dear. I've noticed Raymond is getting more and more forgetful these days about that sort of thing."

She took the shopping bag with the gift in it from Zola. "Besides, I wouldn't want to carry this bag around all day, anyway. Books are heavy."

Zola watched her leave with relief. Sometimes it proved easier, passing the words along, especially when people were receptive like Mrs. Springer.

Seeing two new customers come into the store, Zola blew out a breath. She could use a short break—but she'd need to wait until a lull between sales. Who'd have thought a Friday would be such a busy day?

Zola greeted the two women, who wanted to browse, and then made her way over to the couple who'd walked in earlier. The man was tall and tan, with sun-dipped brown hair, and the woman, a Marilyn Monroe blonde, with a bust to match, her arm tucked possessively through his.

"Welcome to Nature's Corner," Zola said, smiling at them in greeting. "Can I help you with something?"

"Perhaps." The blonde shifted blue, sulky eyes over Zola, scanning her in evaluation.

Zola met her gaze calmly, unruffled by the assessment, watching the woman shift uncomfortably before turning bright eyes to the man.

"Ask her about the scarves." She leaned against him. "See if she knows how to do them."

He turned deep, thoughtful eyes toward Zola— thinker's eyes, artist's eyes. An interesting man. Zola noticed the contradiction of a neat white oxford shirt and trendy loafers, coupled with old jeans and long hair tied back with a leather strip. He didn't know with a certainty who he was, she thought.

The man lifted his eyes to hers, and a swift moment of recognition flashed as they connected on another plane before he dropped his gaze. Zola felt a shiver.

Picking up a square of turquoise patterned fabric, he held it out, his eyes moving to the framed display picture illustrating how to tie the fabric into a garment. "We saw the picture showing how to wrap this into a dress and wondered how it worked—or if it worked—and if it was easy to do."

The blonde fingered the silky, floral fabric. "It's such beautiful material."

"Yes. It's a pareu." Zola smiled at her. "In many island cultures, like in the South Pacific, the women, and the men, wear pareus freely. They're cool and comfortable."

On familiar ground now, Zola slipped off her Nature's Corner apron as she talked. "All pareus are traditionally a fabric piece approximately two yards long and one yard wide, like this one. The material is hand-blocked or hand painted in traditional floral, or *tapa*, patterns." She took the fabric from the woman's hands to spread it out. "You can wrap a pareu into a dress, skirt, turban, or shawl. There are hundreds of designs, but I can show you one that is especially easy."

Zola wrapped the fabric around her back and brought the fabric ends forward to the front. Then she began to cross and tuck the fabric nimbly around her body and above her breasts until the garment took the shape of a tropical dress, dropping to mid calf.

"Oh, it's gorgeous!" The blonde looked charmed. "I think I could do the wrapping, too."

"Of course you could." Zola encouraged her, taking the pareu off herself in a few quick movements and moving toward the blonde to slip the fabric around her back. "Here, I'll show you."

In a few moments, she helped the woman to create her own dress, this one with a silky strap tucked over one shoulder.

The blonde surveyed herself in the wall mirror with admiration. Glancing over her shoulder at the man, she dropped her eyes seductively. "It would look even better without the clothes under it."

As the woman's gaze slid over him with familiarity, Zola turned away to slip her store apron back on again. She answered a final question and then excused herself to go speak to her other customers.

A short time later the man came to the counter carrying the turquoise pareu and another in vivid yellows and red.

"I'll take both of these," he said, his voice rich and deep.

Zola rang them up, wrapped them in tissue, and tucked them into a dark green Nature's Corner bag. She looked up to find the man quietly watching her. Their eyes met, and Zola frowned—listening to the words that rose up in her spirit.

She put out a hand to touch his without thinking. "She isn't for you. Be careful of her."

His eyes widened. "I beg your pardon?"

Zola shook her head and leaned toward him. "Be careful of her. The woman you're with. She's a thief. She's not for you. In fact, she will rob you tonight after . . ." Her voice dropped away, and Zola felt a flush rise up her neck.

The man jerked his hand away from hers. "Who the heck do you think you are to judge me—or her?" His eyes flashed. "You don't know either of us."

Zola met his gaze without flinching. "It's what I heard. Sometimes I simply know things. Keep it in mind, that's all I ask."

She watched him scrutinize her from head to toe with angry eyes. Then he smiled cruelly. "So, what's your next prediction, shopgirl? Do you think maybe *you're* the one for me—since you think she's not? Is that your next line?"

Surprised, Zola caught her breath, crossing her arms over her breasts defensively. She didn't like the way his eyes raked her up and down.

She took a shaky breath. "I didn't get any knowledge about that, sir," she said softly, meeting his stormy eyes with calm ones. "I only got what I told you. If you're wise, you will remember it later."

His eyes narrowed, moving to the name sewn on her apron front. "What do you think you are, Zola—some kind of gypsy fortune-teller? You certainly have the appearance of one and the name to match. Black hair, dark eyes, with an exotic look. Is it cultivated? And is draping yourself seductively in those scarves, like you did, part of your drama act?"

Zola felt her face flush. She pressed down a surge of anger and met his eyes with honesty. "I am half Tahitian by birth, sir. My looks, and my name, are my birthright, not contrived. I grew up in the South Pacific. Wearing pareus is as comfortable and natural to me as wearing jeans is to you. I show all my customers how to drape and tie garments because it is a part of my business as a store owner."

The blonde slithered up to put a hand through the man's arm. "Is anything wrong?" She looked from one to the other.

The man's eyes challenged Zola to reply.

"Nothing is wrong." Zola smiled at the woman. "We just had a momentary disagreement on a small subject."

As the woman drifted away, attracted by a basket filled with shell necklaces on a nearby display table, Zola spoke quietly again. "Keep in mind what I said." She handed the man the Nature's Corner bag over the counter.

He snatched the bag and gave her a final angry stare before turning to leave. She watched the blonde tuck her arm into his again as they left the store.

Oh, well, she thought with resignation, turning with a friendly smile to her next customer.

A little later, Zola finally got a chance to slip into the back of the store for a quick break. She carried a bottle of flavored water and an apple out to the front with her and sat down on a stool behind the counter for a rest. It had been a long day, and there were several hours yet to go before close.

The bell on the door of Nature's Corner jingled once more, and a familiar figure appeared in the doorway. Zola's face broke into a grin. "Maya Thomas, you're not supposed to be here. It's your day off."

"*Yeh,* and how else would I get to see your face if I didn't come to find you here?" The brown-eyed Jamaican woman started across the room toward Zola. Tall and lithe, she wore her gray hair short around her regal, warm-toned face.

She came close to Zola, framed her cheeks with her hands, and studied her with pleasure. "It is good to see you, Zolakieran. You've been away to those far islands too long a time. It is a fine thing to see your face again. *Jah know.*"

Zola loved Maya's occasional lapses into Jamaican terms. "The Lord knows it is good to see your face again, too, Maya."

The older woman kissed both of Zola's cheeks before releasing her to step back. "So when did you plan to come and see your good friend, *yeh?*"

Zola put her hands on her hips. "I only got in last night, Maya. Should I have driven to your place at midnight? I was tired and I needed sleep. It's a long flight from the South Pacific to the mountains of Tennessee."

Maya shook a finger at her. "That it is. And you should have let me work your hours today. I have come now so you will go home to get some rest." She studied Zola's eyes. "You look tired. You know Viola would have worked again today to fill in for you with gladness. She worked your hours all these weeks. Another day longer wouldn't have mattered to her."

"I know. Viola is good to fill in for us when we need her."

Viola Bartlett, a full-figured, warm-natured woman with a grown son and time on her hands, loved to pick up hours at the store part-time whenever Zola needed her. She gladly worked Zola's hours when Zola took her yearly trips home to the South Pacific to be with her family and to do buying for the store.

Maya crossed her arms and lifted a corner of her mouth in a smile. "The truth of it is you couldn't wait to get yourself back in here, and that's a fact."

Zola smiled at her. "You're probably right about that. I've missed it."

"Is that all you're having for your dinner?" Maya eyed the apple on the counter.

"I've been busy." Zola shrugged.

"Well, I'll run behind the store to the Garden Café and get us both a little bite to eat. We'll visit around the customers." She started toward the back door. "You save that apple for later. I'll get us homemade chicken potpies for dinner. You know George's cook has a gift for making those."

"What about your girls?" Zola asked. "Shouldn't you get home for Carole and Clarissa?"

"Ahhh, those girls." She waved a hand dismissively. "They've gone to Pigeon Forge to shop."

Zola leaned her elbows on the counter. "You must love having Carole back home again."

18

Maya's oldest daughter had graduated from college and come back home after Christmas. "Hmmmph. It's little enough I see of her since she started working in Tanner Cross's accounting office." Maya made a face. "And, of course, it will only get worse as the tax season starts coming in." Despite her fussing, Zola knew Maya felt pleased that Carole found a job here in Gatlinburg and moved back home after graduation. Since Maya's husband Nigel died several years ago, the girls were Maya's only family in the States.

After Maya left, Zola looked over the posted work schedule for the coming week, where she'd penciled herself back in for her regular hours at the store again. Maya and she had alternated days at the store ever since Zola bought and opened Nature's Corner three years ago. Zola's other part-time employee was Faith Rayburn, a family friend. Faith was a caring, slightly wispy mother of four who worked around her children's school schedule for extra money. She wasn't good with bookkeeping or with running the register totals, but the customers loved her warmth and local charm.

The bell jingled again, and Zola was soon busy with a new sweep of customers. She rang up six more sales before Maya returned.

During the next lull, the friends sat at the front counter on two stools and ate chicken potpie. They talked about the new products Zola found for the store on her buying trip, and Maya caught her up on store news.

Then Zola told Maya about the man who came in the store earlier. "I wish he had been more open to hear."

Maya frowned. "He's a *bootoo* to take no heed of a useful warning like that."

Zola grinned. She knew a *bootoo*, in Jamaican, was an insignificant or dumb person. "Perhaps," she said. "But I always feel bad when someone gets mad and doesn't understand. I always think I might have expressed things better."

Maya shook her head. "It is not your responsibility in the Lord to see to it that people like His Words. It is simply your job to offer the words as you are given them."

"I guess." Zola sighed as she spooned out the last remnants of her supper. The Garden did have the best homemade chicken potpie.

Maya cocked her head to one side. "Is it better back in Mooréa—how your gift is received?"

Zola laughed. "No. Sometimes it's worse. Some of the natives make an obvious effort to walk around me or make a sign when I go by."

"*Wutless!*" Maya lapsed into another Jamaican phrase, meaning *worthless.*

"Sometimes I get gifts left at my doorstep, like offerings. Hibiscus blossoms, shells, breadfruit, or mangos. Once I actually got a black pearl a diver found. It was a thank-you gift for a word of knowledge that helped to save the man's child." She gathered up their dishes thoughtfully. "I was only seven years old when that happened. Mama made the pearl into a necklace for me. I still have it and wear it."

"Your mama respected your gift and she encouraged it." Maya dumped their dishes and plastic spoons into the paper sack from the café. "She was a good mother. I'm sorry you lost her so young."

"Me too." Zola fingered the pearl around her neck as she remembered her mother. "She told me it was like receiving a pearl of great price to be given the gift of being a seer. She said never to misuse it or to take profit from it or I could cloud its beauty and dishonor God."

Maya made a spiritual sign Zola didn't recognize. "May she be blessed for encouraging you."

Zola nodded. "I've been fortunate, too, that my grandparents are accepting of my gift. It would have been hard if that hadn't been so, since they raised me most of the years after Mama died. I know I told you she lost her life in a small plane accident, coming back from a trip to her sister's in New Zealand when I was twelve. Nana Etta became sort of my substitute mother after that."

"Ahhh. And well you know I am fond of Mother Etta." This was what Maya always called Zola's grandmother, Etta Garnett Devon.

Maya carried their trash out to the back

Dumpster, along with the store trash that had accumulated behind the counter. When she returned, the two caught up on the little things of their lives—as friends love to do.

Zola glanced at the clock on the wall. It was almost seven now, only two more hours until she could close the store. "You go home now, Maya," Zola said, patting her on the arm fondly. "You have to work eight hours tomorrow. And your girls will be back soon. I'll finish up here and close the store."

Two hours later when Zola had counted out the register and was locking the store to leave, she thought of the man again. She had seen clearly he would be robbed tonight by the lovely blonde on his arm.

Zola frowned. She wondered if the man would remember the warning she gave him or if he would be taken advantage of. The woman was very beautiful, but beauty on the outside was not always an indication of beauty on the inside.

Zola shook her head. "As You will, Lord," she said as she flipped out the lights to go home. "As You will."

Chapter 2

It was impossible for Spencer not to think of the odd Tahitian woman off and on through the evening. Leena wore the turquoise pareu wrapped seductively around her lush curves during their dinner together. Just looking at it brought the episode at the gift shop constantly to mind.

Now Leena sat draped across Spencer's couch in the big living room of his mountain home, tapping her red-tipped fingernails to the music lilting out of Spencer's stereo. He watched her from the kitchen, where he was cleaning up the dishes from their dinner of grilled shrimp, Cajun rice, and salad.

"It's such a sweet thing having a man to cook for me." Leena's voice was sultry and seductive. "I'll have to think of some *sweet* way to reward you back. You've been particularly good to me today."

The undertone of her suggestion was certainly not subtle. Spencer frowned, remembering the words of the shopgirl again and recalling the slow flush that had crept up her face and neck when she alluded to a more intimate encounter between him and Leena.

"Darling, do bring me another glass of that lovely Riesling, would you? It would be nice after our dinner." Leena patted the sofa beside her as she caught his eye. "And come and sit with me. We can talk and watch this lovely fire together."

Spencer poured out two glasses of the white wine. He had planned this dinner with Leena Evanston for some time, and he hated that events occurred to put a damper on it. Leena was a decorator out of Atlanta who bought his prints for her business customers when they wanted naturalistic photography in their décor. She appreciated Spencer's work and often recommended him to important clients. Spencer felt flattered when Leena suggested she might come for a visit, and he'd offered to host her for dinner at his newly completed home on the mountain. A subtle flirtation had flickered between them for some time, and Spencer hoped their relationship might move to another level during her visit.

He brought the glass of wine over to Leena and sat down beside her on the couch. She was a handsome woman. Any man would be happy to be in his shoes with her tonight. The fact that she insisted on wrapping herself in the new pareu, with evidently no other clothing underneath, boded well for the evening to follow.

She smiled lazily at him and traced a finger down his arm. "Most men who are as successful as you, Spencer Jackson, are either old or have inherited their wealth. You do impress me with what you've already accomplished with your photography at only thirty years old. You've established a national reputation as a naturalist photographer, have published five coffee-table books that my clients simply drool over, and own your own gallery here in the mountains."

Leena looked around the room. "This is a lovely mountain home you built up here on the ridgetops." She gave him a wide smile, showing perfect white teeth. "But it must get awfully lonely here. Personally, I think I'd need the pace, noise, and happenings of the city to stay happy, but this would certainly be a nice little retreat when I wanted to get away from it all."

He scowled. It vexed him how Leena so readily dismissed his new home. He'd planned and saved for it for a long time, and it had taken him many hikes and exploration trips before he found the perfect spot to construct it on.

She stretched languidly. "If your reputation continues to build, Spencer, you could open another gallery in Atlanta. I think it would go very well. I would certainly help you to promote it. And we could find you a stunning apartment or town house downtown, perhaps in Buckhead." She traced a red-tipped nail up his arm again. "We might see each other a lot more often if you lived closer to me."

Her message was obvious—that she could hardly see herself living happily here. Spencer stood up, slightly irritated that she kept flippantly devaluing the life he loved. "I've got to run back to the bathroom, Leena. You enjoy your wine until I get back."

She giggled and ran a hand down his thigh as he stood up. "I think you'll find what you're looking for in the drawer right beside your bed-side table, darling."

As Spencer walked back through the house into his spacious master bedroom, he thought about her comment. How did she know where he kept anything? Was that a guess or had she rummaged around in the drawers in his bedroom?

Spencer felt a shiver crawl up his spine. The shopgirl's words from earlier in the day floated through his mind again. In the bedroom now, Spencer began to methodically search his drawers, closets, and possessions.

When he returned, he walked casually toward Leena with a smile, leaned over to kiss her, and then picked up her designer briefcase and purse to carry across the room with him to a side table.

"I doubt those would have been in the way, darling." Her eyes followed him, filled with amusement.

As he put both on the table, he started to rummage through them.

Leena's eyes flared. "Whatever are you looking for, Spencer?"

He pulled out a roll of hundred-dollar bills from her purse and then two gold chains he discovered in her makeup case. In a side pocket in her briefcase, he found the small velvet box he'd been looking for.

Spencer held them up. "Are you short of money, Leena, or do you simply have one of those psychological compulsions to steal from people?"

She shrugged, unruffled by his accusation. "I thought I might get a little of your jewelry valued. People seldom realize what their things are worth."

Spencer rolled his eyes in exasperation. "And did you intend to get my money valued, too?"

She gave him a haughty glare. "What makes you think that isn't *my* money, Spencer? I always carry cash with me. Many small businesses still don't accept credit cards."

"Nice try." Spencer opened the roll of hundreds and peeled through them. "Except that I always keep a lucky two-dollar bill rolled up in my cash roll." He held it up for her to see. "It's not likely you would also do that, Leena."

She gave him a pouty look. "Fair is fair, Spencer. You're getting something for yourself tonight. I didn't see any reason why I shouldn't take away a little something for myself, too."

"A call-girl fee?" Spencer blew out a breath. "Usually that is agreed on up front when it's appropriate."

"So fine. Be difficult." She flounced off the sofa with a sulky expression. "It's too bad you had to go snooping and mess everything up. We might have enjoyed a really nice time tonight. I've found artists are generally good lovers."

Spencer winced. "I could call the police, Leena. Theft is a serious problem, especially if you do it often."

She walked over smoothly to pick up her briefcase and purse. "I'm usually generously compensated without needing to add any extra. But I wasn't sure with you. You seemed like the quiet, ethical, frugal type." She shrugged. "I'll go change and you can take me back down the mountain to my hotel. I'll get the limo to the airport on my own in the morning. We'll just let this little episode be forgotten between us."

Leena studied him with candid eyes. "We both have too much to lose to do anything else, don't we, Spencer? I have rich clients you need, and you have a rich talent I can present to them."

Spencer watched, stunned, as she walked back toward his bedroom.

She turned and smiled at him. "Don't worry. There isn't anything else I want in there." She gestured toward his bedroom. "You don't really have much of value here, you know, darling. You're a rather Spartan man from what I can see. It's doubtful we would have done more than enjoyed a night of fun together."

Leena began to untie the pareu as she walked back to change her clothes.

Anger and resentment flickered through Spencer's system at her words. He clenched his fist as Leena nonchalantly closed the bedroom door.

Zeke, Spencer's German shepherd, picked up on Spencer's emotions and growled softly. Zeke never growled unless there was real danger threatening his owner.

Spencer turned to the dog, who'd risen from his bed by the fire, his fur beginning to bristle. "It's all right, boy. We've just entertained a high-class thief here tonight."

Spencer put the bills, necklaces, and ring box into the drawer of the side table. The only thing he would have deeply regretted losing was the ring. His maternal grandmother, Lillian Chatsworth, who he stayed with through his college years in Savannah, had given it to him. She said she wanted him to give the ring to the woman he would marry one day. The ring was an old family piece that could hardly be replaced, whether Spencer ever married or not.

An hour later, Spencer had driven Leena back to her hotel and he now sat brooding by the fire in the dark, thinking about the evening. He could have called the Gatlinburg police chief, Bill Magee, and had Leena Evanston picked up and booked. He still could. He wasn't sure why he hesitated to do so. Perhaps because of the situation. It was embarrassing to have entertained a thief for dinner. And to have hoped for further intimacies with the same thief.

Truthfully, Spencer felt like a royal ass. He obviously had shown no discernment of character in this situation. Yet some little shopgirl had seen it all coming. That rankled, even though Spencer knew he had the girl to thank that he'd become suspicious of Leena Evanston at all and not lost his money, jewelry—and possibly more—to Leena before the evening was said and done. It wasn't true that he didn't have other valuable things in the house. She just hadn't found them.

He motioned to Zeke to come over for an affectionate scratch. Seeming to read his master's disappointment, the shepherd wagged his tail with friendly enthusiasm and gave Spencer a consoling nudge. He petted the big dog with pleasure, grateful for the animal's genuine devotion and loyalty. These qualities seemed to be a rare commodity in this world today.

The phone rang, interrupting his thoughts. Spencer picked it up and heard his brother Bowden's smooth voice on the line. Great. Just what he needed tonight.

"Hey, Two Spence, what's up with you?" He used one of the old derogatory nicknames he'd always used for Spencer. This one had come from a time when Spencer's grandfather, Stettler Jackson, said Spencer was a smart kid but not worth two cents in sales and public relations. Of course, he'd turned immediately, laid his hand on Bowden's shoulder, and said Bowden was a regular chip off the old block and a born natural with the public.

Spencer sighed. "To what do I owe the honor of this call, Bowden?"

"No need to get testy, Spence. I am your big brother, after all. I should be able to call my little brother to say hi—and I ought to get a warmer welcome in return."

Spencer struggled to make an effort to be cordial. "How are Mother and Dad, Bowden? Is everyone well?"

"We're all fine. Not that you would know since you never darken any of our doors." He paused. "That's why I'm calling, Spence. Mother and Dad are having their big fortieth anniversary this summer, and it would mean a lot to them, to all of us, if you would come."

Spencer hesitated.

He heard Bowden blow out an irritated breath. "Brother, it's time to let bygones be bygones with old grudges. We are your family, after all. You need to act like a grown-up and come home to wish your parents happiness on this occasion."

Easy for you to say, Spencer thought. *You always fit into the family business like a glove. You were Grandfather Jackson and our parents' favorite child. And you married Geneva. You could have had anyone, but you had to marry the*

31

one girl I loved. Had to steal her away from me while I was away at college. And now you expect me to come home and act like everything is still the same? I don't think so.

Bowden seemed to sense his thoughts in the silence. "Mother and Dad will send you an invitation for their anniversary later, but I wanted to call and ask especially that you would come. It would mean a lot to them, Spence. To all of us. It's been twelve years since you've really been home for a visit with the family. It's time, buddy."

A peculiar thought went through Spencer's mind that Bowden would have been impressed to see him with a girl like Leena Evanston tonight. To see a girl like that coming on to him, interested in him. She was the kind of girl who used to always notice Bowden and completely overlook Spencer. He had an odd wish that Bowden could have been here to see Leena slinking around in her turquoise wrap, running her fingernails up his arm. He'd have liked for Bowden to see that.

"I'll think about it, Bowden," he said. "I'll see what my schedule is like later. Check whether I can get away from the gallery."

He heard Bowden laugh. "You mean you'll try specifically to see that you're too busy to come, don't you? That's been the pattern so far through every Christmas, Thanksgiving, and family occasion since."

Spencer was silent.

"You shouldn't make Mother and Dad pay for your being mad at me, Eagle Boy." It was another of Bowden's taunting nicknames, based on Spencer's young dream to become an Eagle Scout. He'd made it, too. He'd fulfilled a lot of his dreams—despite his family's lack of support or encouragement.

Spencer shook his head in the dark room. None of them ever seemed to realize how hurt he'd been when Bowden married Geneva. Or even cared how he felt. It had always been about Bowden. Whatever Bowden the golden boy wanted, Bowden the golden boy got.

A flame spurted up in the fireplace and then died down. Spencer watched it thoughtfully. Nothing had changed. He saw no reason to go home again.

"When is the anniversary?" Spencer asked, knowing he had no intention of going to it. "I'll make a note of it and see what I can do."

He mentally noted the date in early June and then, after a few more words with Bowden, managed to get off the phone.

There was a full moon out, and Spencer wandered onto the porch at the front of his house. Hungry to get a closer look at the moon, he started down a short trail by the house, whistling to Zeke to follow.

The trail led through a grove of trees and then out onto a rocky ledge overlooking the valley

33

below. Even in the dark, he could see the shadows of the mountains in the distance. The views from the ridgetop here were spectacular. It was a special place. The night was clear, and a world of stars lay scattered across the sky like shimmering crystals against black velvet.

Tucked up against a rocky cliff at a point the locals called the Raven's Den, Spencer found the makeshift structure. It had attracted him from the first day he explored this property. A series of rough beams held up a simple roof of wood boards, sticks, and thatch. At the front of the structure, a crude, stone wall had been erected, and over it lay a wide shelf of boards. From the rafters above the wall hung a motley array of bird feeders and wind chimes. Rickety benches and chairs had been brought into the hut, along with a rough worktable.

Spencer smiled as he saw it again in the moonlight. A child's playhouse, he'd decided. But the animals and birds loved it. They obviously held happy memories of being fed here in times past. As soon as he bought the property, Spencer began to put out seed, suet, and dried corn for his visitors. When the house builders measured off the property and asked if he wanted the shed torn down, he said no. It looked too much like the playhouses of his own youth he'd built and treasured.

"I escaped out of doors many times to a

hideaway like this to think and dream," Spencer told the dog, who followed a few steps behind him.

Zeke pricked up his ears and looked at Spencer, waiting for him to give the signal that meant he could enter the hut. Spencer nodded, and the shepherd galloped gladly into the structure, nosing around and sniffing the corners for the scents of animals that might have come before them.

Spencer settled down in an old rocker he'd bought at a woodcraft shop. He'd added two rockers to the hut's motley collection of furnishings, since most of the other chairs could hardly support his large frame or that of a visiting friend. Spencer grinned as he settled into the rocker and propped one foot up on the wall. He'd talked the store owner into selling him two used rockers from the shop's front porch since it had seemed wrong somehow to add new chairs to the worn and weathered furnishings already here.

The rustic hut was a soothing place. Spencer couldn't say why it seemed so, but he came here often. Tonight he rocked quietly in the dark and gazed out over the mountains, trying to regain his peace after a stressful evening. Soon, Zeke came to settle down at Spencer's feet. The two enjoyed the night sounds of insects and frogs, and the occasional hooting of an owl. A soft wind rustled the needles of the pine trees nearby, and the moon drifted lazily in and out of the dark clouds.

Spencer sighed, realizing he felt more upset from talking to his brother again than from nearly being robbed by Leena Evanston. He shook his head at the idea. Some pains just never seemed to go away—no matter how much life moved on.

Chapter 3

Zola slept late the next morning. By habit, she awoke at her usual time, but it was an indulgent pleasure not to get up then, to snuggle back under the covers instead. Her cat, Posey, after snubbing her for a day for leaving her for so many weeks, had finally come around. She slept curled up against Zola's side now, purring contently. Zola's hand drifted lazily over her soft fur every few minutes.

She'd enjoyed hearing all the farm sounds earlier as the day began—a rooster crowing to announce the new day, the distant sound of cows mooing and of a tractor starting up. It was good to be home. Zola had lived more of her life here in the rural mountains of Tennessee than in the South Pacific, where she was born. And her roots lay here.

"We'll have to go over for a visit with Nana Etta after we get up," Zola told the cat. "She'll be watching for us. I told her I'd come. But I needed this sleep-in to catch up from the last of the jet lag. That long flight and the time zone changes always take a toll on my system."

Zola stretched and looked around the room. "This is the same bedroom I've slept in ever since I was a little girl," she told Posey. "I still remember when Daddy and Mother remodeled the house. Before that we always stayed at Papa and Nana Devon's place."

She laughed. "This house was always called 'Hill House' or 'Old Farm,' and my grandparents' house was called 'New Farm.' But their house, nearly fifty years old, is hardly new now."

Zola's grandparents' place, a rambling white farmhouse, lay about a mile away—across the creek and down the Devon Farm Road. Zola's house, which had been her great-grandparents' place, was much older. A marking in an old slab of concrete in the foundations of the house read 1902.

"When Daddy was given the land here as his part of the farm, everyone assumed he'd come and tear down my great-grandparents', Wayland and Retha Devon's, old house. But Daddy turned sentimental, and even Mother thought the old place should be preserved. Papa Vern sputtered over the money Daddy spent fixing up the house, but he and Nana felt secretly pleased that he did."

The cat meowed politely in comment.

Zola scratched her neck. "This upstairs room was always mine."

She looked around fondly. She still slept in the same twin bed that had always been her favorite; it was placed beside the window, looking up to the mountain.

"Maybe I love this house so much because the

only time I got to stay here was when my parents visited from Mooréa for summer vacations or at Christmas." Zola stretched lazily. "When they weren't in the States, I lived at Papa Vern and Nana Etta's. I was too young to stay here alone. But after I came back from college, Daddy said I could live here—and fix up the house however I wanted."

Despite the offer, Zola had made few changes to the house since she moved in. The place felt right, somehow, decorated in its mix of American and Tahitian colors and décor.

"It's kind of like me," she said with a smile. "A mix of Mooréa island native and Tennessee mountain girl."

Zola got up and went into the bathroom to brush her teeth and wash her face. The cat followed, leaping up onto the commode top to watch her.

As if reminded of the need to wash up, Posey began to carefully lick one white paw. She was a long-haired white cat with decorative markings of caramel-yellow.

"You know, you shouldn't snub me when I need to go away for a while." Zola popped her toothbrush back into its holder. "After all, you owe me. I saved you from being drowned in a gunnysack when you were only a tiny kitten."

Zola frowned remembering that. "They wanted to drown you simply because you had one blue eye and one brown eye. One of the farmer's best milk cows died unexpectedly and he and his wife got the notion you were bad luck with your mismatched eyes. Silly, superstitious people! You've turned out to be a treasure and one of the smartest cats I've ever had." She scratched Posey's neck and then went into her bedroom to search for something to wear.

A short time later, dressed in a favorite pair of overalls, a white T-shirt, and a plaid-lined denim jacket, Zola, along with the cat, set out to Papa and Nana's house. Posey knew the way through the woods and across the creek to the Devon homeplace as well as Zola did. Taking the lead, the cat pranced down the well-worn path and raced agilely across the split-log bridge over Buckner Branch. In a half mile, the two had cut through the last of the woods, crossed a mowed field, and were heading down the Devon Farm Road. It was a mile walk between the two houses, but a comfortably familiar one on a well-worn trail.

Zola could see smoke curling out of the old farmhouse chimney this morning and knew Papa Vern had made a fire to take the chill off the cool February morning. In the summer, Zola would have found Nana waiting for her out on the porch, but today she found her inside, settled in her favorite chair by the fire, piecing a new quilt. She laid down the quilt to rise and give Zola a hug.

"Did you rest well, child?"

Zola nodded.

Nana started toward the kitchen. "I've saved you biscuits from breakfast and Papa put you out a jar of his fresh honey he took from one of the hives. He said you could take it home with you."

Zola didn't need to ask how her grandmother knew she hadn't eaten breakfast. A smattering of the same gifting Zola possessed dwelt in Nana Etta. It simply served a more practical nature in Nana and was seldom remarked on.

As the two walked into the homey kitchen of the old Devon homeplace, Zola heaved a sigh. A wash of memories flooded over her from a lifetime of meals in this welcoming, sunny room.

Zola settled down at the table, knowing her grandmother would fuss if she tried to help with the breakfast fixings. Nana was eager to express her love by cooking and feeding her this morning.

In her seventies now, Nana Etta moved more slowly around the kitchen. But her hair was still black, like Zola's, with only a threading of gray. She'd let her daughter, Becky Rae, start putting a little color on it a few years ago. It was becoming to her.

Zola watched Nana slip an old print apron over her neck and tie it at her waist. For as long as Zola could remember, Nana always wore an apron in the kitchen. Most of the bib aprons she made herself or they were given to her as gifts.

As the years passed, Nana had grown a little

stockier in build—but not much so. In her fifties, she'd added glasses to her familiar look, and in her sixties, she finally conceded to wear pants around the house instead of dresses. Zola had been a young teen then. The latter transition had *not* been accomplished without a lot of grumbling over the changing fashions of the time.

Zola smiled at her. "You look good, Nana."

Nana snorted softly. "You're looking with eyes of love, then, child."

"That's true," Zola admitted, playing with the chicken-and-rooster salt and pepper shakers on the kitchen table. "But you do look good. Really. Is that a new pants set?"

Nana nodded while she placed the fresh egg she'd scrambled onto a plate and pulled a biscuit and a strip of bacon out of the oven to add to it. "Becky Rae took me down to the outlet mall last week to shop in the sales. They hold good sales in late February, you know. I got this outfit for seventy-five percent off."

"It's nice, and blue favors you." Zola received the breakfast plate from Nana with pleasure and began to spread butter and honey on her biscuit.

"The coffee from breakfast is gone, but I heated some water for tea. I hope you don't mind tea bags. I've still got some of those fancy ones from Christmas someone gave me." She got the decorative tin down from the shelf. "I think it was Judy Ann and K. T. Upton who gave these to me."

She put the box on the table and sat down. Zola sorted through the selection and picked a cranberry zinger flavor. The smell wafted into the air as the tea bag hit the hot water.

"That smells good." Nana sniffed appreciatively and then began to sort through the teas herself. "Tell me which one that is. I think I'll try one, too."

Zola paused with a bite of egg on her fork. "How come you haven't opened these teas before today?"

Nana shrugged. "Oh, they seemed too fancy for everyday. I thought I'd save them for company some time."

Zola laughed. "And since when have I become company?"

"Well, you feel a bit like company when you've been away so long." She settled into the kitchen chair across from Zola's. The cat jumped up on her lap, and she petted it idly. "Even the cat's started to feel too much at home with me."

"Thank you for taking care of her, Nana."

Her grandmother smiled. "I've always liked a cat around. Besides, she caught two rats while she stayed here that I was right glad to be rid of. I praised her real nice for those."

"Tell me all the family news," Zola said between bites of biscuit.

"Well, let's see." Nana Etta looked thoughtful for a moment. "Your Uncle Gene and Aunt Becky

Rae's girl, Doreen, turned fifteen and is wanting her learner's permit. Gene's been trying to teach her to drive on the farm road." She stopped to chuckle to herself. "Doreen mowed down about a whole row of fencing last week when she stomped her foot on the accelerator instead of the brake."

Zola laughed.

Nana Etta continued on with her news. "Your Uncle Ray's put a nice, new neon sign up at Ray's Place on the highway. The other one kept shorting out. This new one looks real fine." She took a sip of her tea. "That's where Papa is today, helping out at the store. One of the clerks is sick."

Ray Devon, the oldest of Nana and Papa's three children, ran a filling station, small grocery, and deli on the parkway going into Gatlinburg. His son, Wayne, worked with him there—as did his daughter, Stacy. Ray had a home only a mile and a half up the Devon Farm Road from Zola's grandparents. Stacy still lived at home, while Wayne had married and built a house practically next door.

Even Becky Rae, Nana and Papa's only daughter, lived on land that had once been a part of the Devon Farm. The more modern house that she and her husband, Gene Gibson, built lay about three miles up Jonas Creek Road, the main road that ran through the Devon farmland. Becky Rae married into money when she married into the

Gibson clan, and their fine home looked a little more palatial than most of the Devon farmhouses.

Zola tuned her thoughts back in as Nana continued her stories.

"Wayne's children, Hilda and Ronnie, are doing a 4-H project of raising some goats. As if all them sheep their Grandma Augusta brought into the farm for her knitting wool ain't enough critters for them to look after." Nana snorted and shook her head. "Those kids, Hilda and Ronnie, keep letting them little goats out and they eat just about anything they can get their teeth into. They chewed up all my purple clematis vines growing on the back fence."

Zola's face fell. "Oh, no, Nana. Will they grow back?" Zola loved those clematis flowers.

"They will, but those goats didn't do them much good, and that's a fact." She shook her finger. "I've warned those kids, and Ray and Augusta, too, that I better not see those goats over here eating my flowers again. You know, goats will eat the clothes right off your clothesline if they take a notion. Haven't got a lick of sense sometimes."

Nana Etta had started sorting through a pile of clipped coupons while she talked. She could never stand to have idle hands for long.

"Are the goats cute?" Zola couldn't resist asking.

"Well, sure, they always are when they're little. Hilda's goat is white and brown, and Ronnie's is gray and already has two little horns sprouting on its head. You'll have to go over and see them."

"I will," Zola promised. She polished off the last of her biscuit and licked the honey off her fingers. "Is there anything else I need to know about?"

Her grandmother paused. "Well, yeah. But I've hated to tell you."

Zola looked up in alarm. "Has anyone in the family died?"

"No, and that's a blessing." She got up to put Zola's dishes in the sink. "But I reckon this will upset you about as much. Someone's bought all the land up at Raven's Den and built a house on it."

Zola dropped the cup that held her tea, sloshing it onto the table. "Oh, Nana, not Raven's Den!"

Her grandmother nodded, coming over with a cloth to mop up the tea spill. "Yeah. I guess we all thought it was such rough land up there that no one would ever want it. But it sold last fall. We didn't any of us hear about it or know about it until the house was up. Then Papa saw smoke up there one day and sent Wayne hiking up the mountain to have a look. We got worried it might have been a brush fire getting started."

Nana tidied up the kitchen while she talked. "Wayne said someone's built a big log house right there on that flat stretch on the hillside. They wound themselves a road down to it from off one of them roads up above Gatlinburg. Wayne's guess is they'd need to get to the place by going up Ski Mountain Road across from where your shop is on the parkway, climb up the hill, twist around a street or two, and then branch down the mountainside. As you well know, there's no road to Raven's Den from down here. I doubt you could build a road up there from this side of the mountain with the steep drop-off slopes and the rocks. Plus there's the creek running down between the ridgetop and our farm. Floods right often."

Zola listened to her, trying not to cry.

"I'm sorry, child." Her grandmother came over to give her a hug. "I know that was a real special place to you ever since you were only a mite. You used to go up there to think and dream and look out over the world. I remember I used to do the same myself a long time ago when I was a young'un. None of us are happy to think that land is sold. It seems like more and more tourists are invading and buying up the land that once was wild around here. It don't seem right somehow, but there's nothing much we can do about it."

She sat back down across from Zola. "I figured it was better I told you than to let you go up there and come across it on your own with no warning."

"Do you know who lives there?" Zola bit her lip anxiously.

Nana shook her head. "No. There wasn't anyone there the day Wayne hiked up, and when he got too close to the house, a dog set up to barking. So, he came on back down here. But he did say they've not torn the land up real bad. Tried to keep things more natural-like, he said. That's a blessing, I suppose."

Zola had trouble concentrating on the rest of the conversation she shared with her grandmother before she finally left to walk back to her own place. She kept thinking about Raven's Den. And, admittedly, grieving about Raven's Den being sold. It was her special place, and she never imagined anyone would buy it.

As she walked back home, with Posey tagging along behind her, she kept looking up toward the mountain that stretched high above the Devon Farm. Like many farms in this part of the country, the Devon Farm lay in a valley laced with creeks. The farmland spread between mountain ridges on both sides.

Jonas Creek Road, which ran alongside Jonas Creek, was the main road that cut through the valley. The two-lane road wound its way from a larger street off the parkway behind Gatlinburg to snake through the rural countryside behind Piney Butt and Cove Mountain until it drew close to the side boundary of the Great Smoky Mountains National Park. Over the years, as the Smokies became a well-loved recreational area, more and more roads began to climb up Cove Mountain from Gatlinburg until they reached the higher ridgetops. Chalets and vacation homes now dotted the landscape on the Gatlinburg side of the mountain, but Zola had never imagined they'd begin to creep down the north side of the mountain toward their farm. The terrain was so rugged and rocky there. So steep.

"Let's be honest, Zola," she said out loud. "Because you laid claim to Raven's Den as a child, and because you could see it from your bedroom window and hiked up to that rocky point so many times, you just thought of the place as your own."

She kicked at a pinecone in the pathway in front of her. "I really hate whoever built there, Posey. It's such a beautiful, natural place. They should have left it that way."

Coming out of the woods behind her house, she glanced up the mountain once again. She couldn't see the new house from down here. But she could feel it there now that she knew about it.

"I'll have to go up," she told Posey. "I'll have to go see what they've done to it."

She felt a shiver go up her spine. "And I'll have to see if they've torn down my place."

Chapter 4

The morning after the episode with Leena Evanston, Spencer was up—and out of doors—early with his camera. Early morning and evening were the best times for professional photography. He took pictures of trees today, still stark from the winter but beginning to bud, and he snapped frequent shots of birds. They seemed especially joyous to see a warm day and signs of spring after the long winter. Spencer had slept fitfully last night, but being out of doors on this brisk, sunny morning soon brightened his spirits. Nature always spoke to him and soothed his soul.

When he returned, he whistled for Zeke. The dog needed his morning walk, and Spence didn't usually take him on his early morning photo shoots. Zeke's scent spooked the wild-life, even though he was obedient to Spencer's commands when they were in the wild together.

Dog and man walked out across the ridgetop now, heading west. Spencer had discovered a woods trail winding away from his land and out across Shinbone Ridge during the fall. Over the months since, Spencer had cleared the trail more thoroughly when he found the time. This hike up the ridge, to a rocky overlook high on Shinbone

Ridge, had become a favorite of his and Zeke's for their morning walks.

Back at the house, after Zeke's walk, Spencer decided to take his lunch, some animal snack bait, and his camera down to the old hut. If he sat quietly for a while, put out some treats and shared his food, he might get some good shots of the birds and squirrels that frequented the feeders. The day was cool yet, but not cold, and the sunshine drew Spencer out of doors. Besides, he needed the therapy of nature after yesterday's events.

He sensed the girl before he saw her as he wound his way down the trail to the hut perched on the rocky ledge. Spencer felt a prickling up his spine as he drew closer to the hut.

Rounding the corner, he saw her—standing by the wall of the natural shed, looking down over the valley. Hearing his steps, she turned. To Spencer's surprise, it was the girl from the shop in Gatlinburg. Tears were streaming down her cheeks in rivers, and he saw her wrestle to stop the flow of her emotions.

Spencer waited, dropping his cooler to the ground beside him and giving her a chance to wipe her face and collect herself. She was obviously upset. However, he saw the moment when she recognized him amid her crying.

"What are you doing here?" She gave him a puzzled look through her tears.

"I live here," he said quietly, spreading an arm around in a broad gesture. "This is my property— about four miles in each direction, maybe a hundred acres at best."

She followed the gesture of his arm, her eyes widening as he spoke. "You didn't take my hut down." She put a hand to her heart. "I could hardly believe it was still standing when I walked up here."

The tears flowed again. "God bless you for that. Truly. God bless you for sparing it."

Her voice was filled with passion, and before Spencer realized what she was doing, she sprinted impulsively across the few yards between them and threw her arms around his neck. When she pulled back to smile up at him in pleasure, she cupped his face in her hands and kissed him full on the mouth.

Spencer couldn't recall if he'd ever received a spontaneous, happy kiss like this before in his whole life. Without thinking, he slipped his arms around her waist and let himself sink into her warmth, kissing her back. She tasted like cherry ChapStick and smelled like fresh apples and apple blossoms. Spencer's spirit soared. It was a moment to remember—like an unexpected photo shoot caught just as the sun came up at the crest of dawn. He snapped the shot into his mental memory, even as he let his hands slide up to tangle in the wild mane of curly black hair that blew around her face in the breeze. Seeming to merge into his haze of pleasure, she pressed against him, letting her hands wrap themselves around his back. Spencer closed his eyes in delight. Life hadn't brought him many spontaneous, warm moments of sheer, genuine affection. And he savored this one.

Her hands patted him fondly as she stepped back from him. He looked down at her, into warm brown eyes flecked with gold from the sun. Her olive skin glowed. She was much more beautiful than he remembered.

She pushed out her bottom lip in a pout then. "Just because I'm pleased with you for not tearing down my hut doesn't mean I don't hate you for buying Raven's Den. It should have been kept natural and wild. There's something special about this place, you know."

Spencer smiled, knowing the truth of her words.

The girl studied him. "You're aware of that, aren't you? You sensed it when you first came here. This place called to you."

Spencer rolled his eyes and shook his head back and forth. "No more of that fortune-telling, island girl. I had enough of that yesterday."

She paused at his words and seemed to shift gears. "I'd almost forgotten about that in our moment here." She stepped back. "You were rude to me yesterday."

He laughed. "And you were polite to me?" He knew his words sounded sarcastic.

She frowned at him, and Spencer regretted causing a cloud to pass over her pretty face.

He held out a hand to her. "I'm Spencer Jackson. I don't think we've been formally introduced. I've lived here in the area for five years. Before that I lived in Savannah."

She looked thoughtful. "You're Spencer Jackson of the Jackson Gallery?"

He nodded and watched her face light up again with that spontaneous glow. "I'm Zola Devon." She slipped her hand into his, and he fought wanting to caress it. She had an odd impact on him, this peculiar girl.

"I own the Nature's Corner store in the same mall with your gallery," she told him. "I've had it for three years. I bought it after the former owner, Eleanor Taylor, died unexpectedly. I guess you remember her." She grinned at him. "Small world, huh? I can't believe we've never met!"

Spencer shrugged. "I don't work in the gallery much. I spend my time out in the field and I travel a lot. Aston Parker runs the store for me."

She interrupted him in an enthusiastic rush. "I know Aston Parker well, and Clark Venable that works with him, too. It's just amazing that we've never met."

"Well, we've met now." He put a hand to her

face and leaned toward her again, remembering how good the kiss had felt earlier, wanting to experience it again.

She stepped back from him, evading the kiss. "Don't make more of that earlier hug than it was, Spencer Jackson. I was enjoying a happy moment when I came up here and found my hut still standing. I'd expected it to be torn down."

Zola walked back toward the natural structure. "I'm so relieved and happy you didn't take this little place down. I know it doesn't look like much, but it has been a very special haven to me."

"You built it?" Spencer asked, picking up the cooler to carry it into the hut. He sat it on the rustic table inside.

She nodded, looking around the little structure fondly. "I built it over the years of my childhood, here a little and there a little. I have a lot of memories about every stick and rock, every wind chime and bird feeder here. Even about each piece of furniture I dragged up here." She pointed down toward the valley. "The trail is steep that goes down to my place below. It wasn't easy getting boards and chairs up here."

He stepped up beside her to look down the hillside with her.

"That gray roof there—on the hillside in the little clearing in the trees." She gestured toward it. "That's my family's place. It's my place right now. My father's in Mooréa all of the year except for an occasional holiday in the States to see his parents and family."

"Mooréa?" Spencer struggled to pull up his geography facts. "That's the island next to Tahiti in the South Pacific, isn't it?"

"It's forty minutes on the ferry across the ocean from Tahiti to Mooréa." She smiled. "Less if you have your own boat. My family lives near Temae on Mooréa, but the whole island is only ten miles across, so it's not far from any one point on Mooréa to any other. If you were born there as I was, and grew up there, every inch of the island feels like home."

Spencer's stomach growled, reminding him of the time. "I brought lunch down here. Have you eaten? If not, I'll share with you. I brought a lot, expecting to feed the squirrels and the birds. I hoped to get a few shots of them while they were occupied with food." He gestured to his camera, draped around his shoulder.

"No, I haven't eaten lunch yet." He watched her consider his offer.

"And I'd like to stay a little longer before I walk back down the mountain. What did you bring to eat?"

He opened the cooler. "A few fried chicken legs left over from a run to the Colonel's place down in the Burg yesterday, some smoked gouda cheese, a couple of apples, bottled water." He grinned at her. "Plus fudge from the candy store down by the gallery."

"From the Sweet Shop?" She grinned back at him. "That did it. I'm staying for lunch."

He laughed, enjoying her spontaneity again.

She explored around the hut while he got the food out. He divvied it up onto plastic plates he'd stuck in the top of the cooler. Spencer often fed the animals with the scraps left from his lunches, putting them out on the rock wall shelf to try to lure the wild creatures in.

"You've added two rocking chairs," she said from behind him.

"Did I ruin the place by adding them?" He turned around to hand her a plate.

"No," she said, considering it. "They fit right in." She sat down in one and leaned back to rock gently, balancing her plate on the arm of the rocker.

Spencer watched the smile of pleasure spread over her face.

"Nice." She looked up at him, her eyes still half closed. "I could never have dragged rocking chairs this large up here. And I love to rock. Always have."

"Me, too." Spencer sat down beside her in the other chair. "My mom once said it was the only way anyone could get me to sleep when I was small. Rocking chairs have always drawn me like a magnet."

She bit into a chicken leg, obviously hungry.

He sat his water bottle down on the ground and attacked his own food. "How far is it from your place up here to Raven's Den?"

"One and a half miles, but it feels like more going up. It's a steep climb after you cross Buckner Branch, and you have to work your way up through the rocks when the trail switches back along the stream later. There's a nice cascade where the stream drops down over a high rocky hill. Have you been there?"

Spencer nodded.

"It's a great place. I like to swim in the pool below the cascades in summer." She finished off the chicken leg and popped a piece of cheese in her mouth. "The downhill return is easier. If you ever come down to the farm, you'll have the hike in reverse. You'll get the hard part coming back."

"I'm in pretty good shape."

She cast a glance over at him. "I can see that." Realizing she'd given him a compliment, she blushed prettily.

They ate in silence then, enjoying their food and the beauty of the day.

Leaning forward, Zola bit off a few pieces of her apple, put them on the rock wall shelf, and began to make crooning, chattering sounds. Spencer soon heard a rustling in the trees above her. He sat totally still in his seat, watching. In a few minutes a gray squirrel came scurrying down a limb, stopping to look at them.

Zola made a few more sounds and talked to the squirrel softly. "Well, little friend, I see you're still around. And that you made it through the hard winter. Look and see what I've brought you." She put a few more pieces of apple out.

Seeming to understand her words and invitation, the gray squirrel scampered down the tree and leaped off a low branch to land on the wood shelf. He stopped and began to eat the apple, obviously comfortable with Zola but keeping a wary eye in Spencer's direction.

Spencer's hand went automatically to the camera around his neck.

Zola shook her head. "Don't try to photograph him this time, Spencer. He doesn't know you yet. Wait until he's come and been fed by you a few times, until he comes to recognize you and knows you're not a threat. Then the little noises of the camera and your movements won't frighten him off. If you try now, you'll only get one shot in before he's gone—if that. He's a fast one."

"You recognize him?" Spencer said softly, still not moving.

Zola chattered at the gray squirrel again. "Yes. I know this one. See that little kink in his tail. I think he got into a skirmish with something once in the past. He's always had that."

"How long have you been feeding him?"

"This one?" She thought about it. "Three years, I think. He's lucky to have lived that long. Squirrels can live six years in the wild but their lifespan is much shortened when they live in more urban areas."

"This is hardly an urban area." Spencer frowned.

"No. But the lure of the tourists and all the food they put out, or throw away, at the chalets and rental houses on the mountain are a big temptation to squirrels. Also where there are people there are cars—one of a squirrel's most dangerous predators."

Spencer laughed.

As they finished their lunch, he watched with increasing delight as Zola drew in squirrels, birds, and even a lizard to the hut.

"You have a way with animals, Zola Devon. I envy that."

She turned to lay a hand on his knee. "So do you, Spencer Jackson. If you did not have a gift for them, they wouldn't come while you're here."

"You think so?" He liked that idea.

"I know so." Zola patted his knee and turned brown eyes to his. "That makes it hard for me to hate you when God's creatures trust you so."

"You're an odd girl."

"So you've said before." She gave him a considering look before lowering her lashes.

He flexed his fingers. "You were right that I

acted rude to you yesterday, Zola. I regret that."

"Thank you for the apology," she said, putting her plate on the ground beside her and settling back to rock gently in her chair.

He rocked, too, looking out over the valley, enjoying the sense of being with her even if they weren't talking. Spencer looked over and saw Zola's eyes closed, a smile on her face.

"What are you thinking?" he asked.

She turned warm eyes toward him. "I was simply communing with my Maker, Spencer. It's hard not to do that when it's so beautiful here, even when I'm with a comfortable earthly companion."

"Well, I guess I won't resent that extra presence."

They rocked for a few more moments in quiet.

Spencer cleared his throat then. "I thought you would ask me about the woman—and about what happened."

She continued to rock. "I already know what happened."

He scowled, and she saw it.

"I don't know *everything* that happened, Spencer." She placed her hand on his knee again and an odd sense of calm spread through him. "I only know that she didn't take anything from you. That she didn't steal from you."

Feeling twitchy now, he caught her eyes with his. "How do you know that, Zola?"

She looked up and smiled. "Your Maker is very interested in you, Spencer, which I know means you belong to Him."

Spencer felt even more fidgety and uncom-fort-able now. He wasn't used to having intimate talks about God or his faith. Faith to him was personal, a deep, inner thing not to be discussed lightly.

She studied him. "Faith isn't diminished by being expressed, Spencer." A smile touched the edges of her mouth. "In fact, most of the time sharing and speaking about faith enhances it."

"Well, I'm not used to that." He got up abruptly and began to load up the cooler.

She didn't say anything else, and when he turned back toward her again she was putting the last scraps of her meal out on the shelf for her friends.

"I owe you a thank-you for warning me about Leena." He watched her to see what she would do.

She smiled at him. "It's not me you need to thank. I've never met you. What did I know about you or that woman? Not a thing. It was God who knew you and God who had an interest in you. I was only the one he used to send the message."

"Is that how you see it?" He scowled. It was a new idea for him to think about.

She got up from the rocker. "That's how it is, Spencer."

He noticed then that she wore denim overalls

over a T-shirt. Her jacket was unbuttoned now, and he could see better what she had on. He hadn't seen a girl in overalls since he'd lived on Daufuskie, a remote island off the coast near Savannah, Georgia.

Zola noticed his gaze.

"They're comfortable," she explained.

He nodded.

"I need to go now." She walked over to look out over the valley one last time.

"Will you come back tomorrow?" he asked impulsively.

"Thank you for asking me." She turned to look at him, and he watched a small shadow of pain cross her face. "I suppose I'll need an invitation to come from now on."

He reached out a hand to touch her arm. "Come anytime, Zola. I knew this hut was someone's special place the day I found it. It belongs to you in that way, but I hope you'll let me share it with you."

She shrugged.

"What time will you come?" he asked.

"After church," she said. "They're baptizing Tanner and Delia Cross's baby, Thomas Walker, tomorrow. I can't miss that."

He glanced at her in surprise. "At Highland Presbyterian on Natty Road?" he asked. "I was invited to that. Delia Cross helped me decorate my house here."

"And you'll be going?" She smiled at him. "If so, then perhaps I'll see you there. Little Thomas is a fine, happy boy, and it's a joyous thing to get to be a party to a baby's blessing in the Lord."

"Yes, I suppose it is." Spencer seldom went to social events, but Zola made it sound inviting.

"Well, maybe I'll see you there," she said, picking up a walking stick she'd left leaning against the hut and starting down the mountain.

He stopped her with a question. "Zola, what do you call this place?"

"Just Raven's Den—as you know it." She smiled her dazzling white smile at him once more. "But this small structure here is a meditation hut. A native friend taught me how to build one in Mooréa. I have one there, too, on the top of a hill looking out over the ocean. It has a grand view, also. A person needs a place where they can go to find peace and get collected in their soul. I have always found that peace in a place like this."

"You're an interesting girl, Zola."

She studied him. "And you're a man who needs peace in his soul, Spencer Jackson." She started down the hill. "I will see you in church tomorrow."

Chapter 5

The next morning, as Zola filed into the Highland Cumberland Presbyterian Church with her family, she wondered if she would see Spencer Jackson at the service. He said he'd been invited to come but he never said if he would actually show.

Noticing many new faces today, Zola realized the church was more crowded than usual. She took her Nana's arm to help her down the aisle.

"There will probably be a fair passel of folks here today to see the baptism," Nana said, obviously noting the extra numbers in church as they worked their way down the aisle to their regular seats. "Tanner and Delia Cross have a lot of friends in Gatlinburg."

Zola slid into the family pew after her grandparents. The Devon family always sat on the sixth row back on the right underneath the big stained-glass window dedicated to the Devons—longtime pillars in the Highland Cumberland Presbyterian Church. As the Devon family had grown, they had spread back into the seventh pew, as well.

Aunt Becky Rae, her husband Gene, their son Jim, and Jim's girls Doreen and Jenny sat in the sixth pew with Zola and her grandparents. Uncle Ray's family filled the seventh pew behind them, with Ray; his wife, Augusta; their daughter, Stacy; their son, Wayne; his wife, Patricia; and Wayne and Patty's children, Hilda and Ronnie.

"We make a right fine crowd when we're all here together." Nana looked around her in satisfaction. Zola also knew she was checking to see that everyone looked as they should—girls in nice dresses, boys in neat suits, everyone's hair properly brushed.

Zola's cousin, Stacy, had the hardest time with Nana Etta's dress code rules. She sat on Zola's left now, cross to be wearing a skirt and blouse.

"Am I mistaken, Stacy," Zola teased. "Or are you wearing makeup this morning?"

"Hush your mouth, Zola." Stacy nudged her with a scowl. "I don't see why we need to dress up or why we can't wear pant suits to church. Look around at all the women who wear pants to church now. You'd think Nana would bend a little on that. I hate skirts." Stacy was an outdoorsy type of woman, and she thoroughly disliked getting dressed up.

Zola grinned. "It's only once a week, cousin. And it's easier going along with Nana than trying to rock the boat."

"You've got that right," she grumbled, as the church music started and the choir and the minister began to file in.

Zola had no time to look for Spencer again until the greeting time in the service. She spotted him as the congregation shook hands and visited, standing near the back of the church. He was making an effort to socialize, but she could tell he wasn't a highly extroverted individual. It seemed an effort for him to make nice. Zola smiled to herself as she sat back down.

When the service ended later, Zola saw Spencer linger as the congregation filed out. Then he made his way down to congratulate Tanner and Delia. The couple had remained at the front of the church with baby Thomas to greet friends and family who came for the christening.

Nana, moving up beside Delia in the line now, patted the baby's cheek. "Little Thomas surely looks pleased with all this attention."

As if on cue, the baby gave her a cute grin and grasped her finger.

Delia smiled. "He was really good today except for trying to push Reverend Madison's hand away when he put the baptismal water on his head."

Delia looked up to see Spencer arrive. "Spencer! I'm so pleased you came. It was good of you." She reached out her free arm, which wasn't wrapped around Thomas, to give him a small hug.

Spencer greeted Tanner Cross, also, and then Nana redirected his attention. "Aren't you the one who bought Raven's Den?" She pushed her glasses up to study his face thoughtfully. "The one who didn't take down Zola's hut?"

He nodded, and his eyes turned toward Zola's with a question.

Zola felt a blush steal up her face. "This is Spencer Jackson, Nana." She turned to Spencer then. "Spencer, this is my grandmother, Etta Garnett Devon."

"And this here is my husband, Vernon Rayfield Devon," Nana added as Zola's grandfather came to join them.

The two men nodded and shook hands, and Spencer shook Nana's hand, too, offering polite greetings to both.

Spencer's brooding gray eyes drifted to meet Zola's then. Zola felt his gaze drop and slide slowly over her fitted shirtwaist dress and down her bare legs to her black patent pumps.

Her heartbeat quickened unexpectedly, and she struggled to think of something to say.

Fortunately, Nana spoke instead. "Well, Mr. Jackson, I guess you'd better come home to Sunday dinner with us, since we're going to be neighbors now."

Spencer shook his head. "That's kind of you to offer, Mrs. Devon, but it's really not necessary . . ."

He didn't get to finish that thought before Zola's grandfather interrupted, thumping him on the back. "We have plenty for lunch, boy, and we'd like a chance to get to know you. Your place on the mountain is the view out our back windows, son, and our farm property borders against yours up on the ridge. It would be good if we came to know each other. I'd be pleased if you would say yes."

Spencer's eyes softened. "I'd be glad to say yes, then, Mr. Devon. Thank you, sir."

Zola grinned at Spencer.

Nana looked between the two of them thoughtfully. "Zola, you go ride with Spencer back to our place. It's hard to find the turn roads out of Gatlinburg and around behind the mountain to our farm. A person can get lost real easy trying to get to Jonas Creek Road if he doesn't know the way."

Zola nodded her agreement, and Nana patted Zola's arm fondly. "I'll only be a bit longer before I leave."

Zola snapped her fingers suddenly. "Oh, I forgot to tell you, Nana. Mary Ogle is here today, visiting with John Dale and Hallie Madison. She said she hoped she got to see you before she left."

Nana smiled. "Well, I'll go looking for her right now before Vern starts pushing on me to leave." She gave him a warning glance. "I haven't seen Mary Ogle in a coon's age and I want to say hello."

She turned away, making her way back through the church. Zola's grandfather followed, greeting friends along the way.

"You're in for it now," Zola told Spencer. "We

have a big family. They'll grill you about Raven's Den—and probably about your life."

"I think I can manage it. I travel a lot, Zola. I'm used to being in the public eye and being asked questions as a photographer."

"I'm glad to hear it." She smiled up at him and linked an arm through his. "Let me introduce you around a little, since you're a guest today, and then we'll go pay our respects to the minister and his wife at the door."

After some visiting, they made their way to the vestibule, where Zola introduced Spencer to Reverend Madison and his wife, June.

June swept Zola with an evaluative look up and down and a slight frown. "I see you're back from your trip."

"I am, June. And I saw your gorgeous little granddaughter here today with John Dale and Hallie. She certainly is cute." Zola watched June's face soften a little. She loved that grandchild.

"Little Mary Grace had her first birthday last month," June said, smoothing her short hair back from her face.

"Well, she's a beautiful child." Zola reached out to take Reverend Madison's hand as she spoke. He was a tall man, dressed in clerical robes, with glasses on a serious face.

The reverend pressed Zola's hand affectionately, making polite greetings. She started to reply but then stopped what she was about to say

70

with surprise, looking up at him. *He's moving to another church,* she heard.

She shook her head sadly. "Oh. I didn't know you were leaving, Reverend Madison," Zola said. "We'll all miss you here at Highland."

June slapped at her and hissed softly. "Hush, Zola. We haven't told anyone yet."

Zola saw Spencer look between them with curiosity.

Seeing his look, June heaved an exasperated sigh. "Our Zola here has a queer way of knowing things which aren't *any* of her business to know sometimes." She frowned. "And she has a real bad habit of speaking them out, too, when most polite folks would keep their mouths shut."

Spencer tried to suppress a smile.

Reverend Madison leaned over closer to Zola before anyone else walked up. "It's a decision we only recently made, Zola. And we haven't told anyone, yet. So do keep it to yourself, if you would. I'll make a formal announcement soon."

"Of course." Zola smiled at him and then paused once more, listening to that inner voice. "Ahhh. Charleston. You're going back to Charleston, Reverend Madison. That's nice. Charleston has always been a favorite place of yours. And June has wanted to go back for a long time. Your daughter and her family live there." She smiled at June. "I'm sure everything will work out just fine."

Zola heard June sputter again, but she ignored it,

still listening within. More was coming to her. She saw a clear picture of Perry Ammons, the church's youth pastor, standing in the pulpit.

She patted the pastor's hand. "You know, I think Perry Ammons would be a good interim pastor here at the church," she offered. "Maybe even a good full-time pastor if he'd consider the job."

June swung her eyes around anxiously to see if anyone was listening to their conversation and then snapped a warning at Zola. "For goodness' sakes, girl, mind your tongue, and quit talking about this matter. Mrs. Harper is coming and she couldn't keep a confidence if her life depended on it."

June was obviously becoming annoyed, but Zola noted, with relief, that Reverend Madison looked thoughtful about what she suggested. She was glad. Zola tried hard to say the things she felt she was supposed to.

June turned to Spencer and shook a finger at him. "I hope you know what you're getting your-self into running around with the likes of Zola Devon. I'll warn you. She's a right queer girl. You keep a watch on her."

Zola watched him suppress a grin.

"Yes, ma'am," he answered politely, taking Zola's arm to walk on out of the church. "I'll keep a watch on her."

He managed not to laugh until he got to the parking lot, opening the door of his car to let her in. His amused eyes caught hers then. "So, it's not only me you play fortune-teller with, huh, Zola Devon?"

"Hush, Spencer." She scowled at him, climbing into his brown SUV.

He went around to let himself in and started up the car, still smirking.

Zola glared at him, but after a few minutes she spoke. "I didn't know Reverend Madison was leaving until I shook his hand." She bit her lip thoughtfully. "I'm sorry to learn it. He's been at the church for a long time. Most of the people will be sorry to learn he's moving away."

She turned to grin at him while she buckled her seatbelt. "However, many won't be too sorry to say good-bye to his wife, June."

Spencer grinned back at her. "She seems kind of outspoken for a minister's wife." He paused thoughtfully. "And is it normal for the minister's wife to stand outside after the service to greet the congregation as they leave?"

"No. That's totally a June thing. She's always done it. Says it helps her to get to know all the people in her husband's church." Zola giggled. "But mostly it gives her a chance to say her piece when she wants to."

"Did you really *see* that the minister was leaving —and that he was going to Charleston—when you shook his hand?" Spencer lifted an eyebrow in question.

"I did. It was very clear." She turned her eyes toward his. "And I don't like you calling me a fortune-teller, Spencer Jackson."

"Aren't you?"

She frowned at him. "No, I'm not. A fortune-teller, to quote Madame Renee's advertising, is a person 'who foretells your personal future—who uncovers your desires, wishes, and dreams, who finds the answers you've been seeking.' " She turned angry eyes to Spencer. "And all for *only* a small fee."

She saw Spencer wince.

Zola blew out a breath. "The tellings of a fortune-teller don't come from God, Spencer. That's the big difference. They come from a person, who may or may not mean well. And who may or may not be right in her fortune-telling arts."

She twisted the straps of her handbag in her lap. "A fortune-teller provides her arts on demand—and for a fee. A Christian seer gets wisdom or knowledge about some current or future event only as God wills it and never takes money for it. The gift of knowing is given as God chooses—and usually for some purpose or reason."

Zola saw Spencer thinking about this. "So, why do you think God told you the minister might be moving?"

She thought for a minute. "I don't know exactly. Perhaps to seed the idea to Reverend Madison that Perry Ammons should be asked to fill in as interim pastor and maybe even become the next pastor." Zola considered this thoughtfully. "Perry Ammons is the part-time youth pastor right now and Perry has a deep faith. I've heard him preach when he fills in for Reverend Madison. I admit, I never considered it before, but I think Perry would be very good for the church."

Spencer steered his SUV artfully around a lane of blocked traffic on Gatlinburg's main highway through town. "I think I've met Perry Ammons at breakfast at the Garden Café with Tanner Cross and some other guys. They have some sort of regular get-together there every week."

He paused to let a pedestrian cross in front of his car. "Isn't Perry Ammons the one who has the wedding chapel on the Cosby Highway?"

Zola nodded. "Yes. Perry and his wife have a nice wedding chapel. But he served as a pastor in a church before he came back here to live. He is an ordained minister, you know."

Spencer looked over at her. "Do you think he has the right ordination? Most churches are kind of picky about that sort of thing."

Zola watched the tourists thronging down the sidewalk of Gatlinburg on a Sunday afternoon. "I don't know, Spencer. I didn't get that." She felt a little silly then.

"You know what?" Spencer laid a hand on her knee and patted it. "I wouldn't worry about it.

If, as you said, God had a reason for you to say what you did, then He'll work it out."

She looked over at him in surprise, comforted. "That's very wise, Spencer. Thank you."

As they came to a turn in the road, Zola gave him directions.

They drove along quietly for a few minutes, and then Spencer spoke again. "It must be hard sometimes, doing what you do. I'm sure people get mad at you a lot and don't understand. I certainly got mad."

He grinned, remembering it, but then turned troubled eyes toward her. "You know, I actually think it might be dangerous what you do sometimes. What if someone tried to hurt you? Got really angry or was threatened by something you knew? It could happen."

Zola considered this and shrugged.

Spencer slowed to a near halt in the Gatlinburg traffic and turned to catch Zola's eyes. "Has anyone ever threatened you, Zola?"

She smiled at him, wanting to lighten the moment. She didn't want him worrying about her. "Madame Renee has threatened me." She giggled. "She says I'm ruining her business. She comes into my shop sometimes to rant and rave at me."

He grinned at her. "You mean there really is a Madame Renee?"

"Oh, yes. She rents a place out on the highway outside of Sevierville. Many of her clients talk to her about me. She showed up in the store one day furious that I told one of her clients a different piece of knowledge than she had." Zola laughed. "She was especially angry I was giving away my knowledge for free. Said I was foolish to do that—and that it made her look bad."

Spencer laughed. "I guess it does."

"Have you ever gone to a fortune-teller?" Zola turned her eyes toward his.

He shook his head. "No. But I remember a woman named Jewel Kilgrew that people called a 'wise-woman' out on Daufuskie Island. Many of the people on Daufuskie lived isolated from the world for a long time. They still hold a lot of odd beliefs and superstitions. I remember Jewel got what she called a 'knowing' about what was wrong with my dog one time when he was sick. Came to tell me about it. I was grateful. Her advice helped to save Zeke's life."

Zola nodded. "Turn left up ahead." She pointed. "At the road sign beside my Uncle Ray's place on the corner."

"Is this your uncle's store?" Spencer asked, turning onto the road between the store and a tourist shop beside it.

"Yes." Zola looked at Uncle Ray's new sign and smiled. "It's hard to make a living off farming alone like in the old days. People often need to have other occupations to supplement. My family uses their farm mostly for their own needs today.

Even my grandfather worked down in Sevierville at the hardware store most of his life. He only farmed on the side."

"But your family has kept the land."

"Yes." Zola smiled. "We all love the land. It's in a pretty valley with the hills rolling up behind it. You'll see. My Nana says our blood is all planted in the Devon land."

Zola pointed out two more turns to Spencer until they drove down Jonas Creek Road along the long, broad, tumbling stream the road was named after.

"Where were you raised, Spencer?" Zola asked.

"Just outside Richmond, Virginia." He loosened his tie with one hand.

"Is your family still there?"

"Yes. All of them but me." He slowed the car to pass over a short, wooden bridge.

She gave him a teasing look. "And does Virginia call to your blood, Spencer? Are you still planted in that land in your heart?"

"No." He nearly bit her head off with his sharp answer.

Zola's eyes widened. "Ouch. I guess I hit a nerve."

"Yes. I'm not very close to my family." He didn't add anything else.

Watching his jaw clench, Zola wisely decided to let the topic go for now.

She pointed to a dirt road up ahead. "Turn there, Spencer. That's the Devon Farm Road leading back to my grandparents' place. It weaves a circle through the major part of the old farm. The big gray house we passed a block back on the left was my Aunt Becky and Uncle Gene's place."

"Is your place on this road?" he asked.

"No, but there's a well-worn path to it across Buckner Branch and through the woods. By the road, you need to continue driving down Jonas Creek Road about a mile." She smiled at him. "You can run me down to the house after lunch if you want. But don't expect much. It's only an old renovated farmhouse."

Spencer turned to smile back at her. "Are you kidding? This whole place around here is a photographer's heaven." He pointed. "Look around you. It's beautiful. Graceful white farm-houses, weathered red barns, fresh green fields dotted with cows and goats, misty mountains rising in the distance on either side. Plus that picturesque old brick church we passed back up the road. I definitely want to come back here to take some shots of that."

Zola reached over to put a hand on his knee affectionately. "I'm glad you like it here, Spencer. I always have. And that old brick church is the Jonas Creek Missionary Alliance Church. I'll take you to visit one Sunday if you'd like. My best friend, Rachel Lee Upton Howard, goes to church there. She plays the piano every Sunday and sings solo occasionally. She's really good, too. Her daddy, Pastor K. T. Upton, is the minister there."

"If I visit, will you go with me?" He slowed the car over a rut in the road as he asked.

She grinned. "Sure. But you'll find it's very different from Highland Cumberland Presbyterian."

"How so?"

"Livelier. Less formal. Louder. More fervent and passionate in the worship style. And the gifts might flow."

He shrugged. "Won't scare me. It sounds like one of the churches over on Daufuskie or like Aston Parker's AME Zion church in Savannah I often visited."

Zola pointed Spencer toward the driveway that pulled off to her grandparents' rambling white farmhouse. She studied him discreetly out of the corner of her eye. Interesting little aspects about Spencer Jackson seemed to continue popping out unexpectedly all the time.

She looked across at him; he was dressed in a neat white shirt again. The shirt was tucked into khaki slacks with a jacket to match for church. Only his long, sun-dipped hair, tied back neatly with a leather string, gave away the artistic, independent streak she knew she'd seen in him.

Zola smiled at him. "Maybe we'll talk some more about your interesting church experiences another time."

"Maybe," he said, parking the car and opening the door.

Chapter 6

Spencer found himself quickly enveloped into the bosom of Zola's family as soon as he entered the Devon house. *Enveloped* was the best word to describe the experience in Spencer's way of thinking. Her family was a boisterous, talkative, hugging sort of group that seemed to encircle him in their warmth. He'd traveled and been around many kinds of people as a photographer—but experiences like this were always striking. It made Spencer want to capture it on film. But he didn't think it possible. It was why he'd never delved more deeply into documentary photography or candid portraiture as some great photographers had done. He didn't feel capable of capturing emotions like this; he couldn't get detached enough from the experience. He liked to revel in it too much, to watch it, to listen to it. It was fascinating.

Zola's aunt, Becky Rae, slapped her knee as she talked now. "Lord in heaven, I couldn't believe that dress Dora Hensley had on today. Those were the most bodacious flowers in that fabric design I've ever seen in all my born days. And on those hips of hers, they jiggled like Jell-O."

"Now, Becky Rae." Nana chided her. "Let's not

be uncharitable. Besides, you're not exactly a skinny woman yourself."

"No. But I do know how to dress for my weight." She heaved a sigh. "I just do *not* understand how some women don't show a lick of sense in the dresses they pick out for themselves."

"If they all wore pant suits most of them would look better," Stacy interjected. She'd changed out of the dress she'd worn to church earlier and now wore old jeans and a plaid flannel shirt. Stacy was what Bowden would have called a tomboy or, in a less kind moment, a geek. But Spencer already liked her. He guessed Stacy and Zola might be near the same age.

The Devon family were all sitting around the big dining room now, enjoying coffee, homemade caramel cake, and ice cream, after a huge Sunday after-church meal. Spencer felt pleasantly stuffed —like after Thanksgiving—and he was still working his way through the cake, drizzled with a sticky homemade caramel icing worth shouting about.

Spencer counted eleven adults around the long dining room table and four children at the kitchen table around the corner. He could hear the children giggling periodically, and their young voices often trickled into the room with the adults.

Wayne's wife, Patricia, a sunny blonde, stood up. "I'm going to start clearing these dishes off,

Nana. And Becky Rae and the girls and I are washing and putting up today. You've done enough cooking. You go out in the living room and visit with everyone."

There seemed to be a rumbling movement as everyone started to get up from the table.

"That was a great meal, Mama," Ray said. He pushed his glasses up on his friendly, smiling face. He turned to Spencer. "And it was good having you with us, Spencer. We all feel a little better about Raven's Den being sold now that we've met you. Sounds, from what you told us, like you're trying to keep the place natural—like God made it."

Zola's grandfather, Vernon Devon, shook a warning finger at Spencer. "You be sure you don't ever cut down that old tulip tree up toward the top of Shinbone Ridge. It must be nearly thirty feet in diameter. I remember I couldn't even stretch my arms around it. There's not many virgin trees around here like that one anymore."

Spencer smiled. "I know that tree. I've photographed it."

"Well, I'd like to see that photo." Vernon licked a last dab of caramel icing off his finger before he left the dining room. "I can't get up that ridgetop quite like I once did."

Spencer thought of suggesting he'd e-mail him a copy of the photo print of the tree but then changed his mind. He hadn't even seen a computer in the house. "Mr. Devon, I'll make you a copy of the picture and bring it by sometime."

Vernon nodded. "Well, that would be right good of you, Spencer. I hear tell you do good photo work. I'll have to come down to your gallery someday. Maybe see some of your pictures."

Spencer smiled. Everyone seemed to be filing into the big living room at the front of the house now. Some of the family carried a few of the dining room chairs into the room with them as they shifted locations.

Zola joined Spencer, still standing by her grandfather. "I think Spencer needs to get home, Papa." She gave her grandfather a hug. "I may let him take me over to my house as he leaves."

He patted her fondly. "Well, you go tell your grandmother good-bye first. She went back to the bedroom."

"I'll be right back," she told Spencer.

"Fine girl." Vernon Devon looked after her. He turned his still-keen hazel eyes to Spencer. "Zola was raised for much of her life in the South Pacific islands. Perhaps you know that. Her mother was Tahitian. My son Stanford's a missionary doctor over there in Mooréa next to Tahiti. Warmhearted people the Tahitians— generous, kind, welcoming. Maybe a little too warmly affectionate."

He eyed Spencer candidly. "You ever take advantage of that affectionate streak in our girl and I'll learn of it, boy. We watch our women real carefully here in the valley. We don't condone none of them new 'goings on' you see on the television and hear about that young folk are doing these days. We still live by the Good Book. Just wanted you to know that right up front."

Spencer wasn't quite sure what to say in reply. "I'll remember that, sir."

"See that you do." He nodded several times as if to affirm the words again.

Zola came back then to save him. "Ready to go?"

Spencer nodded gratefully.

She gave him an odd look as they got into Spencer's car out in the driveway. "What did Papa Vern say to you? You looked kind of stunned when I came out."

He grinned at her then. "He just warned me off."

Her eyebrows flew up. "He what?" She thought for a minute and then shook her head knowingly. "Oh, you mean he gave you the morals talk."

"He does that often?"

She looked thoughtful. "He usually only does it with boys I've been dating for a while." She grinned at him. "He didn't show you his shotgun, did he?"

"Thankfully, no." Spencer shuddered.

"Well, then you got off easy." Zola laughed that warm, spontaneous laugh of hers.

"Will you still come up to my place?" he asked.

She stretched lazily. "Yes. If you'll wait and let me change clothes first. I'll want to hike back down, and I don't want to do that in a dress."

Spencer started to say she looked nice in a dress but decided to keep that thought to himself. With the grandfather's warning still rumbling in his mind, he wasn't sure he wanted to get too close, too fast, to this girl who saw things in others' lives all too clearly. He remembered then that the Daufuskie wise-woman's husband left her while he lived on the island, said she caused him too much difficulty with her "knowing."

It wouldn't be easy being close to a woman like Zola. And Spencer had dealt with enough difficult people in his past. He wanted his peace now.

Perhaps the two could just be friends. Zola was an interesting girl.

She changed clothes quickly while telling him to explore around the house. Zola lived in a rustic white farmhouse with a gray tin roof. A small, open front porch sat in the angle between the two sections of the farmhouse, and a screened porch opened off the kitchen in the back. Inside the house, a riot of rich colors and an eclectic blend of both Appalachian country and South Pacific island décor filled every room. Spencer grinned to see what looked like richly printed pareu fabric in the living room drapes and throw pillows right beside a Shaker table with Early American ladder-back chairs. He picked up a giant seashell that sat beside an ancient, antique clock on the mantel.

"I found that shell on the beach at Mooréa," Zola said, coming back into the room in jeans and a long-sleeved T-shirt. She carried a lined jacket over her arm.

He noticed she'd made some effort to pin up her froth of naturally curly hair into a clasp behind her head, but it was hopelessly drifting out of the clasp already.

She pointed to the old clock. "That clock was my great-great-grandfather Devon's."

"Nice mix of items everywhere." He looked around him.

"I'm a mix, too." She shrugged. "It seems to suit me."

"It does suit you, and I like it." He resisted a desire to reach out and touch her face. "Every spot in the house is interesting and seems to yearn to tell a story."

"Ahhh. There goes that artist in you speaking. I like that." She led the way out the door. "We'd better go. The dog is wanting to get out at your house."

Spencer rolled his eyes. "Zeke has a dog door to an outdoor run, Zola."

She turned her brown eyes to his. "Yes, but he wants his walk. And he's listening for your car."

As Spencer followed her out to his SUV he worried again about spending time with a woman who constantly popped out little personal details like she did. After all, a guy liked a little privacy. What if she read his mind when he was thinking something he didn't want to share? Or when he was thinking something . . . well, sort of intimate. Would she just come right out and say what he was thinking? It creeped him out to even consider it.

They wound their way out of the Jonas Creek valley and back to the parkway leading into Gatlinburg. Zola pointed out local spots of interest along the way and told him humorous stories. She was entertaining company.

"Tell me how you ended up coming to Gatlinburg via Richmond, Virginia, and Savannah, Georgia." She turned her bright face toward his with interest.

"I was raised in Richmond, as I think I mentioned before." Spencer tapped his fingers impatiently on the steering wheel as he replied. The traffic in Gatlinburg was heavy and slow today. "My parents own a rural place outside the city near a seventy-five-hundred-acre park called Pocahontas State Park. It's about twenty minutes from Richmond. I grew up in a house near the park's border and explored nearly every inch of it with my best friend, Peter Bradley."

"Do you still stay in touch with him?"

"I do." Thinking of Peter brought happy memories to mind. "Peter is a park ranger out in Yosemite. Whenever I go out West to do photography, I stay with him. He's moved around a time or two to other national parks, so I've had a chance to visit each of the ones he's worked with."

"And do you have brothers and sisters?"

"I have an older brother and a younger sister." He frowned. "As I've told you, I'm not very close to my family. My father inherited the Jackson Studio, a photography business that my grandfather Stettler Jackson started in downtown Richmond. It's well-known there for weddings, special events, and portrait photography. All my family work in the business. My mother added a catering end, called Jackson Catering, after she and my father married. She and my sister and my brother's wife work in different aspects of that. My brother works with my father and my grandfather."

Zola smiled. "Your grandfather still works in the business?"

"He will until they drag him out with his toes up, if you know what I mean. He loves that business." Spencer felt himself gripping the steering wheel tighter while he was talking about his family. Zola didn't seem to notice his discomfort. It was good to know she couldn't always know what he thought or felt.

She looked out the window, watching the tourists milling around the sidewalks of Gatlinburg on a Sunday afternoon. "I guess you learned your photography skills from your family."

"My father taught me," he admitted. "He always loved the out-of-doors and I liked to go on walks with him as a boy. He told me once he'd hoped to be a biologist, to teach biology in college. I learned a lot from him about nature. It didn't interest my brother. That love of nature was the one thing my father and I had in common."

Spencer realized he'd told her more than he meant to.

"It's good you and your father had something in common you could share." She smiled at him. "Those are good memories."

They were, and it was odd how Spencer found himself remembering those good times suddenly.

"What took you to Savannah?" she asked, interrupting his thoughts.

Spencer maneuvered the car into the turn lane and negotiated his way off the parkway to start up Ski Mountain Road before he answered. "I went to college there. The Savannah College of Art and Design has a fine photography program. I wanted a change, and my parents were supportive—after some argument—for me to go to Savannah. My mother's parents, the Chatsworths, lived in the city then. That's where my mother was from. My grandparents had a small apartment over their garage. It was agreed I could go to school in Savannah if I lived with them."

Her eyes brightened. "Did they live downtown in one of those gorgeous row houses?"

He grinned. "Oh, yeah. In an old house steeped in history. It was a great place. I didn't mind living there. I doubt I'd have cared much for dorm living. Not my thing."

"So why didn't you go back home and join the family business?"

Why do women always ask so many questions? Spencer thought. He put his car into low gear to climb the steep hill.

She waited patiently for him to answer, looking at him with interest.

Spencer considered what to say. "I discovered nature photography while in college. It captured me. I loved it in a way I'd never liked doing portraiture work or weddings back home. It answered some need in me. I went with it, grew in it, and never looked back."

Zola smiled. "I love that book you did of all the scenes of the coastal marshes. It was called *Up Close on Georgia's Barrier Islands.*"

Spencer felt pleased she knew the name of the book. "That was my first publication. I'd been showing my photography at the gallery in Savannah where Aston worked, and he had a publisher come in one day saying he wished he knew a photographer who might do some coffee-table books of natural sights around the area. Aston told him about me; he asked me to write up a proposal and send some photo samples."

Cresting the mountaintop, Spencer started

down the winding drive to his house. "The books are what really began to build my reputation as a photographer."

"You've done several, haven't you?"

"Five, and I'm working on the sixth. The money from the books helped me buy the gallery here in Gatlinburg. But now my photography is beginning to make good money on its own, as well."

"What is the new book you're working on?" she asked.

He considered whether to answer. He wasn't a man prone to share his personal life freely. However, glancing over to see her waiting on his answer with such a rapt face dissolved his reluctance. "I think I'm going to call this new book *Small Pleasures in the Shadow of the Mountains*. I'm trying to find the unique and unusual to put in this book—the small unexpected pleasures you come across here in the Smokies."

"I love that idea," she said.

"Well, here we are." He stopped the car in his driveway. "I hope you won't feel angry to see the place I've built up here. I tried to design a home that fit into the setting. I wanted it to feel like it belonged here."

"We'll see," she said quietly. Spencer looked over to see her eyes squeezed shut and her hands clenched in her lap.

Spencer gave her a worried look. "You're not going to cry again, are you?"

"I don't know." She heaved a sigh. "This is a pretty emotional thing for me."

Spencer rolled his eyes. "Well, let's get it over with. Whatever you're going to feel about it, Zola, the house is here. You can't turn back time."

"I know." Her answer was soft.

He came around to open the car door for her. "Here, come and look. It's just a mountain house, Zola, not some pretentious mansion."

Spencer took Zola's hand and led her around toward the front of the house. He watched her squint open her eyes.

"Ohhhh."

Spencer waited, but that was all she said.

"Oh, what?"

She walked up the stone walk to the rustic log cabin, with its roughhewn timbers, settled naturally into the mountain setting. "It doesn't look new. It looks like it's been here for hundreds of years." Her voice sounded slightly awed.

Spencer let out a small sigh. "It was built with logs from several old houses and barns that the builder, Cooper Garrison, found around Tennessee, Kentucky, and Georgia. That's real chinking there between the logs and he used natural rock for the chimney. Cooper made a genuine effort to create a house that was authentic. And I fought to save every tree I could around the place."

She followed the stone walk to the broad front porch of the cabin. It looked out over the mountain ranges beyond and down to the valley below. She laid her hand gently on one of the rustic beams that held up the porch roof and then walked across the porch to stand and look out over the expansive vista. A fog lay draped over the lower mountain ranges, its wispy fingers shrouding some of the view.

Spencer followed her. He stopped to stand beside her, looking out toward the mountains beyond with her, enjoying the feel of the crisp air, savoring the panorama of overlapping mountain ranges against a blue sky.

She put a hand on his arm. "It's nice, Spencer. You've kept the feel of Raven's Den. You haven't spoiled it."

He felt his heart sing inside him.

Zeke barked then, reminding Spencer of his presence. He opened the door, leashed the big shepherd, and then brought him out to meet Zola.

He shouldn't have worried about how Zola and the dog would hit it off. She squatted down on his level, said a few words to him in some language Spencer didn't recognize, and then held out her hand for him to sniff. Soon, Zeke was running his head under her hand and rubbing his big body against her legs. She laughed joyously, as pleased with Zeke as he seemed with her.

Spencer took her through the house then, pointing out the chinked walls inside, the hard-wood floors retrieved from a hundred-year-old house being torn down, telling her about the stone taken from a mountain quarry to create the big fireplace in the main living room. He told her how his decorator, Delia Cross, decided on mossy greens, russet reds, and earth browns for the colors in the house—to enhance the cabin's natural materials and complement the outdoor vistas.

"It's homey and beautiful," she said, running her hand over the stone fireplace in pleasure, laying her hands on the wood walls to feel the texture of the old logs.

Her appreciation for all he'd done to create a special place was so reverent and genuine that Spencer found himself bodily responding to her —getting physically excited. Strange. He began to notice Zola's lips, her scent, and to be conscious of the swell of her breasts under her shirt.

His heart beat more rapidly when she looked across at him shyly and asked to see the bedrooms. "I've only furnished one of the bedrooms upstairs for guests. The other two I'll get to in time. But the master downstairs is fully complete." He led her down the hall to his bedroom.

It was very spacious, and she walked through, not seeming to notice the big bed, which dominated the room and Spencer's thoughts. Instead, she focused on the photographs on the wall. "Your work is everywhere." She ran her fingers over the rough frame of one of Spencer's photographs on the wall. "And I love the natural framing you've used on them."

"I make a lot of my own frames. I actually used wood scraps left from the builders for most of the photographs here in Raven's Den."

She stopped to examine the photograph in front of her that showed a small, weather-beaten white house set under a large oak draped in Spanish moss. "Where was this taken?"

"It's the little house I rented on Daufuskie." He walked over nearer to her. "It's a pretty primitive little place, but I got attached to it. I ended up buying it. I got Zeke when I moved to that house. We lived there and explored the island and marshes together for three years."

"Did Aston live there with you?" Zola asked. She already knew Aston and Spencer lived together in a mountain chalet after they first moved to the Smokies.

Spencer laughed. "Not hardly. Aston *came* from Daufuskie. He helped me find the place on the island, helped me make contacts I needed there. But he wasn't interested in moving back. He stayed in his upscale city apartment the years I lived on Daufuskie."

She turned soft eyes to his. "Weren't you lonely out there by yourself?"

Spencer looked back on that time, remembering how healing it had been to live on his own, to come to know himself on Daufuskie, to work on his art with all his heart. He'd come to terms with himself there on the island. "No, it was a time I needed. The solitude helped to shape me."

"It can do that." She nodded with understanding, not seeing his reply as odd.

He moved to stand behind her, putting his arms around her, leaning her back against him. Spencer knew his physical condition would be evident to Zola, but he wanted badly to touch her, to be close to her for a moment. He rested his chin on her head. She was shorter than he, and Spencer could tuck her head right against his neck and heart. She smelled of that light, woody, fruit scent again—like apples and a whiff of apple blossoms. He fought his hands so they wouldn't stray from her waist to the soft area under her breasts.

"Is Zola your real name?" he asked, his lips against her hair.

She laughed and pulled away from him. "It is my real name and more so, Spencer. My full name is Zolakieran Sidella Eley Devon."

Zola started back toward the living area, leaving him to follow. "*Zola* means 'ball of earth,' *Sidella* means 'prophetess,' and *Eley* means 'light.' My mother researched *Devon* once and it means 'poet.' Quite a lot of name for one young girl, I used to think."

Spencer tried to settle his emotions so he could think of an appropriate response.

"It's a mouthful, isn't it?" She laughed that warm laugh of hers again. "My mother's family goes back to Tahitian royalty and it was a tradition in her family to give three names plus a surname to each child. She gave my brother and I both the kinds of names expected by her people. My brother is Wayland Aidan Stephonera Devon. He is ten years my senior. My mother thought for a long time she wouldn't have any other children. But then I came."

Out in the living room again, she knelt to scratch Zeke. He rolled onto his back to give her better access to his belly.

Spencer envied the dog her touch.

"Why don't you and Zeke walk me part way down the mountain?" She turned her dark eyes to his. "I need to go home now. I haven't been back from Mooréa long and I have a huge list of things I need to do around the house and the farm."

He nodded and went to get Zeke's leash. Zeke had already perked up at the word "walk," which he well recognized, and had headed eagerly toward the door, wagging his tail.

Spencer laughed in spite of himself. "You've said the *w*-word now, Zola. And I think Zeke is ready to go."

"So am I," she said, picking her jacket up from the back of the sofa.

They walked out the ridge trail together. Spencer began to feel better as he walked in the cool mountain air.

He showed Zola how he'd cleared the trail to make it more accessible. At the junction where the trail split, they started downhill toward the valley. The other path led up the familiar trail to Shinbone Point. Their trail switched right after a quarter mile and began to descend toward Buckner Branch.

"Stop and listen," Zola said at one point, putting a finger to her lips. "You can hear the falls from here if you're really quiet and the wind is right."

She was right. Spencer could hear a faint sound of rushing water on the air.

They found the falls a quarter of a mile later. Buckner Branch fell in a long spill over a rocky embankment to splash onto the rocks below before swirling into a deep pool. Beyond the pool, it tumbled over another rocky ledge in a small series of cascades before continuing down the hillside. The trail down into the valley picked up on the other side of the stream.

"I'll go the rest of the way alone," she said, starting to step out on the broad rocks in the pool to cross the stream.

Spencer watched her, wondering what it was about this sprite of a girl that drew him so, even when he'd determined not to be further interested in her.

Stopping on a big rock in the middle of the stream, she looked back at him and flashed him a big smile. Then she motioned for him to hop out to the rock where she stood.

Spencer dropped Zeke's leash and spoke to him to sit and stay. Then with two or three strides over the rocks, he joined her. The sound of the falls and the spill of the cascades filled the atmosphere, and the air felt fresh with the scent of rushing water.

The February air was chill, and Zola's cheeks were rosy from the cold and the exertion of their hike. She put a cold hand to Spencer's cheek. "Thank you for showing me your house. It's wonderful. I don't mind it being on Raven's Den."

Spencer felt a slow smile of pleasure start to spread across his face.

She grinned at him. "At least not too much!" She stood on her toes and kissed him then. The sensations were a glorious mix of cold and heat —cold from the crisp air and heat from the emotions stirring between them.

Spencer tangled his hands in Zola's hair, pulling her against him as they stood on the giant boulder in the stream. He took their kiss deeper than the sweet, little kiss Zola had begun, moving it into a passionate one that soon had both their hearts thudding as loud as the waterfall behind them. How did she always manage to create these photographic moments—these incredibly memorable, emotion-filled incidents? He didn't know and he didn't care. He just lost himself in her.

She pulled away from him to smile at last. "I think I'm beginning to like you a little instead of hating you." Then she patted him on the cheek and leaped across to the next rocks in the stream and over to the opposite shore.

"See you soon!" she called, starting off down the path toward her house.

Spencer stood and watched her until she went around a bend into the woods, turning to wave a last time before she did. Then he picked his way back over the rocks the way he'd come.

Zeke wagged his tail happily to greet him. Then the dog looked longingly down the trail toward the direction in which Zola had disappeared into the trees.

"She's really something, isn't she?" Spencer picked up Zeke's leash and started back up the trail. "We're going to have to watch it around her that we don't both lose our heads."

Chapter 7

Zola didn't see Spencer for several days. She was busy settling back into her work hours at the store after her trip. Being away through most of January and February always put her behind. In addition, shipping orders had arrived from the buying she did while in the islands.

She fell asleep with exhaustion on Wednesday evening, listening to the rain falling on the metal roof of the farmhouse. A nudging of the Spirit woke her early on Thursday morning. She could see the sun coming out with brilliance in a clear blue sky when she crawled out of bed to get into her clothes.

Thirty minutes later, she'd hiked up the mountain trail to Spencer's house and was banging on the door. Zeke, already up, quit barking when he recognized Zola's voice, but it took more banging before a sleepy-headed Spencer padded out to the front door to peer out at her in surprise.

He opened the door. "What are you doing here?" He muffled a yawn behind his hand. "It's really early."

"I know." She pushed her way into the house, trying not to notice Spencer was dressed only in plaid boxers and a loose T-shirt. Zeke greeted her with doggy enthusiasm, obviously not concerned that she'd arrived at seven a.m.

Zola leaned over to pet the big dog's head. Scratching Zeke's ears, she could feel the woolly undercoat beneath the dense, prickly outer coat of the shepherd.

She saw Spencer suppress yet another yawn.

"Get dressed and get your photo gear, Spencer," she said. "You have a shoot to do."

"What?" He scowled at her. "What the heck are you talking about?"

Zola put her hands on her hips impatiently. "Look, Spencer, you need to trust me here. We have a really short window for this, and you need to get ready fast. You hear? I promise you, you'll be glad you listened to me later."

"I don't like you one bit right now," he grumbled. "I stayed up until two last night going through digi pictures I'd taken. It took a long time. I planned to sleep in today."

"So did I." She glared at him.

He rolled his eyes in resignation. "All right. All right." He started toward the bedroom and looked back. "Do we get to eat first?"

She shook her head in the negative and heard a mumbled expletive in reply.

He came back in a few minutes, dressed and pulling on a jacket. He grabbed a hat and gloves from a tabletop and then headed toward his office and workroom to get his photography gear.

"I assume this will be outdoors?" He looked back at her in question.

"Yes. But you'll have to figure out what photographic stuff you need. I didn't get any information about supplies."

A mumbled "Thank God for that" filtered out behind him.

Surprisingly, Spencer and Zola were out the door and on the road within ten minutes after Zola arrived.

He felt irritated she'd walked to the house. "You could have driven, Zola." He frowned at her. "It's cold out early in the morning. Especially in late February."

"It was faster to walk up. And time was every-thing."

"Where are we going?" Spencer raised an eyebrow her way as he headed down the mountain road from his house to the parkway.

"Up Newfound Gap Road. You'll know the right place when we get there." She leaned back against the seat and closed her eyes.

He nudged her. "What do you mean, *I'll* know? I don't have any of that seer gift in me, Zola."

She yawned. "You won't need it. It will be obvious."

She slipped into a quiet sleep as the car traveled up the mountain highway, but she woke quickly when she heard Spencer's exclamation.

"Oh, my gosh. Look at that! Unbelievable!"

She opened her eyes to see the entire mountain-side covered in a white hoarfrost. Every branch and tree trunk was glazed in a dazzling coat of ice and snow, all sparkling brilliantly in the morning sunshine.

"I've never seen anything like this in all my life!" Spencer slowed the SUV to a crawl to look at the natural show in front of them.

As they rounded the next corner, they could see that the glistening frost continued for miles. Here at this point, it flowed up the mountain as far as they could see and down the ridges into the deep valley below. Everywhere they looked was a white, dazzling wonderland—radiant against the blue sky, shining in the brilliant sunshine.

Spencer stopped the car at a pull-off and began to unload his camera equipment.

"How did you know?" He looked at Zola in amazement as he began to set up his tripod and pull his 35 mm SLR camera, zoom lenses, and filters out of his camera bag.

"I didn't." She yawned again. "Evidently God is interested in your work."

He looked at her with wonder in his eyes. "Well, thank Him, would you?"

"You thank Him. He'd like that better." She walked over to a rock wall to stand closer to the edge of the glory before them. It was unbelievably beautiful.

In the mountains, it was rare for a hoarfrost of

this magnitude to occur, and even rarer to be fortunate enough to see it. Once the sun popped out, the ice would begin to melt away. The splendor of a frost like this was short-lived indeed.

Zola turned back to see Spencer lost in his work now. He moved quickly around the area, snapping shots at different angles. He used the tripod, or got on his knees propping one elbow on a knee to keep the camera still. She watched him working with the viewfinder to locate the best composition, thinking carefully about which perspective he wanted to take the picture from. He played with different lenses and added filters; she assumed that was to cut off some of the glare. It was bright out.

He used a digital camera today. Zola watched him stop every now and then to look at a shot he'd taken. Other times he simply moved around, shooting without examining what each picture looked like at all. Instinct, she guessed. He probably knew intuitively what to do, how to shoot to get the results he wanted. She guessed he could simply feel when the shot was right.

Spencer looked up to see her watching him at one point. He motioned for her to come over to see the photograph he'd just taken.

She studied the digital image. "It's incredible. You managed to catch that hawk soaring over all this." She looked up toward the ridgetop to see if it was still there. "I didn't even see it."

He smiled and dismantled the tripod to tuck it back into the straps of his camera bag. "Let's drive up the road a little further. See how far this goes."

They did and found more vistas around the next bend. And the next.

It was several hours later when Spencer seemed to be satisfied with his morning's work and started to pack up his equipment.

He leaned over to kiss Zola impulsively, his lips cold from the time out of doors. "I will never say a derogatory word about your gift again." He smiled at her.

"You'd better not." She traced a hand down his face affectionately. She couldn't admit to him what a rare joy it had been to watch him work. The creative energy flowed off him as he did. It was exciting.

"Your hands are cold." He turned one of her hands over to blow his warm breath across her palm.

Zola's heart skittered a beat.

"Where are your gloves?" he asked.

"In my pocket. I took them off to eat an icicle. I was thirsty."

He seemed surprised at that and looked at his watch. Obviously, he'd lost track of time, absorbed in his work.

"Come on," he said, opening the car door to let her in. "I'll take you to a late breakfast. It's the least I can do. Where do you want to go?"

"The Pancake House." She grinned at him.

He started the car. "The Pancake House it is."

They started down the mountain, Spencer stopping occasionally to take a few more shots. He was like a man obsessed when working.

"Tell me what it's like to see as a photographer," Zola asked him later as they sat over breakfast, drinking hot coffee and eating eggs, sausage, and hot pancakes drizzled with fresh blueberries and blueberry syrup.

He looked thoughtful. "A photographer has to learn to see in a new way. He needs to learn to see scenes in lines, shapes, and textures. Like an artist, he learns to manipulate and set his scene, use the influence of light and the force of color to his advantage." He took a sip of his coffee.

"The camera becomes a tool for exploration. With experience and a right heart, a good photographer can gain a picture that captures nature's soul." He gestured as he talked. "Like any artistic endeavor, the goal is to share your experience with others, to make them see as you see. To touch them in a new way."

She leaned forward, fascinated with his words.

"If I photograph a picket fence," he continued, "I want the viewer to not only see the fence in its rural setting but to feel the rhythm of the fence." He spread his fingers in an arc as if drawing the fence in the air. "Sometimes I think photography achieves its uniqueness by expressing what is impossible to express in words."

Zola licked blueberry syrup off her fingers. "I like the messages and stories your photographs portray, Spencer. You're very good at what you do."

"Thank you." He stretched his shoulders back, obviously tired. "Do you mind stopping by the gallery with me, Zola? I'd like to leave my photos with Clark—so he can begin to look through the images. He's an expert on the computer and has an eye for just which shots will make the best print images."

He dug money out of his pocket for the tip. "I often let him go through the images to give me his take and then I go through them on my own later, comparing my ideas with his. When Clark and I get it down to the wire and decide on a handful of shots, then Aston has this incredible knack of knowing which images will sell. Sometimes what is the best art and what is the best image to sell are two totally different things."

Zola had never thought about photography as a group process. "The three of you make a good team."

"We do. That's true." He got up, dropped the tip on the table, and picked up their breakfast ticket before reaching out a hand to help Zola from her chair.

It dawned on Zola then that Spencer was

consistently a gentleman in this way. He opened car doors, took her elbow crossing a street, helped her up and down from her seat.

She looked at him as she took his hand. "You have good manners."

He grinned at her. "It's the Southern gentleman bred into me. My sister Rita would say it's my good Southern Chatsworth blood showing."

Zola noticed a warm tone when Spencer mentioned Rita's name. "You're fond of your sister?"

His face darkened. "We were close once. When we were small."

Zola left the subject wisely alone then. Spencer would tell her about his life one day when he was ready.

At the gallery, Spencer enthusiastically shared the adventures of his morning photo shoot with Aston and Clark. Zola wandered around the well-lit gallery spaces studying Spencer's work. She hadn't been in the gallery in several months, and she saw the pictures with new eyes now that she knew the photographer.

Clark soon went into the back office to work on the computer, and Spencer and Aston walked over to where Zola stood, observing a close-up photo of a purple aster with a bee on it.

She pointed to the framed photo. "Did you know honey bees, like this one in your photo-graph, often travel four miles to collect pollen and nectar from flowers and blossoms to make honey?"

Aston grinned. "That's a huge distance for a little bee. Wonder if they take the weekends off or ever take a rest?"

"Actually, they do rest some days." Zola turned to him with a smile. "They also take a break on rainy days from collecting."

Aston laughed with a hearty sound. "So when we're moaning over a rainy day, the bee guys are having a happy dance for getting a day off."

"I guess so." Zola liked Aston. He was an easy, comfortable black man, wonderful with the public and very competent and smart. Spencer was lucky to have him.

Aston gave her a small hug now. "It's good to see you again, Zola Devon. It's been a long time."

"Yes, it has."

He stepped back, still holding her hand affectionately in his. "I'd have invited you and Spencer to go to lunch with me but Spencer tells me you just finished a late breakfast."

"We did. Our morning got rather busy and we were late eating."

Aston smiled. "So I heard." He shook his head then. "I'm envious of Spencer getting a whole morning to himself with a beautiful woman. I'd like to have someone special to be taking to lunch."

Spencer interrupted them, looking at his watch. "Listen, I'd better take Zola home. I know she's tired. Her little mission got her up at the crack of dawn today."

Zola wandered over to look at a few more photographs while Spencer and Aston said their good-byes. Then Spencer came to help Zola back into her coat.

As they started to leave, Zola stopped abruptly and turned back to look at Aston. She was hearing a word for him. It floated up clearly into her consciousness.

"Aston, if you'll go to lunch right now you might not have to eat lunch alone." She grinned at him. "Go to the Garden Café and look for the woman alone at the table by the window in the right front corner."

Aston stepped forward eagerly, his face lighting up. "Will she be a black woman, this lady by the window?"

Zola laughed. "I believe that's what you've been praying for, isn't it, Aston? God likes a specific prayer. I also think you'll find she grew up near the ocean, like you. I think you mentioned that would be nice, too."

"And is she tall with a good smile?" Aston was probably six foot four.

Zola smiled at him. "God isn't hard of hearing, Aston Parker."

"Glory Hallelujah!" He grabbed up his coat from behind the counter and started toward the front door.

"Hey!" Spencer caught his arm. "You're not going to believe God is in the matchmaking business—just like that—are you?"

"Brother, you're a slow man to believe, aren't you?" Aston punched him on the shoulder. "And slow to see. We serve a good God, you know."

He pushed through the door, and then reopened it to look back. "You didn't get a name, did you, Zola?"

She shook her head with pleasure at his enthusiasm. These were the best of times with her gift. "It's Carole," she said, wondering what Maya would think of this. The woman she *saw* in the café was Maya Thomas's daughter.

Spencer watched Aston sprint across the courtyard of the Laurel Mountain Village Mall. He shook his head in amazement.

"Unbelievable. Aston was so excited he forgot to even tell Clark he was leaving for lunch. Let me run back and tell him that he needs to cover the front of the store before we go."

Spencer started toward the back of the gallery. "I'll be right back."

The door opened while Zola waited, and Ben Lee came in, loaded down with an armload of framed prints.

Zola ran to hold the door for him. Benwen Lee, whom everyone simply called Ben, was a Chinese man who ran a framing shop in the Gatlinburg area. Zola knew he framed most all of Spencer's photographs, and she often had Ben frame nature prints for her when she needed a framer for Nature's Corner. He did excellent work.

Zola smiled at him. "Hello, Ben. How are you?"

He walked over and leaned the stack of framed photographs, all wrapped neatly in brown paper, against the counter before answering. "Ahhh. I am not good, Miss Zola." He frowned. "You have been away and perhaps have not heard about my daughter."

Zola put a hand to her heart. "I hope she's not ill."

"No. Missing. No one know where. One day she here, one day she gone." He shook his head sadly. "Police have looked and looked since the first of the year when she went missing and have found no trace of her. There is no peace in that, no peace at all. It is a great sorrow."

Zola put a hand on Ben's arm in sympathy. She knew Seng Ryon was Ben's only daughter. In fact, it was Seng who'd brought Ben to the States. She had married Juan Hee Chen, who owned the Chen Palace Chinese Restaurant in Gatlinburg, and after Ben's wife passed away in China, Seng encouraged Ben to come live with them. He did live with them for a season, but then started his framing business and moved into an apartment over his shop, wanting his own independence.

Zola was truly sorry to hear about Seng. "What happened?"

Spencer came out as she asked this, interrupting their conversation. He spoke to Ben and signed the receipt for the delivered merchandise. Then Spencer looked across at Zola. "Ben's daughter disappeared while you traveled to the South Pacific, Zola. She went out to the bank at the end of a business day one evening and never came back. The police have been unable to find even a trace of her."

"Did she get to the bank?"

Ben jumped into the story. "No. Bank say she never come. Money from the day at the restaurant gone, too."

"The police think it must have been a robbery." Spencer looked at Ben sympathetically. "They don't hold out much hope Seng is still alive. But it's hard for Ben and the family. They have no resolution."

Ben pushed his beat-up, tan fedora back on his head. Zola couldn't ever remember seeing him without that hat on.

"Are they still investigating?" Zola knew all of Ben's family, and it was hard to imagine how grievous this time had been for them.

"Police say there is not much clue, but they are still looking." Ben shook his head sadly. "Juan Hee, Seng's husband, he not same man since she been gone. Seng was right hand partner in the business. She is missed there even though Frank Jie and Zia do much of the work."

Frank was Juan and Seng's son, and he and his wife, Zia, had worked in the business for years. However, Juan and Seng's daughter, Nina, worked for Ben. Zola had known all the Lee family since girlhood and gone to school with Nina.

"I am so sorry about this, Ben." She leaned over impulsively to hug him.

"Someone did this bad thing to my Seng." He looked at Zola pointedly. "We need to know who it is. You see if you can know, Zola. You have gift to know."

Zola chose her words carefully. "Ben, you know I don't know things of myself. I am just some-times used by God to share things as He desires. It's His knowing and not mine. But I will pray the police will find the people who did this awful thing to Seng."

He gave her a stubborn look. "You pray God show *you*. You *make* Him show you."

Spencer stepped in then. "Listen, Ben. I know you are troubled, but this situation isn't Zola's responsibility. She isn't a fortune-teller. Be careful that you don't threaten her."

Ben shuffled his feet.

"I truly am sorry about Seng." Zola patted his arm fondly. "She was a wonderful person."

Ben left then, and the awkward moment passed.

Zola looked over to see Spencer scowling. "That's the sort of thing I was talking about, Zola.

People pushing on you and pressuring you, knowing you have a gift. It could be dangerous for you."

She spoke softly. "And should I have stayed in bed and not come to wake you this morning to photograph the hoarfrost?"

He laughed. "I'm not even going to consider answering that! Come on. I'll take you home, Zola."

Chapter 8

The photographs from the hoarfrost turned out to be spectacular. Spencer knew he would use at least one of the photos in the new book he was working on. Already, several photographs had been enlarged and framed to sell in the gallery as well. Aston said people always stopped to talk about the prints.

February slid into March, and soon April arrived. Spencer saw Zola now and then at the hut behind his house at Raven's Den. He had revisited the church one Sunday and seen her there, too. But he had not asked her out. She was a complicated woman, and he didn't know if he wanted to become more involved with her.

Sitting sprawled on the big sofa in his living room, Spencer realized he was thinking about Zola again. Despite his continual mental reasonings, he thought about her far too often. And whenever he saw her, his blood pumped. He hoped it would go away in time. He didn't want a deeper relationship with her.

In annoyance, he paced back to his office.

I'll check my e-mail, catch up on my correspondence, Spencer thought, seeking a distraction. He sat down at his computer and booted up the system.

Zeke padded into the room to plop down at Spencer's feet.

Spencer reached down to scratch the dog's back with affection. "We just need to get our minds on something else, don't we, buddy?"

He scanned down the in-box list of new e-mails. It was lengthy. He needed to catch up. But then his eye spotted the e-mail from Bowden.

Hesitating, Spencer thought about deleting it— considered not reading it at all. But then he clicked it open.

Hey Two Spence,

Thought you'd like to see this family photo Granddad snapped at Rita's birthday. You haven't seen all of us in a long time and I thought you might enjoy a family shot.

Bowden proceeded to chat away about family doings and the Jackson business. He wrote as though he and Spencer were friends who communicated frequently, when the opposite was so and always had been. They never e-mailed congenially like this.

Spencer drummed the desk with his fingers in irritation. What did Bowden want? Why was he suddenly calling and e-mailing like this? His eyes went back to the e-mail.

Look how my two boys are growing, Spence. Trevor is nine now and Austin is seven. Trevor looks a lot like me, and Granddad. Acts like us, too. Everybody says so. Austin looks more like Geneva. Blond, fair. He's a quiet, gentle kind of kid. Granddad said he should have been a girl. Acts a lot like you used to. Likes strays and weird girls for friends, can't catch a football for crap, and likes to roam around out in the woods.

Spencer scowled. Why was he doing this? Talking about Geneva? Talking about his kids? Spencer had never even seen his nephews. Didn't even know them.

He'd cherished no desire to see Geneva cradling Bowden's babies against her breast. Children that should have been his.

I'm trying to catch you up on the family so you'll feel easier with us when you come home later for the folks' anniversary. I told Mom and Dad that you were going to try to make it. They're really looking forward to seeing you.

Let's look back on all the good times. Bowden

What good times? Spencer's fingers itched to delete the picture and message. But he couldn't bring himself to do it. Instead, he printed it out. He even stuck a piece of photo paper into the printer for better quality.

Flicking off the computer with annoyance, Spencer carried the photograph back over to the couch to study it. The dog padded after him, sitting down and gazing up at Spencer with concern. Zeke could always tell when something was bothering him. Shepherds were good at reading emotion.

"My parents look older, Zeke." Spencer talked to the dog to calm him. "My father has more gray hair and there are streaks of gray in my mother's hair now." Spencer smiled, touching the picture. His mother had her hair pulled back in the traditional bun she favored, and she was wearing her pearls. She'd always loved those for formal occasions.

Spencer's eyes moved over the picture. "Rita looks good. I guess she must have turned twenty-six at this birthday." He did the math in his mind and nodded.

Zeke pricked his ears up, as if carefully listening.

"Rita was only fourteen when I started college." He paused, remembering. "She threw her arms around me and cried when I left. I didn't see her again until she turned eighteen. She came down with Mother and Dad for my college graduation in Savannah. But she couldn't come when my parents came a few years later for the big Chatsworth reunion. She was in the middle of her culinary school."

He petted the dog, letting his mind drift. "Rita always loved to cook—and especially to bake and decorate cakes. That's what she does now with the business. I hear she's greatly prospered that aspect of the catering business working with Mother."

Spencer studied the photo again.

Despite the years that had passed, Rita still had that fresh, happy face. Being the youngest and the only girl, she hadn't felt the pressure from the family to continue in the family business as Spencer and Bowden had or to excel in every endeavor. He'd even heard his mother say that if Spencer had been a girl instead of another boy, she wouldn't have borne any more children. It seemed like he'd always been introduced as "the middle son." *Here is our oldest son, Bowden, our little charmer, and our youngest daughter, Rita, and this is our middle boy, Spencer.*

Not able to avoid it any longer, Spencer studied Bowden, Geneva, and their two boys. Bowden still looked smooth, confident, and handsome. But then, he always had. His boy Trevor did look like Bowden when younger. And the other boy, Austin, looked gentle and less confident in comparison—eager to please. Spencer felt a wrench in his gut. Poor kid. He hoped he toughened up.

His eyes slid to Geneva at last. She was still beautiful, yet she looked less soft now, and she'd cut her hair off. It hung short, just brushing her chin. He studied her more closely. She looked older, too. Spencer realized she must be thirty now, as he was, and Bowden thirty-four. It *had* been twelve years since he'd seen either of them.

Spencer tossed the photo down. He fought tearing it up as raw pain lanced through him and a shaft of old emotions hit his heart. How it had hurt when he learned they planned to get married. When he realized, once again, that his brother had taken one more thing he wanted. Had flaunted one more victory in his face.

He got up restlessly to pace to the window.

"Let's go out, Zeke." Spencer watched the dog jump up in anticipation, offering an enthusiastic bark of excitement. "Let's get out of here for a while."

Spencer took the path down to the hut in long strides, hungry for the peace he always found in that odd place Zola built on the rocky point of Raven's Den.

Rounding the corner toward the edge of the ridgetop, he heard a throaty voice and a soft peal of laughter. Zola. He stopped, frowning. He didn't want her to be here today.

She looked up, catching a glimpse of him, and her face broke into a wide smile. Her dark, curly mane of hair tossed in the April breeze and her warm brown eyes sparkled. She wore jeans today with colorful embroidery stitched down the sides. A bright yellow shirt peeped out from under her old car coat, and a green lizard sat perched on her hand. She'd been feeding the squirrels and birds when he arrived, and all the birds scattered when he and the dog drew near. The two squirrels, however, stayed on the feeder, watching him and Zeke carefully.

As Spencer studied Zola, he couldn't help but see Geneva beside her in his mind. Geneva was so different from Zola. She'd always been poised, polished, sleek, and blond, her movements, her coy smile, and her voice smooth and practiced, her clothes always impeccable. She was the kind of girl that had always liked Bowden and usually ignored him. But she'd fallen in love with him and not Bowden when he was eighteen and a senior in high school. He still remembered how thrilled he'd felt at her interest in him.

Spencer shook his head and focused on Zola once more. Zola in her bright, scruffy clothes, her hair a tangle, her old hiking boots covered with a thin film of dirt, a stray leaf caught in the tangle of her hair. And holding a green lizard on her hand. Bowden's words from the e-mail came back to him: *Acts a lot like you . . . Likes strays and weird girls for friends.* Spencer could almost see Bowden's suppressed smile—could imagine him rolling his eyes over Zola and smirking in amuse-ment if he were here.

Spencer stood hesitant in the pathway. He'd

worked hard to be successful, to be well-thought-of. To be admired rather than ridiculed and put down. When he was with Zola, his past came back to haunt him. He felt like the young boy with the stutter that the svelte girls, who cruised into the house on Bowden's arm, giggled at. Zola made him feel conspicuous and awkward again. She was like what Bowden typically termed "the geeky girls" who always liked him in high school.

She cocked her head to one side now. "What's the matter?"

"Don't try to read my mind, Zola." His voice was edgy and curt.

"You know I don't do that. I *can't* do that." She shrugged her shoulders and walked over to put some more bits of food out on the feeder for the squirrels.

He thought about leaving. Going back to the house. But the hut and the stunning view over the mountains and the valley drew him.

Spencer made his way down the rock path and walked into the wood shelter. He went over to stand by a support beam, gazing out into the blue sky. Puffy clumps of white cumulus clouds floated across the horizon.

He felt Zola walk up beside him after she greeted Zeke. She put a hand on his arm. "That one there." She pointed to one of the clouds. "It looks like a wolf. See? There are the pointy ears at the top and there's the snout raised up getting ready to howl. It even looks like he has teeth." She giggled.

Spencer could see the wolf shape clearly in the clouds as she said it, but it annoyed him to see it. It seemed like the games he'd enjoyed when only a boy. It reminded him of the pleasure he'd always taken in nature because relationships with people had been so disappointing.

"Do you like always being weird, Zola?" He gritted his teeth.

She lifted her eyebrows. "I'm simply myself, Spencer. Not afraid to be who I am. Not afraid to be individual. And not wanting to pretend to be something I'm not."

He scowled. "Only kids look for shapes in clouds."

"Is that so?" She laughed a tinkling laugh, annoying him. "I wouldn't say that to my grandpa. He's very fond of cloud watching. He likes to brag that he gave me 'my eye' for clouds." She punched at his arm in fun, her nose wrinkling as she smiled up at him. Happy. Relaxed.

He pulled away from standing close to her, trying not to let the apple scent of her drift into his nostrils and play with his mind. At Zeke's eager request to explore, Spencer snapped off the leash and gave him the okay to head out into the trails and woods around the hut. Zeke, well-trained, wouldn't go far.

Zola tilted her head to one side, studying him. "What's wrong with you today?"

"Nothing." He snapped the word out as he crossed his arms. "I've just got a lot of adult things on my mind. And I don't have time for foolishness and fancy."

"I see." She went over and sat down in the rocker to rock, closing her eyes and soon smiling. Obviously blocking him out.

It provoked him. He searched for the peace he saw on her face within himself, but it evaded him. Spencer propped a hip on the wall and looked at her.

"I heard Madame Renee came into your shop and threatened you again." He knew he was purposely trying to rattle her peace, but he didn't care.

She opened one eye to look at him and then closed it. "She is often upset with me. We serve somewhat different masters."

"That's kind of pompous of you to say, isn't it?" He wanted to pick a fight with her. "How do you know she's not a Christian, too?"

"Oh, she says she is." She continued her rhythmic rocking. "She tells me she prays before she reads her cards or looks into her crystal ball."

"So maybe she hears from God that way. How do you know?"

She opened her eyes to study him. "You don't call God up on demand like that, Spencer. Perhaps

Madame Renee means well. And I often think she does. But the fortunes she gives people for a fee are not from God, Spencer."

"And so who made you the great authority on who hears from God and who doesn't?" He frowned at her.

She stopped the rocker and sat forward. "Do you always try to pick a fight with others when you are in a bad mood, Spencer? I doubt it makes you very popular, if you do."

"And what would *you* know about popularity?" He felt his face redden. "I'm sure you weren't very popular at school when you were younger— with all your odd ways and that seer gift of yours."

He saw a flash of pain cross her face as she looked out over the mountains. "There are always a small percentage of individuals who seem to rule in every level of schooling. Perhaps even in later life. And, of course, they insist on a specific loyalty and conformity to the popular leaders and their prescribed norms. I may have had my moments when I wanted to fit into those minority groups but I always knew I'd have to compromise my individuality to conform. So I could never do it for any length of time."

Spencer felt bad for a moment that he'd made her remember earlier hurt and rejection. He understood that. "It hurts to be different. To be ridiculed. To always be one step behind and to never be able to step out ahead. To never be respected or liked."

She looked up at him. "Is that how you always felt?"

"We were talking about you." He barked the words at her.

"If you say so." She sat back in the rocker to rock again.

Provoked at the turn in the conversation, he introduced at new topic. "I hear Ben Lee has started telling everyone you are going to get a *knowing* about who hurt his daughter. That you're going to find her."

She sighed. "I guess I need to talk with him again about that."

Spencer paced over to look out at the view again. "It could be dangerous for you having idle talk like that milling around about you, Zola. What if the killer is still around? He might feel threatened about you. He might decide you know something. Might want to silence you. Did you ever think of that?"

Zola stretched her shoulders. "It would be nice to think you could be worried about me, Spencer. But I think you're only trying to provoke me or anger me today. To take my peace because you can't find yours."

He took a step toward her, scowling. "I told you not to read my mind, Zola. To try to analyze me."

"Just a lucky guess this time." She stood up. "I kind of wish you hadn't come out here today, Spencer. I was having a good time before you did. Enjoying all the signs of spring beginning to pop out. Reveling in new beginnings. Thinking of how nature—and people—can always reinvent themselves. Become new. Shed the old."

He stepped toward her aggressively, clenching his fists. "You're preaching at me."

"No. But it wouldn't hurt you to shed some of your old garbage." She shook her head. "It's as easy to be happy as it is to be miserable, Spencer."

"So now you're saying I'm miserable and full of old garbage?" He felt his anger rising.

"You're taking everything I say and putting it in the worst possible light." She put a hand on his chest. "I've certainly seen a new side of you today, Spencer Jackson. A moody, broody, dark side."

She tilted her head to one side, considering him. "It's like you have a foot caught in the past, like an animal with its foot caught in a trap."

"So what should I do, oh wise Zola, chew off my foot like the old fable?"

She pushed at his chest then. "No. Simply open the trap and let yourself out. Free yourself. I believe you are capable of doing that."

He searched for an answer, caught off guard by her words.

"God will help you if you ask Him, Spencer." Her words grew soft.

"Don't mess with my faith, Zola." He clenched his fists again. "I have my own kind of relationship with God and it suits me just fine."

"Does your faith help you? Can you draw strength from it?"

He pulled away from her now. "Stop it. I don't want you digging around in my life, Zola. I have as much a right to my ways as you do to yours. Besides, who are you to say I'm not happy with my life? I don't like you always probing at me."

She watched him quietly for a moment. "You seem so angry at me today. Perhaps you'd like for me to go home. Would you like that, Spencer?"

He could feel the soft peace radiating off her again, and it made him prickly and churlish. "Yeah, why don't you do that, Zola? Just go home and leave me alone."

She studied him, gave him a small wave, and then left. Not adding any more words. Not asking any more questions.

He watched her walk down the hill and then slip out of view as the trail switched north and disappeared into a stand of evergreens. She didn't turn back to wave good-bye at the turn as she usually did.

Zeke sensed her leaving and looked after Zola with questioning eyes, whining with agitation and making Spencer feel worse. He whistled for the dog not to follow after her. He and Zeke often walked part way down the mountain with Zola, and the dog had learned the pattern. The shepherd came back to the hut, obviously disappointed.

Spencer sat in the rocker and tried to find and savor his own peace. But it evaded him. He got up and paced the hut, his thoughts a torment. Surprisingly, he felt worse after Zola left than he had before. He hadn't expected that.

He knew he'd been unkind to Zola. He wasn't usually such a jerk.

Spencer kicked at a pinecone on the floor near the rocker. It was all Bowden's fault. He never should have opened that e-mail.

Spencer brooded for two days after receiving Bowden's e-mail. There had been a time earlier in his life when he yearned for his brother's attention, when he'd have been thrilled to hear from him. But over the years Bowden's teasing, his subtle putdowns, and biting criticism had finally caused Spencer to pull away. When Bowden married Geneva, Spencer lost the last threads of hope for having a warm, loving relationship with his brother. Now, he found it easier to stay away from his family in Richmond—to keep his distance from Bowden.

He unlocked and pushed open the door of the Jackson Gallery on Thursday morning, still feeling broody and preoccupied. Restless and edgy.

"Hello, my brother." Aston Parker got up from

the bench behind the counter in the gallery. As always, he crossed the room to wrap Spencer in a warm hug. Spencer had grown used to Aston's easy affection over the years. But it had taken time. His own family were not the type to hug each other affectionately.

"I've brought Clark some more images to go through." He laid a stack of digital memory cards on the counter. "I put them on cards so he can load them."

"He'll be in later. I'll see that he gets them."

Spencer ran a hand through his hair. He hadn't slept well again last night.

Aston gestured to the little sitting area in the gallery. "Stay for a while. I'll get us a cup of coffee. The gallery won't open for another thirty minutes."

Spencer slumped into one of the sofas, glad for a little company this morning.

Aston brought the coffee back and draped himself across one of the chairs beside Spencer. He was a tall black man, his skin a warm brown, his dark eyes friendly, and his smile a mile wide. Aston and Spencer had been friends for twelve years. They met the first year Spencer started college in Savannah.

"I think I miss having you around, friend." Aston propped his long legs on the magazine table. "The chalet feels lonely some days." Aston had stayed on in the chalet he and Aston previously shared further down the mountain.

"Is that right?" Spencer smiled and realized this was the first time he'd felt a surge of happiness in days.

"Hmmm." Aston studied him. "You look kind of rough, friend. Either you've been out in the field too long or something's troubling you."

Spencer sipped his coffee, not sure what he wanted to tell Aston.

Aston leaned forward. "I'm your brother, man. There's not much we haven't shared. You know about my alcoholic father, my unwed mother, and my brother who spent two years in prison. We've had some long nights of sharing our past, you and I. We've let down our hair about our past lives and rejoiced in the many ways we've overcome." He elbowed Spencer's arm. "It's hardly a time to keep things from me now."

He spoke the straight truth. That's one of the things Spencer had always liked about Aston. That, and the fact that he could trust him.

Spencer heaved a sigh. "I got an e-mail from Bowden on Tuesday. A nice, friendly, brotherly e-mail." He felt his fists clench as he talked and knew his tone was sarcastic. "He even sent me a family picture."

Aston raised an eyebrow. "Hardly the norm for Bowden. My guess is there were some subtle digs tucked into the commentary. What was the main point he gave for writing?"

"My parents have an upcoming fortieth anniversary. Bowden says he's working on me to come." Spencer drank some more of the hot coffee, grateful for the surge of caffeine this morning.

Aston snorted. "Well, I'm sure Bowden didn't present the invitation in a way that made you yearn to be present." He laughed. "But it is an important event. Maybe you should consider going, man. You can face what's there now. You're strong and time has passed."

"We've had this talk before." Spencer knew his voice sounded surly.

Aston crossed his arms. "Yes, and we'll have this talk again until I can persuade you to face the past and deal with it. It's hard to move on until you do."

Spencer looked at Aston over his coffee cup. "Like you did with your dad?"

"Yes. Like I did with my dad." Aston's face darkened for a moment. "It was a hard meeting, but I got freed by having it. It was needed."

Spencer pushed his coffee cup around on the table. "It's not like I haven't seen my parents since I left home."

"Yes, but, man, you haven't been home once in twelve years. It's not normal or natural to stay away for so long."

Spencer snapped his answer. "My home life wasn't normal or natural."

Aston waved a hand. "Ahhh. It wasn't so bad. You were loved, raised with all the advantages, sent away to college, had all your needs met."

Spencer interrupted him. "No, I didn't have all my needs met. And my parents always excused the way my brother acted. Even when it was wrong."

"Your brother is a slick and sly one." Aston shrugged. "And from what you've always said, he's much like your grandfather Stettler Jackson, another less than admirable character. Your brother's flaws probably seemed comfortable to your father—and to your mother—having lived around them so long with your grandfather. Excusing the flaws of family members becomes a pattern in some families."

"They always favored him, too." Spencer felt himself scowl.

"So? My father always favored my sisters, Letitia and Damika. And he was fond of pounding on Jamal and me when he was drunk." He spread his hands. "Was it their fault? Should I dislike them for it?"

"It's not the same thing." Spencer barked out the words.

Aston gave a deep laugh. "Those girls teased and provoked me, too. Made my life a misery sometimes. You've got to be an overcomer, Spencer. Let the past go. And don't worry so much over tomorrow. Live in today. Enjoy the present."

He nudged Spencer's knee with his foot. "Find a nice woman. Kiss a pretty girl. Like Miss Zola Devon." Aston wiggled his eyebrows at Spencer, grinning.

Spencer shifted uncomfortably. "That's unlikely. I messed that up while I've been in this funk."

"Ahhh. So there's more than Bowden Jackson behind this mood of yours." Aston finished off the last of his coffee and set the mug on the table. "You might as well tell me what happened."

Spencer told him about the day at the hut. "I ran her off, Aston. I was rude. I found myself comparing her to Geneva in my mind. And thinking about what Bowden would say about her."

Aston laughed, annoying Spencer. "You need to smarten up, man. If you found another woman like Geneva, you should run hard and fast the other way, not go after her. Don't you know that by now? And considering the good character of your brother, any woman he'd like might be one to steer clear of."

He shook his head. "Good friend, you've spent too many years looking for another Geneva and wishing for some girl your brother would be impressed with. When are you going to stop doing that? It is foolishness."

Aston put a hand on Spencer's arm. "When are

you going to see who you are and seek what is right for yourself—and say the heck with what others think?"

Spencer scratched his neck. "I don't know. I seem to stay locked in the past in some dark way, even when I don't want to stay there. Even after Leena Evanston thieved from me I found myself thinking about how impressed Bowden would have been with her looks, her polish, and her position."

"Man, how can you see that, acknowledge it— and not want to move on?" Aston gave him a disgusted look. "Especially when you've got a nice girl like Zola showing an interest in your sorry self."

"I doubt she'd want to see me again." Spencer sagged back into the sofa dejectedly. "She hasn't even come to the hut at Raven's Den since I ran her off."

Aston looked at his watch and stood up. "Then, man, you go after her. Find a way to tell her you're sorry." He paused. "You do like her, don't you?"

Spencer nodded.

"Then hike your sorry ass down that mountain and find a way to let her know how you feel. Give yourself a chance to have a little happiness, man. You deserve it. You don't deserve any more Genevas and Leenas. Stay away from the kind of women Bowden would want. Why would you want the kind of woman who would like him anyway?"

Spencer knew Aston was right, and somehow it felt cleansing to have admitted what an idiot he'd been. He clapped Aston on the back with affection as he stood up.

"You need to open the gallery," Spencer said, looking out the window. People were already milling around in the courtyard of the mall, probably having just finished breakfast at the Garden Café.

Thinking of the Garden reminded Spencer of Carole. "How are things going with Carole Thomas?"

A broad smile spread across Aston's face. "Very good, man. She is a fine, fine woman. It is time for us old bachelors to be looking around for a good woman at this stage. A man needs that."

Chapter 9

Zola sat on the porch of her farmhouse in a big white rocking chair watching Rachel Lee Howard's toddler play. Rachel Lee sat on the steps below her, where she could hop up and get to Ava quickly if needed.

"She's really grown while I've been gone." Zola smiled.

Rachel Lee blew out a breath. "She keeps me running, I can tell you that."

Little Ava laughed with childish glee as she walked in and out of the door of a big cardboard box Zola had put in the yard for her to play in.

"That box was a great idea, Zola. It's so big it seems like a house to Ava."

"One of my shipments came in it yesterday. I knew you planned to come today and I thought Ava would like it."

"Bye-bye, Mommy. Bye-bye, Zee." Ava waved at Zola and Rachel Lee as she went inside the box again, taking her rag doll with her. She plopped down on a blanket inside the house to play with the doll and a box of blocks Zola had brought out.

Rachel Lee pushed her blond hair back behind her ears. "Thanks for keeping Ava for me this morning while I had my doctor's appointment. I appreciate it. Mama had that ladies' circle meeting and I hated to consider taking Ava with me to the doctor's."

"It was my pleasure." Zola meant it. She enjoyed playing with Ava. They'd dragged toys out of the old toy chest in the house earlier, and then brought the box outside after lunch as the day warmed. The novelty still hadn't worn off the box.

Rachel Lee's voice broke into her thoughts. "What's going on with you and that photographer who's moved up on the hill?" She raised her eyebrows at Zola in question. "Are you still seeing him?"

Zola wrinkled her nose. "I've never exactly been *seeing* Spencer Jackson. I met him when I heard he bought Raven's Den. He still lets me go up to the hut, and I see him there every now and then."

"I heard he came to the house for dinner."

"Nana and Papa Devon invited him home to dinner after he came to church to attend the baptism for Tanner and Delia's baby."

"Well, that visit got people to talking. I'll tell you that. You don't have men over to meet your family very often, Zola." Rachel Lee leaned her back against the porch rails and stretched out her long legs.

"Well, the invitation *wasn't* mine." Zola scowled. She wasn't sure she really wanted to talk about

Spencer Jackson today. Even with Rachel Lee. She hadn't slept well the last two nights since he'd been in that broody mood up at Raven's Den when she last saw him. And she'd avoided going to the hut since.

Rachel gave Zola a confused look. "I kind of thought you'd started to like Spencer. You know." She wiggled her eyebrows. "You said there had been some sparks and that the two of you enjoyed some good times."

"Well, that was *then*." Zola emphasized the last word. She waved at Ava as she went in and out of the box again, the child giggling at herself in the process. Zola grinned watching her. It was hard to stay in a bad mood with a happy toddler around.

"So. What happened with Spencer?" Rachel pressed.

Zola gave in to the inevitable. There was little that Zola kept from Rachel Lee. They'd been best friends since before kindergarten.

"I don't know, Rachel." She shrugged. "He seems to like me. We feel natural and easy together. And then he pulls back. Retreats from me."

Zola leaned back in the rocker and propped her feet up on the porch rail. "He's a very complex man. I know he has some sort of unresolved issues with his family. He gets all testy talking about them. But he hasn't shared."

Rachel Lee picked up one of Ava's rattles and turned it over in her hands. "Well, you're so warm, open, and easy to be around. Maybe you'll be good for him."

She shook her head. "I don't know. He was really broody and dark the other day. Acted like he disliked me. Picked at me critically. He actually told me he wanted me to go home. It was odd."

"Sounds downright rude to me." Rachel Lee made a face. "Maybe something happened to set him off. Sometimes David is moody when he's had a bad day at the college or when he's had to deal with a difficult student or a cranky administrator."

Zola's eyes caught hers. "Yes, but David *tells* you about it. He talks to you about it. He doesn't shut you out."

"I guess." She shrugged and smiled. "And if he doesn't, I can usually wheedle it out of him if I work at it. I have my ways of honeying him into a better mood." She giggled.

Zola tossed the leaf she'd been worrying in her hand at Rachel Lee. "I'll bet you do!" They both laughed. "You and David are good for each other." Zola smiled at Rachel Lee. "I'm glad you found each other."

"Well, I'd like to meet Spencer some time. See what I think of him." She stretched and stood up. "Will you keep an eye on Ava for a minute? I'm going to run into the bathroom and then pack up

Ava's things. I need to get her on home for a nap."

Zola nodded. She got up and walked out in the yard to play peep-eye games with Ava one last time. Zola loved hearing the baby squeal with laughter when she looked into the window of the box at her and said "peep-eye."

She was squatting by the door of the house, handing blocks back and forth to Ava, when she heard Ava say, "Big man."

Feeling a shadow fall over her, Zola looked up to see Spencer.

Speak of the devil, she thought. "Hey, what are you doing here?"

Instead of answering, she saw his eyes widen at the sight of Ava. His face paled. "Is she yours?"

Zola rolled her eyes. "Honestly. What do you think, Spencer? She's fair, blonde, and blue-eyed—and as you've said yourself, I look like a gypsy." She stood up.

Spencer shuffled his feet in embarrassment. "I just asked."

Rachel Lee came out on the porch then to interrupt the awkward moment.

Zola pointed toward her. "Ava belongs to my friend Rachel Lee."

She motioned to Rachel, who was standing with raised eyebrows on the step. "Rachel Lee Howard, come and meet Spencer Jackson. You said you wanted to meet our new neighbor who lives up at Raven's Den."

"Pleased to meet you, Spencer." Rachel walked out to take Spencer's outstretched hand in greeting. "Zola's grandparents have said some nice things about you. And everyone is pleased you aren't overdeveloping Raven's Den."

Zola watched Spencer take in Rachel's fair blonde looks with appreciation.

He looked up toward the mountain. "Did you go up there, too, when you were small, Rachel?"

She followed his gaze. "Sometimes. But Raven's Den and roaming in the mountains was always more Zola's thing than mine."

Zola could see Rachel sizing Spencer up while they talked.

"You know, I'd love for you to meet my husband, David. He isn't a photographer, but he's a history professor at Maryville College and likes to snap shots of historical places. He has a fascination with old photographs and might have some you'd enjoy seeing."

"I'm interested in history and I enjoy old photographs. Perhaps we will get a chance to meet some day."

Zola noted Spencer was being gentlemanly and congenial today. The bad mood seemed to have blown over.

Rachel's face brightened. "Why don't you and Zola come over to the house for dinner tomorrow night? I haven't had a chance to invite Zola over since she got back. It would be fun. Our house is real close by—just down Little Cove Church Road. It's the turn beside the old brick church."

Zola watched Spencer's interest perk. "I've been wanting to photograph that church."

"Well, aren't you in luck?" She gave him a provocative grin. "My daddy is the pastor of that church. And David has some old photographs of the church I'm sure you would love to see."

Spencer swung his eyes to Zola's in question.

She nodded and saw him smile. *My, how the wind has turned!*

Spencer actually smiled. "I think we would be pleased to come, Rachel."

"You just call me Rachel Lee. Everyone else does." She beamed at him. "And I'll look forward to seeing you and Zola tomorrow night."

She reached inside the box house to pick up Ava.

"Is six o'clock all right?" she asked, adjusting Ava to one hip. "We'll have to put up with Ava for a little while, but then she'll go to bed and we can have an adults-only time." She giggled, obviously pleased with herself.

Zola accepted the inevitable. "What are you cooking so I'll know what to bring?"

"Hmmm. Let's see." Rachel Lee put a finger to her chin thoughtfully. "I think maybe a pork loin roast, my grits casserole, green beans I canned last summer. Then maybe a little sweet corn and some of those cooked apples I put up. I'll do biscuits and bake a pecan pie, too. Mama gave me some of her pecans she froze that I can use. I'll stir up some fresh whipped cream for the top."

Zola watched Spencer's eyes brighten.

She grinned at him. "All the Upton women are excellent cooks. You won't be disappointed in dinner, Spencer."

Rachel Lee reached over to give Zola a good-bye hug. "You don't need to worry about bringing anything this time. I know you're working tomorrow."

She sent Spencer a troubled look then. "You're not one of those vegetarians or anything, are you? I always forget to ask those things."

"No, ma'am."

She sighed. "I'm happy to hear that. I've never been good with those tofu and bean things." She headed for her car.

Ava waved at them as Rachel Lee strapped her into the car seat. "Bye-bye, Zee. Bye-bye Man." She looked wistfully toward the box. "Bye-bye, Ava's house."

Zola spotted Ava's rag doll still lying on the blanket in the house just as Rachel Lee started the car. "Wait! Ava's left Sue-Sue behind. I'll get her."

Zola snatched up Ava's beloved doll and tucked it into the child's arms through the window. She leaned over impulsively to kiss her. "Bye-bye, you sweet thing. Zee will see you tomorrow."

As they backed out of the driveway, Zola heard Spencer chuckle. "Sue-Sue?"

Zola frowned at him. "Ava is only twenty-one months old, Spencer. She's hardly going to name her doll Susannah Delores. She couldn't pronounce it."

He grinned. "Who said I didn't like Sue-Sue?"

She walked over to get the blanket and blocks out of the box house. "Carry that box around and put it in the back shed, will you? My niece and nephew might want to play with it later. It's a great box." She walked up the steps of the porch. "I'm going to put these things in the house. Then I'll meet you out back on the screened porch. I'll bring some iced tea."

She came out the back door a few minutes later to find him sitting on the porch glider, pushing himself back and forth with one foot.

"I thought you'd snag the rocking chair for sure." She grinned at him as she handed him a glass of tea and settled into the battered green rocker herself.

Spencer continued pushing the glider back and forth with his foot. "This moves back and forth, too." He slugged down about half the tea, sat the glass on a side table, and then stretched his arms out on the back of the glider.

Zola watched him. "You certainly seem to be in a better mood today."

He winced. "I was kind of a bear the other day."

Zola waited.

He looked out through the screen toward the trees, green with new spring buds. "I thought I'd see if I could find some photo shoots around the farm. And I figured I'd better swing by and offer an apology for my bad manners."

"Any particular reason for your bad manners the other day you want to talk about?" She saw his jaw clench.

"No. Nothing I want to talk about. Can't we just let it go?" He shifted uncomfortably.

Zola looked out into the sunshine of the day. It was a glorious day—so welcome after the winter cold. Everywhere blooms were getting ready to bud. Early flowers had started to peek out around the farmyard. Baby animals were beginning to arrive. She had no desire to dwell on negative, unpleasant memories.

She looked over to see Spencer watching her.

"I see you brought your camera. I assume the other things you need are in that vest with all the pockets."

He patted several of the pockets on the old tan fishing vest he wore over his brown T-shirt. "For short photo trips, or when hiking, I've found I can fit most of the things I need into the pockets of a fishing vest—film, a small zoom lens or two, a couple of filters."

"Makes you look very much the sportsman." She grinned at him. "You want some company on this photo shoot or would you prefer to go alone?"

He sat up alertly. "Are you getting anything about where I should shoot?"

Zola rolled her eyes. "No, I'm not. It's really rare I get things like that, Spencer. Don't start thinking of me like Ben Lee does. That's only an occasional part of who I am."

She leaned toward him with enthusiasm. "But I know some places myself that might have possibilities. I notice things sometimes and think: *That would make a great picture*." She dropped her eyes. "Sometimes I notice things now and think: *Wow. That would make a great shoot for Spencer*."

When she looked up, she found him watching her with his serious hazel eyes. "I see things on my walks sometimes and think of you, too. I'll see something unique or special and think: *Zola would like that*."

His voice had dropped, and the intimacy of his gaze made her shiver. But Zola found herself wanting to pull back instead of responding to him. He might be sweet today but cruel tomorrow. Zola wasn't so sure she wanted to open herself back up to the hurt she knew he could bring.

She got up from the rocker and started toward the porch door. "I'll walk around the farm with you for a while, Spencer. I'd like to get out and explore. See what spring things are popping up.

See what little delights we might find. Are you ready?"

He nodded, seeming to accept that she didn't want to bite at the teasing bait of intimacy he'd thrown out. Zola wondered why he invited affection from her anyway after the other day? He'd seemed to almost despise her then. Zola hadn't liked the ways his eyes looked at her that day, as if she fell substandard to some gauge in his head and came up lacking. It hurt. He'd pushed her away that day. Now here he was again.

Zola could have hurt him back in kind today. Said she was busy. Flipped him off. Sent him on his way. But despite it all, he interested her. And there was something about him that tugged at her. She'd risk a little more time with him to figure it out. After all, he had come by and apologized. That was something.

She led the way out into the sunshine. "Let's go behind the shed before we start down to the farm. If we're lucky, the spider's web I saw earlier may still be there."

They walked around behind the old shed, and then Zola pointed. The web hung between the shed and a tree trunk that grew against the side of the weathered building. It was a gorgeous spider haven, the white webbing intricate and sparkling in the sunlight.

"It looked prettier early this morning with the

dew sparkling on it in the early sunshine." Zola smiled in remembrance.

Spencer took out his camera. "Mornings and evenings are always the best time. But I wasn't sure I'd be welcome too early, and I was afraid to wander around the farm without an escort or invitation." He grinned at her. "I kept remembering you mentioned your grandfather Devon had a big gun."

She ignored him, directing his attention back to the spider web. "This is an orb web, the classic web many spider species build. Usually Mrs. Spider is waiting patiently in the hub, or center, of her silky network. If a juicy insect blunders into her web, she'll rush out, bite him, and carry him back into her hub. She can feel vibrations of anything that hits her web."

Spencer was already taking pictures, leaning a shoulder against the shed to stabilize the shot.

"Look!" Zola pointed. "See that silken thread strung out from the web to that tree nearby? That's Mrs. Spider's dragline. She lays a silky line like that when she leaves her web and then uses it like a safety line to glide back home on."

He looked at it with interest between shots.

Zola stood by the wall of the shed, watching him work. "Did you know a spider can roll up a leaf and fix it in place with silk to make a little leaf hammock to take a nap in? Sometimes if you look carefully in the trees near a spider's web you can find a leaf hammock—and sometimes with Mrs. Spider sleeping in it."

He studied the shot he'd just taken and then looked over into Zola's eyes. "I love the way you see nature, as though everything had character and personality. You make me see things with new eyes."

"Nature delights me. I have no trouble picturing Mother Nature governing her world and its principles like a bucolic monarch. I don't think most people reverence nature enough today. They just plow through it or drive right by it."

"And don't have eyes to see the magic." He finished the sentence for her.

Zola loved it when he was like this. Sensitive, poetic, artistic—alive to the world, with an inner warmth radiating out of him. So different from that dark, brooding man of the other day.

She waited, keeping her thoughts to herself, while he finished his photos of the web.

He looked up. "Could I come back early one morning to try to get a shot when the dew is on the web?"

She smiled. "Sure—if you'll give me some warning the night before. Then I won't freak out to have a man wandering around in my backyard before the sun is barely up."

"I'll call you." He closed the camera and put a small zoom lens back into a pocket of his vest.

"Where does your next inspiration lead us, Zola? To the end of the rainbow?"

She gave him a playful push. "No. We'll head down to the farm. It's spring and baby animals are popping up in different places. There are baby sheep in Uncle Ray and Aunt Augusta's barn. They may be out in the field today; it's so warm. And I want to go by the pond to see if the tadpoles have started to jump out on the land yet."

"To become little green frogs?" He fell into line behind her as she led the way down the woods path from her house toward the main Devon Farm.

She looked over her shoulder at him and nodded. "I noticed the limbs were starting to break through on some of the tadpoles the other day. Most still had their tails, but I bet those are going to be absorbed into their bodies soon. My guess is some fine, alluring little insects have already tempted them to hop out of the water for a snack."

Spencer jumped in to add to her story. "Those little guys really become eating machines once they get to that stage. I read once that a frog can consume over nine thousand insects in a season."

"Yes. And the good thing is that they eat mostly nonbeneficial insects. They're a natural pest-control help to the farmer."

At the farm pond, they found frogs in several

stages—some still at the spawn stage, looking a lot like green fish, some at the tadpole stage, with a more frog-like body now, and others bouncing around in froggy joy in the mud and grass by the pond's edge. Their garumphing noises occasionally broke the silence of the warm day.

Zola sat down on a log to watch the scene while Spencer took photos.

He looked up at one point. "You said the spider was a Mrs. Spider. What about these froglets?"

She gave him a saucy smile. "I definitely think of that little frog there as *Mr.* Frog." She pointed. "He swallows his food whole. He obviously has no manners. And he actually ate one of his fellows—a smaller tadpole—only a few minutes ago. Really tasteless, aggressive behavior. Certainly not the nurturing type."

Spencer laughed—a warm, rich laugh. "Yes, these guys are definitely active, reckless fellows. I can see how the frog in the Beatrix Potter series could have been envisioned by the author spending time watching green frogs like these hatching out."

Zola nodded in delight. "Oh, you mean Mr. Jeremy Fisher!"

"Yes." Spencer looked up from the camera. "I'd forgotten his name."

"Mr. Jeremy Fisher was a lively character. I remember he wore that cute little red waistcoat and patterned vest, and he loved to get his feet wet but never caught a cold. I loved Beatrix Potter's stories and characters."

Spencer chuckled as he took a few more shots. "Great memory. So who was the reckless toad in the *Wind in the Willows* books? Do you remember his name?"

"Of course. Toad of Toad Hall." Zola flopped back onto the grass in the warm sunshine, a little distance from the muddy banks of the pond. She closed her eyes, enjoying the sun baking down on her and the symphony of young froglets in the background.

She felt Spencer drop onto one knee beside her. "Here. Look at this one." He held the digital camera toward her so she could see the shot of the frog leaping in midair.

Zola laughed. "Oh. He looks joyous, doesn't he? Like a storybook character."

There was no quick reply from Spencer. She looked up at him and saw attraction simmering in his eyes. "You make me joyous, Zola Devon. You light up my world like sunshine."

She opened her mouth to answer, only to have it covered with his. An eager kiss. A passionate kiss. A deliberate kiss. How could she resist?

Zola opened her mouth to him, letting him in, and stretched her arms up to wrap them around him. He dropped down to partially cover her body with his, his hands reaching up to thread through her hair. She heard his breath catch and could feel his heart beating rapidly against hers.

Spencer pulled up to look down at her. He traced a finger down her cheek and across her lips. "You are a remarkable and beautiful woman, Zola Devon."

A cloud passed over her thoughts. "You didn't seem to think so the other day. You wanted me to leave. You seemed angry at me."

His eyes looked away from hers for a moment.

Zola reached up to touch his face. "It confuses me when you're so changeable. Sometimes I think the past has you in its grip and you forget to see the joy of the present."

He smiled down at her. "That's it exactly, Zola. And those are my dark moments."

She put her hands on his chest. "But this is not a dark moment, Spencer?"

"No. Not at all." He leaned over to kiss her again.

They were soon lost in kissing and hugging until a loud *Moooo* startled them both into laughter. The farm cows had wandered down to the pond to drink, and one large brown milk cow stood right over them looking down at them curiously.

Coming back to their senses, Spencer and Zola struggled to their feet, Spencer gathering up his camera and the vest he'd taken off.

"Come on." Zola started off across the field.

"I'll race you down to the barn. We can get a drink at the hose and you can photograph the sheep."

The rest of their afternoon was a picture-perfect postcard blur of happy memories. Zola almost forgot the moody side of Spencer from earlier in the week as they laughed together and explored the farm.

Spencer took photos of baby sheep and the children's 4-H goats. He snapped shots of Papa Vern working with the beehives, of the old barns around the farm, and of new flowers peeping up through winter leaves. Zola loved to watch him work.

At the end of the afternoon, Spencer walked her back home before he started up the mountain.

"Zeke will be missing you." She said this to cover her desire to reach out and touch him again. He was getting to her—this deep, artistic man.

"Actually, Zeke has been missing you, Zola. Do you want to come up to see him?"

Zola felt glad she had a reason to say no. The heat was a little too intense between her and Spencer today. "I can't. I have to work for Maya at the store tonight until close. She and her daughters, Carole and Clarissa, are going into Knoxville to see the Disney on Ice show at the coliseum."

"That sounds like fun." Spencer's eyes continued to watch her.

"Yes. It does." She put her hands into her pockets to keep them from reaching out to him. "I'd better go and get dressed and get a bite to eat before I go to the store."

"Okay." He looked down at her, moved a little closer to her, running a hand down her cheek. "I had a good time today, Zola."

"Me, too," she said, keeping her hands firmly in her pockets.

He grinned and kissed her nose. "I'll pick you up tomorrow night to go to Rachel Lee's house at a little after six. Do we need to dress up?"

"No. Just dress casually."

He turned to start up the mountain.

Zola walked up the porch steps to go into the house, but then stopped, listening.

She could hear Spencer whistling in the distance. She grinned as she recognized the melody. He was whistling "Zip-a-Dee-Doo-Dah."

Zola shook her head. Yes—my, oh my—it had been a wonderful day.

Chapter 10

The next evening, Spencer found himself remembering Aston's words as he drove to Zola's house to pick her up. He was glad Aston had encouraged him to make up with Zola—and glad she'd been willing to forgive him yesterday. As Aston counseled, he had taken his sorry ass down the mountain with that intent.

The day had turned into a better time than Spencer could have envisioned, too. Zola was truly a remarkable woman—if a little unusual. Like Aston, she was warm and open. And joyous to be with. He'd never shared a time with her that hadn't brought him some unexpected delight.

When Spencer allowed it, Zola made him feel young and carefree. She made him feel happy. And she stirred him deeply as a man with her spontaneous, generous nature. His kisses with her in the sunny field still haunted his thoughts. He didn't deserve Zola's affection, and yet, he craved it.

She waited for him on the porch of her house, sitting in the old rocker.

"Am I late?" he asked, opening the car door.

"No. I was just sitting out enjoying the twilight."

A big white cat sat on her lap in the rocker,

curled up in sleep. It opened sleepy eyes to look at Spencer as he started up the porch steps.

Spencer stopped with one foot still on the stairs to look at the cat. "He has one blue eye and one gold one."

"He is a she, and her name is Posey." Zola stroked the cat. "Her former owner planned to drown her for being different, because her eyes didn't match. The world is not always kind to nonconformists, to those who are different."

Spencer frowned, wondering if she was talking about him.

"I related to Posey's situation." Zola sat the cat over on the chair beside her and stood up. "I am different, too. Will you drown me for it, Spencer?"

He wondered where this thought had come from and felt uncomfortable.

She reached up to pat his cheek. "We'll see, won't we?" Zola unwrapped the strap of her purse from the back of the rocker and draped it over her neck, an interesting gold cloth purse, covered with colorful sequins and stitchery. She wore a long skirt, in a dark red, with a peasant blouse tucked into its waist. He could see tucks and fancy stitching on the blouse. She looked like a gypsy tonight, and her scent of apples and sultry blossoms drifted in the air around her.

They chatted about mundane things on their trip to David and Rachel Lee Howard's house. Spencer craned his neck to look at the old brick church as they passed it at the turn off Jonas Creek Road. It was so interesting in its architecture.

"How did Rachel Lee meet a professor at Maryville College?" he asked.

"She worked at the college while going to school." Zola trailed an arm out the window like a child might, enjoying the feel of the wind against it. "When David transferred to the college to teach history, he said he felt attracted to her right away. He might have felt free to date her if she'd only worked at the school, but when he learned she was a student he had to back off."

"The prof-student thing?"

"Yes." Zola smiled and nodded. "However, the week before Rachel Lee graduated, David asked her for a date for the weekend after." She giggled. "The rest is history, I guess you'd say. They're happy together. You'll see."

It didn't take long with David and Rachel Lee Howard for Spencer to see what Zola meant. There was an easy harmony between the two. David was obviously older than Rachel Lee, perhaps midthirties. He was a thinker and a typical academic in many ways, his desk and office piled with books and papers, his conversation sprinkled with stories about his teaching and his passion for his subject. But Rachel was his match in many ways, complementing him with her natural, down-home warmth.

It touched Spencer to see the obvious affection between David Howard and his wife—and between David and his small toddler. The child obviously adored him, and David played with her with pleasure, tossing her into the air to make her laugh, riding her on his knee to a nursery rhyme.

The child remembered Spencer, too. "Big man," she said, pointing at him when he came in.

Spencer was never able to induce her to call him Spencer. She couldn't pronounce it, but before the evening finished, she'd started calling him "Pence."

The Howards lived in a new home, built to look like an old farmhouse. It was warm and spacious inside, with an open arrangement between the kitchen, dining room, and living area that made for nice entertaining.

Zola had been right about Rachel Lee having a gift for cooking. Everything tasted delicious, and she made it all seem easy and effortless.

After dinner, David showed Spencer some of his old photos of historical spots around the area while Rachel Lee and Zola cleaned up from dinner and got Ava to bed.

"There are some great places in the Smokies to photograph that many people don't know about." David flipped open some pages of a book. "This is an old church and house back in the Cataloochee Valley on the North Carolina side of the Smokies, off the interstate as you head toward Asheville. Both the church and the house sit on the Little Cataloochee Trail that used to be an old settler's road. It's like an undiscovered, uncrowded Cades Cove over there. Have you been there to shoot pictures?"

"No," Spencer answered, looking at the photos with interest.

"Well, these aren't recent pictures, of course. They were taken a long time ago, but the park has kept this church and house, several other historic houses, and a school well preserved." He tapped his fingers on an old photo of a schoolhouse. "Rachel Lee and I spent a whole day over there exploring a couple of years ago before Ava was born. You should go over there. It's less disturbed than some areas of the Smokies. You could probably get some interesting shots."

Spencer enjoyed an easy rapport with David Howard from the first. He liked the man, and he liked Rachel Lee, who bubbled over with natural warmth and enthusiasm.

"I'd like to photograph the church that Rachel Lee's father pastors." Spencer sat back on the sofa, draping his arm along the sofa back. He'd eaten too much and was more than pleasantly full. "Zola said I could visit one Sunday. I think she said Rachel Lee plays the piano at services. Do you go to church there?"

David smiled. "I do. But it's a vibrantly

charismatic church. A very different experience from my former Episcopal background."

Spencer sensed a story in David's tone. "Was there a problem in that?"

"I doubt I could have married Rachel Lee if I hadn't been able to bend a little in my faith. All of Rachel Lee's family goes to the Jonas Creek Missionary Alliance Church." He grinned. "I was suspect enough being a college professor and having come from up north."

Spencer laughed. "How has that worked out?"

"Well, I guess Pastor Upton's warning was an accurate one." He scratched his chin. "He warned me that if I got around that slippery creek bank of a deeper walk in the Lord long enough, I might fall in. Or the Holy Ghost might push me."

A big grin spread over Spencer's face. "I know what you mean. I churched in the AME Zion church outside Savannah with my friend Aston Parker for most of the years I was in college and living near Savannah. I'm used to that kind of talk about the slippery creek bank."

"Well, that may help you with Zola." David closed the books he'd been showing Spencer and settled back into a comfortable chair.

Spencer waited.

"Zola's special. Unique. Walks to a different drummer." David looked over at Spencer. "But then so do you. You should understand that."

"You think so?" Spencer shrugged. "There's

nothing different about me. I'm only a regular guy."

David laughed. "You forget I've been in your gallery, Spencer. I've seen the way you look at life from your photographs. The last thing I'd call you, Spencer Jackson, is a regular guy."

Spencer felt suddenly annoyed.

David studied him, and Spencer knew David had seen his expression change.

David smiled at him. "When I was growing up, I was always a bookish kid. Wore glasses by the time I was ten. Sucked at football and baseball. Rode my bike three miles every Saturday to go to the library to get books. I was fascinated with history, with old places, old stories. But I'm a professor of history now. I've come into myself."

Spencer shifted uncomfortably.

Leaning back in his chair, David continued. "I wasn't a regular kid, and I'm not a regular guy. I quit wishing I could be only a regular guy a long time ago. And, over time, I've learned that deep down inside most regular guys wish they were more like me and you, Spencer. Or like Zola. But, of course, they wouldn't say so."

Spencer wasn't sure he liked David's words. "Maybe I want to be just a regular guy."

David grinned. "Oh, come on. Be honest with yourself. Look back in the annals of history. Who do you admire? Who comes to mind? The stand-out guys who were different and accomplished something or the regular guys? Your real hunger is to be a guy who stands apart from the crowd—at least, if you'll admit it."

Spencer thought about his words. "I have the feeling you're giving me a familiar lecture."

"Maybe." David crossed one leg over his knee. "I work a lot with college students who are learning to appreciate their uniqueness, who are beginning to get over wanting to fit in with the norm and starting to develop their own individuality."

A flash of annoyance streaked through Spencer. "You think I haven't gotten over that? That desire to fit in with the norm?"

"What do you think?" David quirked an eyebrow at him.

Spencer threw a sofa cushion at him. "I think you remind me a lot of my friend Aston Parker."

David fended off the cushion with a laugh. "I met Parker once in the gallery. Nice guy. I'd like to know him better."

Spencer considered this. "Maybe I'll host a dinner soon up at Raven's Den. Pay you back for the meal here. Invite Aston and Carole, the girl he's dating, Rachel Lee, you, and Zola. Maybe Clark Venable, the other guy I work with, too."

Zola and Rachel Lee came into the room as Spencer stated this thought.

"Oh, that sounds like fun!" Rachel Lee said. She and Zola came to sit down in the living area. "Who does Clark date?"

"No one in particular." Spencer scooped up the sofa cushion he'd thrown playfully at David and put it back on the couch.

"Well, maybe we can fix him up with someone." Rachel Lee put her finger to her chin thoughtfully. "Let's see."

Spencer raised an eyebrow toward Zola and grinned playfully. "Maybe Zola might have an idea. She sort of introduced Aston and Carole."

"I can't think of anyone right off." Zola sent him a forced grin, knowing he was baiting her.

"I've met Clark," Rachel Lee went on. "Kind of a geeky guy, into computers and the outdoors. Doesn't dress up like Aston does to work in the gallery. Lives in jeans. Hmmm." She snapped her fingers. "Let's fix him up with Stacy."

Zola sat up in surprise. "My cousin, Stacy?"

Rachel Lee crossed her arms. "How many Stacys do we know, Zola?"

"Well, I don't know. Stacy doesn't date much and I don't know if she'd come."

"She'd be perfect. And if you can't get her to come, I will. She owes me for something."

"What?" Zola asked.

Rachel Lee waved a hand. "Never mind. But she does." She turned a warm smile toward Spencer. "So when can we all come up, Spencer? I'm dying to see what you've done with Raven's Den."

By the time they left for the evening, a potluck

dinner was arranged for a Friday evening later in the month at Spencer's place at Raven's Den. Rachel Lee planned the event so quickly that Spencer wasn't even sure how it all happened.

"She's good." Zola said this with a smirk as they got in the car.

"What?"

"Rachel Lee. She's good. She can talk anyone into just about anything."

Spencer grinned. "So, was she a bad influence on you growing up?"

"No. She was actually a good influence. Rachel Lee was always one of those genuinely nice people. All the things she talked people into doing were usually good for them."

"Like getting you to eat your spinach?"

Zola laughed. "You saw her getting Ava to eat her peas by singing her a little song about peas tonight, didn't you?"

"I did." Spencer laughed. "They're good people, Rachel Lee and David. I had a great time."

"I'm glad." Zola leaned back and closed her eyes.

The quiet of the evening settled around them.

"Listen." Her voice grew soft. "You can hear an owl."

Spencer heard it then. He hadn't noticed it before she mentioned it. But now, he enjoyed listening to it calling in the darkness.

"What kind do you think it is?" he asked.

"Probably a barn owl." She cocked her ear. "You can tell by the sort of screaming sound it makes, really different from a hoot owl's call."

He thought about that as he started the car and backed out of the driveway. "A barn owl is the one with a sort of white, heart-shaped face, isn't it?"

"Yes." She smiled. "There is a barn owl nest near the old barn behind my farmhouse. Maybe it's one of those owls we're hearing, out hunting mice and voles tonight."

Spencer's interest was sparked. "Do you know where the nest is? Do you think I could get some photos sometime?"

"Maybe." She laughed. "Owls aren't easy to photograph, Spencer. Especially barn owls. They're hard to see. They blend in, look like tree bark. But you can come and try sometime. I'll show you the place where I saw their nest."

When they got back to Zola's house, she didn't ask him in. She stopped at the steps to turn and tell him good-night. "Thanks for taking me to David and Rachel Lee's with you."

"It was a date, Zola. I was supposed to pick you up."

She looked at him in question, cocking her head to one side. "Was it a date? I thought Rachel Lee asked us to come. You didn't ask me out."

He leaned toward her, feeling the hairs on his arms prickle as he got close to her. "Do you want me to ask you out, Zolakieran Sidella Eley Devon?"

Her eyes widened in surprise. "You remembered my whole name."

"I remember a lot about you." He reached out to run his hands down her arms and felt her shiver under his touch.

She swallowed and tried to remain casual. "What is your full name, Spencer?"

"Spencer Gordon Jackson. I'd carve our initials in a tree, but it would be a lot to carve."

"And it would hurt the tree," she finished.

He smiled and leaned in closer. "Let's have a date tomorrow night, Zola Devon. One where I'm asking you out. It's a Saturday night—a good night for a date."

He heard her suck in her breath. "It is a good date night. But I'm scheduled to work at the store until six tomorrow."

"Then I'll pick you up there at six and we'll go out to eat somewhere in Gatlinburg. Wouldn't that be nice?" He slipped a hand up to touch her face.

"All right." She pulled back a little. "I can ride in with Faith tomorrow; then I won't have my car to bring home. Faith works for me and lives nearby. She's Rachel Lee's sister, you know."

"I didn't know." She was babbling and nervous around him. He liked it. All too often Zola seemed to hold the upper hand with him.

He cupped her face in his hands and leaned in closer.

"I probably need to go in," she whispered.

His answer was to brush his lips over hers, to slip his hands underneath her mass of curly black hair, to whisper her name against her mouth.

Spencer looked at her then. She'd closed her eyes to savor it.

It was always like this with her. Magical. Memorable. She always did something to make each time with her one he would never forget.

She reached her hands up to catch the front of his shirt, not opening her eyes. And then she traced her fingers up his neck and over his lips and face.

"I want to know how you feel without seeing you." Her voice was a soft whisper between them.

He closed his eyes and reveled in the moment with her, touching her, letting his fingers roam over her face without looking at her, too. It was heady stuff, and both of them were soon breathing more rapidly.

Impatient then, Spencer caught her against him and kissed her with urgency and passion. It was all the better for the teasing before. Beginning to simmer with sexual excitement, Spencer let his hands start to roam down to cup her hips.

She pulled back, taking his hands into hers. She looked at him then with very serious eyes. "I can't go there, Spencer. I want you to know that right now. In the place I walk in the Lord, I can't go there. The gifts don't flow where there is sin. And I respect too much what is entrusted to me to disrespect the One who gave me His gifts."

"You're trying to tell me you don't sleep around." Spencer tried to steady his heartbeat.

She sighed. "A lot of my dating ends pretty early because of that."

He studied her, looking at the passion still shining in her eyes, seeing her lips still soft and wet from his kisses. She wasn't saying these words because she didn't want him.

She dropped her eyes and then looked up at him again. "You don't have to go out with me tomorrow night now if you don't want to."

He saw the worry in her eyes, the edge of regret and disappointment already beginning. He knew feelings like that.

Spencer kissed her fingers, still laced in his hands. "I want to go out with you, Zola. I'll pick you up at six." He leaned over to kiss her nose, not trusting himself to dive into her mouth again.

"Okay." She stepped back, turning to start up the porch steps, searching for her keys in her handbag to unlock the door.

Spencer framed his hands and took a mental shot of her as she turned back toward him to say good-night. The light from the open doorway framed her in a soft glow—backlighting her— enhancing her special beauty.

"Good-night," she said quietly, starting in the door.

"Good-night, beautiful Zola," he replied.

She turned back at his voice.

Spencer smiled at her, feeling an unexpected tenderness touch him. "You said earlier you were different, Zola. I'm different, too. You won't drown me for it, will you?"

"No." She smiled back at him. "I will cherish you for it. I believe it is God's intent for us each to be unique and different."

He watched her wave and shut the door.

Walking back to his car, Spencer worried if he might drown in a different kind of way with Zola Devon. And he wondered how she might change him in the process.

Chapter 11

Zola sat at the counter in Nature's Corner the next day looking through a stack of purchase orders, while Faith Upton Rayburn visited with two store customers. Zola smiled to herself to hear Faith at work. She had a natural Appalachian gift for getting to know a stranger quickly.

"Well, isn't that something?" Faith nodded her head at the older woman she talked with. "Your husband being a Bales probably means the two of us are related back somewhere."

She flashed the woman one of her sunny smiles. "My mother was a Bales before she married. Her people go back to Ephraim and Minerva Bales. Their old cabin still stands on the Roaring Fork Nature Trail. Have you and Mr. Bales been there yet?"

The older gentleman pricked up his ears, eager to learn more about how to find the Nature Trail just outside of Gatlinburg.

Faith gave the couple directions to get to the Ephraim Bales cabin. "The Jim Bales cabin is on that road, too. You can pick up a little auto tour book to tell you all about it. Who knows? They just might be your great-great-grandparents."

A chat about genealogy ensued.

Faith walked over to the pile of homemade quilts stacked on a shelf near the silky pareus.

"You know, two of these quilts were made by Minnie Bales Jenkins. She lives right here in the region. She's probably kin to you, too. You really ought to look at her work. She might be one of your Bales cousins."

The couple from Ohio oohed and aahed over the quilts, and they ended up buying two to take back to their married children in Cleveland. As the woman exclaimed, "I'm sure our children will be thrilled to get a handmade quilt probably made by one of their Appalachian relatives."

They left the store, delighted with their purchases and eager to drive the Roaring Fork Nature Trail to see the two Bales cabins.

"Good job." Zola smiled at Faith. "That was a big sale for us today."

"What?" Faith always seemed genuinely surprised at the idea that she'd benefited the store. It was part of her charm that her natural interest in people dominated her sales instinct.

Maya grumbled only yesterday about Faith. "That woman could talk the legs off a jackrabbit. She makes a friend of every stranger she meets."

"Yes, but she often outsells all of us," Zola replied with a grin.

It was the truth.

Faith walked over to lean on the counter near Zola. "Isn't it incredible," she said, "that a couple of tourists would walk in here today, coming all the way from Ohio, and probably be kin to me?"

"Yes, it is." Zola smiled at her.

Faith frowned instead of smiling back. "You know, it worries me, Zola, that Ben Lee keeps telling people you're going to find the person that hurt his daughter."

It was typical of Faith to rapidly change subjects, too.

She shook a warning finger at Zola. "Ben's daughter has probably been murdered and that's a dangerous business. I don't like Ben spreading rumors like that." Faith put a hand over Zola's. "What if people really believe you can somehow know who the murderer is? That criminal might still be out there somewhere and come after you."

"I doubt that." Zola put the stack of orders back into a file, satisfied all were correct.

Faith fingered the seashells in a basket on the counter thoughtfully. "Well, it really is sad about Seng Ryon, Ben's daughter. She was a non-talkative, no-nonsense sort of woman, but she was a good person. And she worked real hard at that restaurant, too. It must be awful for her family not knowing what even happened to her."

Zola listened to Faith's chatter with affection. Faith was Rachel Lee's older sister by ten years, and she'd often looked after both girls when they were smaller. She was now happily married to Dalt Rayburn, a fiddler and one of the members of the Rock Hill Boys bluegrass group. Dalt's people lived in Wears Valley and Dalt, like his father, was a fireman at the Wears Valley Fire Department. His mother was head cook and kitchen administrator at the Buckeye Knob Camp.

"How are your children, Faith?" Zola asked. The store had grown quiet for a few minutes, so it was a good time to catch up.

"Heavens, Logan's in that shooting-up adolescent stage and all his pants are suddenly too short. And Lila's growing up, too, and getting all fussy about her clothes and wanting to wear lipstick." She rolled her eyes. "I told her not to let her Granddaddy Upton see her in lipstick! You know what he would say!"

Zola smiled, remembering Reverend Upton's strict rules about makeup and dress for girls. "I remember he wouldn't let Rachel Lee wear lipstick until she turned sixteen. She used to put berry juice on her lips."

Faith laughed. "Lila does that same thing. And Alicia copies her. She's in first grade now. Let me show you her new school picture."

Faith dug into her purse to get out pictures of her four children. "Taylor, my third," she said, tapping his photo. "He's gotten his daddy's fiddling gift. He just won the junior championship for his age group. Lordy mercy, he can surely play the fiddle."

"I'll bet Dalt is proud."

"Well, sure. But he's proud of all his children. They've each got their own gifts."

The phone rang, interrupting them.

Faith answered, "Nature's Corner, this is Faith."

She listened without comment to the caller, and then hung up slowly. "Now that was a right odd call, Zola. Some man mumbling in a muffled voice about a bomb. Isn't that peculiar?" She looked at Zola in confusion. "It sounded like he said it was all your fault for his bad luck and that you needed to pay."

Before Zola could consider a reply, the front door opened, and a man dressed in black, wearing a ski mask over his face, threw something into the store. He slammed the door behind him afterward, and then started racing frantically across the courtyard of the Laurel Mountain Village Mall.

A canned-looking object rolled across the floor of the store and then began to emit smoke and make a whistling noise.

"Oh, my gosh!" Zola felt her heartbeat escalate. "Quick, Faith, out the back!" Zola grabbed Faith's hand and raced for the back of the store. They both heard the explosion as they pushed their way out the door into the alley. The store alarm went off, shrieking into the air, and total chaos ensued at the mall.

Thirty minutes later, Zola sat patiently filling out a report with the Gatlinburg police chief, Bill Magee, when Spencer pushed his way into the store.

"Are you all right, Zola?" he asked, elbowing his way around the policeman trying to block the doorway.

She nodded, while the young officer began to protest about Spencer pushing past him.

"Let it go, Raymond," Bill Magee said. "Jackson owns the store a few doors down. He's naturally concerned and he obviously knows Zola."

The officer let go of Spencer's arm then, allowing him into the room. Spencer made his way to Zola, searching her face, looking her over anxiously.

A soft warmth rolled through Zola's being. He was worried about her. "It was only a smoke bomb," she assured him. "Sounded and looked scary. Made a lot of noise. But was essentially harmless."

Bill Magee looked up from his paperwork. "Faith and Zola got a threat call and right afterward some man ran up and threw a smoke bomb into the store. The women acted smart— they ran out the back. And when the bomb exploded it set off the alarms. We're looking for who did this right now."

"What kind of threat was made?" Spencer's face grew angry. "And who would threaten Zola?"

Magee shrugged, his attention on his paper-work. "Something about Zola causing bad luck."

Before Spencer could comment, the young officer interrupted. "I just got a call, Chief. They picked up the man who threw the bomb. Caught him from the description of his car and the license number a tourist gave."

Zola turned her eyes to his. "Do they know who it is?"

The officer nodded. "Yeah. It was Aldo Toomey, the kid that does the local deliveries around town. You know, the one who works for the Beardsleys." He scratched his head. "Don't reckon he's ever been in much trouble before."

The chief phoned in to the station as the officer finished answering Zola's question. He stepped away from the counter for a little privacy while being filled in on the arrest.

"I know Aldo," said Zola in surprise, her mouth dropping open at the officer's words.

"Yes," added Faith. "He's that froggy-looking kid who's always coming in here running his mouth about how he's going to win the lottery or the Powerball. Always full of pipe dreams."

She gave Zola a puzzled look. "Aldo doesn't quite seem like the bomber type."

"No." Zola agreed, trying to remember what she knew about Aldo.

The chief hung up the phone. "I think we're about finished here. I may need you to come down to the station later. To see if you can identify Toomey."

Faith looked up. "He wore all black and a ski mask but he seemed the right size, now that I think on it." She scratched her head. "I just can't figure out what got into Aldo to do such a thing. I mean, he ain't the brightest bulb on the Christmas tree, but he isn't normally mean-spirited."

"No, he's not." Zola frowned. She tapped her fingers on the counter as she thought about this and then looked up at the chief with determination. "I'm going down to the station with you, Chief Magee. I want to hear what Aldo has to say about this."

"I don't think that's a good idea," Spencer put in with a scowl. "It might be dangerous. He threatened you."

Zola sent a warning look his way. "I think I'll do as I see fit, Spencer Jackson. And we can take a rain check on that date we planned."

It was about six p.m., the time they'd agreed to go out to dinner together tonight. Zola knew this was why Spencer happened to be in the area.

She turned to Faith. "Do you think you can clean up here and then close the store by yourself, Faith? I think we ought to close early after this. There's still smoke in the air but it ought to settle out by morning. Besides, most of the visitors we'd get now would probably be curiosity seekers versus buyers."

Faith nodded in agreement. "I'll sweep up and

spritz some air freshener around before I leave."
She waved a hand at the gray soot till floating in
the air. "This smoke might irritate folks' eyes if
we stayed open, too, but it'll be gone by the
morning."

Zola reached under the counter to find her
purse.

"You sure you don't want me to come with
you?" Faith asked. "I'm a bit worried like Spencer
about you confronting Aldo if he's still upset or
acting demented."

Zola shook her head.

"I'll go with her." Spencer stepped forward.

Zola turned to him, ready to argue.

He put up a hand. "We've got a date, remember," he reminded her. "After this situation is
cleared up, we'll go out to eat like we planned."

Spencer sent her a smug look before she could
protest. "Besides, you don't have your car. You
drove in with Faith. I can drive you home afterward."

Zola remembered he was right. She had ridden
in with Faith.

"If you're sure you don't mind," she replied,
having too much on her mind to put up further
arguments.

Bill Magee started toward the door. "I'll see
you both down at the police department." He
turned to look back at Zola. "And you'll *only* get
to talk to Aldo if I think it might do any good or

183

shed some light on this. Be sure you know that, Zola."

As it turned out, she did get to talk to Aldo Toomey. She told Spencer about it over dinner. He'd taken her to Howard's on the parkway, a fine steak house that had been in Gatlinburg for over fifty years.

"I hope you like steak," he said, as he parked the car.

"I do." She ventured a smile, although she still felt edgy and keyed up.

"Good." He grinned boyishly at her. "Howard's is my favorite date place."

She sent him a pouting look. "So that means it's not a place you chose especially with me in mind?"

"I didn't know anyplace Tahitian in the Burg." He grinned back at her.

Zola giggled, dissipating some of the tension she felt. "Well, I'm going to be an expensive date," she said, offering him a sassy reply. "I want those wonderful fried mushrooms they have as an appetizer."

"Umm." He took her arm as they crossed the street. "I like those mushrooms, too. We'll share."

After the events of the evening, Zola wasn't sure why Spencer seemed in such a good mood, but she felt grateful for it. The afternoon had been stressful, and she'd been rattled and frightened by the bomb being thrown into the store. Even though it turned out to only be a smoke bomb, she and Faith hadn't known that at the time.

Settled in a cozy booth now, she and Spencer sat working their way through two of Howard's fresh dinner salads. The dim lighting and the hum of soft conversation around them felt soothing.

Zola licked raspberry vinaigrette dressing off her finger, thinking about her talk with Aldo.

"Ready to talk about it?" Spencer asked, picking up on her thoughts.

Zola blew out a breath. "I guess. You heard Faith say Aldo is always getting whipped up, saying he's going to win the lottery or Powerball. Well, he said he had a dream about some numbers and then the next day the numbers in the dream exactly matched the packing number on a box he was getting ready to deliver."

She shook her head. "Well, Aldo became convinced that he held the winning numbers for the big Powerball giveaway going on. The prize amount had risen to several million dollars—a lot of money. He babbled all this conviction to Madame Renee, the fortune-teller on the highway coming in to Sevierville. Evidently, Aldo took a delivery to her store and they got to talking."

"Is this the same Madame Renee you've had run-ins with before?" Spencer asked.

"Yes," she answered. "And Madame Renee looked into her crystal ball and told Aldo she saw that he would win the Powerball on those numbers. She called it a series of fortuitous signs."

"So what happened?" He forked up a bite of salad as he asked.

"Aldo got even more excited and started making winning plans—that he'd drop out of school, quit his job, and get into NASCAR racing. He decided he'd buy a Corvette to start, for local races, and then move up." She shook her head, remembering. "He actually came into the store a week or so ago telling me all this. I listened but I told him I saw that he should not buy a Corvette or quit school or his job. I told him that I knew he was excited over the coincidences of the numbers, but that I believed his numbers were not the winning numbers."

Zola sighed. "I saw clearly they weren't."

Spencer leaned forward, propping his elbows on the table. "And that's what made him come after you?"

"No. There's more." She took another bite or two of her own salad before she continued. "Aldo didn't listen to me. He bought the car, dropped out of his college classes, and turned in his notice at Beardsleys. The officers said he went all over town telling everyone how rich he was going to be."

"I gather he didn't win," Spencer said, before popping a fried mushroom into his mouth.

"No, he didn't win, and he was angry. Now he couldn't pay on the Corvette and he didn't know if he'd be able to get back his old job." She sighed. "He went to confront Madame Renee in a snit and told her he should have listened to me instead of her. He claimed it was all her fault he'd gotten himself into this trouble because she told him he would win."

Spencer considered this. "Well, it didn't help things with a guy like Aldo."

"No, it didn't." She sipped at the white wine Spencer had ordered.

"What did Madame Renee do?"

"Well, that's the worst of it. She convinced Aldo I'd 'cursed' his luck and caused him not to win the Powerball."

Spencer raised an eyebrow. "I gather she's one of those people that can't admit to being wrong?"

"Evidently." Zola fidgeted with her napkin. "Aldo fits a pattern, too. He's one of those people who always sees the messes he makes in his life as being someone else's fault—and never his. So, of course, he got angry at me."

Spencer interrupted in annoyance. "And he decided to punish you by scaring you and throwing a smoke bomb into your store?"

Zola nodded. "That's about it."

"He told you this?" Spencer tapped his fingers on the table with annoyance.

"Yeah, I think Aldo regretted what he'd done as soon as he did it." She spread her hands.

Spencer snorted. "And regretted it even more after he got caught and realized he might serve time over this."

Their steaks arrived and conversation paused as they talked to the waiter who brought their dinner. They'd ordered Howard's T-bone steak for two with baked potatoes.

Zola put pats of fresh butter on her potato and then looked across the table at Spencer. "I didn't press formal charges against Aldo. He'll have some issues to work out with the police on his own, but I didn't add to them."

Spencer laid down his steak knife after cutting the meat. "You felt sorry for him." His mouth quirked into a slow smile.

She studied his face. "I thought you'd be critical of me for not pressing charges."

"No. How could I? I didn't have the police arrest Leena Evanston when she tried to rob me. How could I be critical of you?"

She smiled. "I forgot about that."

He shrugged and took a bite of his steak. "Eat." He pointed to their steak. "This is great. And I hear red meat is good to help with stress."

She watched his mouth twitch. "You've never heard that about red meat in your life," she accused, spearing a bite of steak with her fork.

He grinned at her. "Maybe not specifically, but it's probably true. I'm sure there's a study out there somewhere that documented it."

She laughed. "I'm glad you stayed around and still took me out to dinner tonight, Spencer."

"Is that right?" he said, raising an eyebrow and studying her with those smoky hazel eyes.

"That's right. You've made a bad evening better."

Later, when he drove her home and walked her up to her porch, he laid a hand on her arm. "Do you think Madame Renee is the type to get vengeful over this and cause you further trouble?"

She wrinkled her nose as she thought about it. "No. I think she'll hear about what happened and worry that some repercussions might come her way over this."

He smiled. "She'll probably take a malicious delight in knowing your store got smoke-bombed."

Zola blew out a breath. "She probably will. She's a very strong-willed and opinionated woman. And highly competitive."

"She sees you as competition."

Zola sighed. "I guess."

He put a hand up to her face. "I'm sorry she sicced Aldo your way with her lies."

"Me too."

Spencer leaned in to kiss her then, and Zola felt herself tense.

He stopped before his lips touched her mouth. "It's only a kiss, Zola. I won't ask for more than you want to give."

She smiled at him in the moonlight. "And what if the more-I-want-to-give is to go on a photo shoot with you one morning again?"

He kept his lips next to hers as he answered. "I'd tell you to be ready at seven o'clock tomorrow morning. I'm going out early."

She threw her arms around him and kissed him then with abandon. "Will you really let me go?"

"Of course," he said against her neck. "You bring me luck."

"I hope I bring you blessing," she said, tracing her fingers down his arms.

"That, too," he said softly, wrapping her in his arms again.

A little later, he pulled away to look at her.

"What are you thinking?" she whispered.

"That you are very beautiful in the moonlight and that I wish I had a camera to capture this moment to remember it."

She touched his face with her hand. "Just snap the photo with your memory. Then you can never lose it."

He brought his hands up and made a clicking sound. "There. It's done. A moment never to be forgotten."

Spencer stepped back, preparing to leave.

"Thanks for being there for me tonight. I appreciate it."

"I owe you a few, Zolakieran. I'm glad I could be there for you."

Zola hugged herself in the chill of the evening as she watched him leave. He had made a bad evening turn into a good one.

She stood on the porch until his car was out of sight down the drive.

"I guess we'll simply have to wait and see how this all turns out, Father," she said on a soft prayer as she let herself into the house at last. "We'll just have to wait and see."

Chapter 12

Spencer went to bed thinking of Zola and woke up thinking of Zola. The woman was getting to him. He still couldn't decide if that was a good thing for him or not.

He padded out on the porch to let Zeke out and to check the light. Day was just breaking, but it looked like a good morning for photos, the sky clear with no rain clouds in sight.

Spencer stretched and thought about his plans for the day. At mid-April, the wildflowers were blooming. Butterflies and newly hatched insects were out. Birds were returning, and many small animals that had been hibernating or holed up for winter were enjoying the spring weather. Spencer's goal had been to randomly hike up some trails and see what delights he might stumble on today. That made it a nice sort of day to take Zola along.

He talked to Zeke as he made his way back inside. The big shepherd trotted along eagerly beside him toward the kitchen. "Zola probably wouldn't like to go along on some of my shoots that take me wading through swampy lowlands or sitting for hours watching duck nests."

Spencer reached down to scratch Zeke's head as he poured out his dry dog food. "You eat up, friend, and I'll take you out for a short walk before I head out."

He pulled up to Zola's house shortly before seven to find her sitting on the porch waiting for him. She picked up a backpack that sat by her chair and grabbed a small cardboard box sitting on the table.

Spencer got out to open the door for her and gave her a teasing grin. "Packing light, I see?"

"Actually, yes." Her answer was saucy. "The pack is all I'll be carrying on the trail. The box has some breakfast food in it, plus some extra bottles of water."

"I brought coffee." He pointed to the thermos and cups in the SUV as she climbed in.

"Good, I like coffee," she said, buckling her seat belt. "But I like food in the morning, too."

"Trail bars?" he asked, climbing into the driver's seat and starting the motor while he snapped his seat belt.

"Better." She dug into her box and brought out warm bagels and a container of cream cheese. She proceeded to spread cheese over a bagel with a plastic knife.

"Girly food." He grinned at her.

"Don't knock it until you've tried it," she said, popping a bite of bagel slathered with cream cheese into his mouth.

The bagel had a warm, wheaty taste and was laced with soft raisins. "Mmm, pretty good."

"Did you eat before you came?" she asked.

"No." He looked both ways before heading out of the driveway and onto Jonas Creek Road. "I usually only bring snack bars and portable food along. I eat as I get hungry."

"I thought of that idea but decided this would be better—since I wouldn't be driving." She began peeling a big navel orange now, and soon broke off a juicy section to offer him.

"I feel like a baby bird being fed by its mama."

"Then open wide." She grinned and tucked the orange section into his mouth.

He caught her hand with his and nibbled on her finger. "It's kind of sexy being fed by a woman."

"Believe me, I do not feel sexy at seven a.m." She pulled her hand away from his to take another bite of her bagel.

Spencer let his eyes rove over her. Zola wore jeans and a snug-fitting T-shirt today. A gray knit hoodie hung loosely over her shirt to ward off the chill of the early morning. She'd pulled back her dark, wavy hair today and caught it up with a clip, but the curls were already escaping to drift down her neck.

"You look sexy to me." He caught her eyes with his and reached over to trace a finger down her cheek.

He saw a wary look in her eyes that surprised him. Evidently, he wasn't the only one wondering about their relationship.

She put his hand back on the steering wheel. "You seem to be in a pretty good mood today."

Intuitively, he knew she was remembering the times he'd acted more broody and moody. She'd seen him in one of his darker moments, too.

He drove silently, thinking on this, while she picked up the newspaper on the seat to browse over the front page. Zola passed him bites of bagel and orange as he drove.

They made quick time through Gatlinburg in the early morning hours. The tourists were still sleeping in, and even the town had just begun to wake. The only places busy at this hour were the restaurants serving breakfast and the hotels checking out travelers heading home.

Zola's troubled voice interrupted Spencer's thoughts. "Oh, no," she said, her eyes still on the newspaper. "A little kid is lost up in the mountains. His parents must be worried sick."

Spencer poured more coffee into both their car mugs. "I saw that piece earlier," he replied, taking another bite of the bagel she offered him.

He watched her eyes scan the newspaper article. "It says here he was with a Scout group camping in the mountains and wandered off." She paused, an anxious frown darkening her face.

"Lord have mercy, Spencer, he's only eight years old and he's been out all night. They've searched for him since yesterday afternoon."

"I heard something about that on the news last

night." He merged into the turn lane to swing a right at the Sugarlands Visitor Center. "The television news reporter said eight Cub Scouts hiked that short trail down from Clingmans Dome Road to the Mount Collins shelter to spend the night on the mountain. Evidently this one kid took off when they were looking for kindling around the camping area. The other Scouts and their leader didn't miss him for an hour or so and when they couldn't find the boy they called the rangers."

"Well, bless his heart. He must be scared to death. I hope they find him today."

Spencer reached over to snag another orange section from her hand and rustle the newspaper playfully. "Got any good news in there?"

She grinned at him. "Why sure. Dolly Parton's in town for some event having to do with her Imagination Library." She paused to sip her coffee. "Isn't it wonderful she gives children free books every year through that effort? She is one fine person."

Spencer changed gears as he started up the mountain.

Zola looked out the window then. "By the way, where are we going for this photo shoot? We've left Gatlinburg far behind now."

"Well, my plan was to try for some early wild-flower shots today, maybe find some spring wonders for my new book. I thought the Little

River Trail out of the Elkmont area might be a good place for photos."

"Oh, that's a favorite trail of mine." Zola turned a sunny smile toward him. "Further up that trail after the bridge is a stunning display of phlox and there are snowy orchids along the early trail if you look carefully for them."

"So I've heard." He smiled at her.

She sighed. "I can climb out onto some of those big boulders in the stream to sit in the sun while you're shooting your pictures."

"Maybe. But we have to stay together, Zola. That's important." He frowned.

"You're thinking of that child. If he'd stayed with the others, or with a buddy, he probably wouldn't have gotten lost."

"Yes. It's one of the first things you learn in scouting—the importance of a buddy."

She patted him on the knee. "Well, I'll be your buddy today, Spencer Jackson. And the lunch I brought is even better than the breakfast."

He resisted the urge to capture her hand and hold it on his leg. "What did you bring us for lunch?"

"Ham and cheese sandwiches, made with some of Nana Etta's fresh-baked ham," she recited. "Chips, pickles, fresh pineapple chunks in a Ziploc bag, and homemade sugar cookies."

"Sounds good."

She nodded.

An hour later, they'd hiked almost a mile up the Little River Trail. Spencer had found a bounty of trillium to photograph, both the white and yellow variety. They'd discovered fire pinks, showy orchis, and a world of different violets along the trail. Spencer even cut down a side path to photograph the remains of an old, rusted-out car left behind from the logging days.

"I read that old car was a fancy Cadillac once belonging to one of the logging superintendents," Zola said as they walked on up the trail.

Spencer grinned. "Doesn't look very fancy now." He hoisted his tripod over one shoulder.

Zola swung her arms happily while she walked. "Have you photographed anything special you might include in your new book today?"

"Maybe. That squawroot you discovered is interesting."

She wrinkled her nose. "It's a parasite, you know. That's why it's yellow like it is and not green like most plants. It steals its chlorophyll from the trees it grows under."

She paused to take off her jacket and tie it around her waist. "You know, squawroot is really common in the Smokies, Spencer. I thought this book is supposed to be about hidden treasure in the mountains and the unexpected. Perhaps we'll run across something more unique."

Spencer put out a hand to slow down her pace. "Maybe we just did, Zola. You might want to walk more to the left side of the trail."

She followed his eyes, and Spencer heard her quick intake of breath. "That's a rattlesnake, Spencer." Her voice came out in a whisper. "You don't want to mess with him. He's a big one."

The large snake lay coiled in a circle on a sunny spot on the side of the trail. His mottled, brown snakeskin almost blended in with the dirt.

"He's just resting in the sun on the side of the trail." Spencer studied him. "I don't intend to bother him or interrupt his siesta, but I think I might be able to get a shot or two of him if we're quiet about it."

Zola retreated backward and climbed on top of a big rock beside the trail. "You don't usually see snakes on well-hiked trails like this. They don't like people, and they try to stay away from places tourists frequent."

Spencer focused his camera. "Yes, but it's early. We haven't seen anyone on the trail except for those two guys hiking down from Jakes Creek when we first got out of the car. He probably thought he could snag a little nap in the morning sunshine before the tourist traffic kicked in."

He heard her blow out a breath. "You know, I really think I could skip this experience, Spencer, and slip on by this big guy. Why don't we simply let him sleep on? I'm not fond of snakes."

"I'll only be a minute." He squatted down now to plan and frame his shot. "This rattler blends in so beautifully with the trail and the rocks behind him. I think he'll make a great photo."

He snapped off a few shots without the rattler even moving a muscle. Then the big snake seemed to sense the light from the camera and lifted his head from out of the coils. A soft rattle followed as he saw them.

"That's a warning. Time to go," Spencer said, skirting carefully backward to catch Zola's hand as she climbed down from the rock.

They walked quickly up the trail, staying as far away from the snake as they could. Spencer heard Zola breathe a deep sigh of relief when they moved out of sight of the reptile.

"I hope he's not there when we come back." She shivered slightly at the thought. "We really should have stayed clear of him."

"Yeah, but I got some great pictures." He stopped to back up the digital camera to show her the shots he'd taken.

"Eeew." She made a face. "You zoomed in really close. It looks like you were right on top of him instead of a safe distance away."

He grinned. "They're great shots. Maybe I can use one of them in the new book."

"Hmmmph." She snorted. "I'd hardly call a rattle-snake an unexpected treasure in the Smokies."

He laughed and swatted her on the bottom. "It's all in the eye of the beholder, Zolakieran."

Farther up the path, they found the sweeps of

purple phlox Zola remembered seeing on an earlier hike on the trail. The flowers spread gaily in a broad, sunny area beyond the bridge that spanned the Little River. In a cluster by the stream bank, Zola also found lush stonecrop, with star-like white flowers, for Spencer to photograph. It was a pretty spot.

"We can sit here in the grass by the bridge and eat our lunch if you like," Spencer told Zola.

He scanned a nearby hillside. "You get our things out while I walk up that hill to get some shots of those ferns around that fallen log."

She nodded and smiled as he started up the slope.

A short time later, Spencer came back to find Zola sitting quietly on a log by the bridge, the picnic still not out of her backpack. She looked tense.

"What's the matter?" he asked, squatting down beside her.

She looked up at him with big eyes. "I see the child."

"What child?" He dropped down to sit beside her, puzzled. "What are you talking about, Zola?"

"The child that's lost. I can see him."

Spencer felt a chill go up his spine. He hoped Zola wasn't seeing a little corpse or something.

"Is he all right?" Spencer finally asked.

"He's hurt." She closed her eyes, looking

pained. "It's his foot, or his ankle or something. I can feel how much it hurts. He can't walk anymore."

"Where is he?" Spencer laid a hand on her arm. "Can you see that, Zola? Can you see where he is?"

"Only sort of." She shook her head. "The Lord said you'd know where he is."

He stood up then, irritated. "Well, that's nuts, Zola. How would I know?" He frowned at her. "You're the one that does this seer stuff."

She took his hand and stood up, too. "No, Spencer. It's the Spirit that sees. We're simply the channels or the vessels for the spiritual gifts. And God is no respecter of persons. Everyone has the gifts deep within. It's only that not many people walk in them."

He scowled. "I don't think I'm going to be of any help here, Zola."

She led him over to a big boulder by the trail. "Here, sit down with me. I'll tell you what I see and then you've got to pray to know the rest. Otherwise, we can't go find him."

He blew out an exasperated breath. "Why can't we just hike out and tell the rangers what you've seen, Zola? I've got a cell phone in the car. We can call this in."

She gave him a small, patient smile. "Rangers and police like facts, Spencer, not what they call 'speculation.' They don't put a lot of credence in the spiritual for answers to practical matters. Think about it and you'll see why that probably isn't a good idea."

He considered it. "Yeah, I guess you're probably right. Even I have to admit the whole thing sounds kind of nutty and I know you."

She shook her head. "We have to go find him, Spencer. He isn't too far away for us to get to. I know that for sure. And he's praying for help."

Spencer heaved a big sigh. "So tell me what you know."

"He didn't mean to get lost. He thought he was taking a little shortcut over this hill back to the shelter where they were staying. Only it didn't work out like he planned."

"People need to stay on the maintained trails in the Smokies." Spencer kicked at a stick below the rock they were sitting on. "They always get in trouble when they get off the trails."

Zola put a hand on his leg. "He didn't mean to get lost, Spencer, and he's truly sorry now that he tried that shortcut."

"You said earlier you saw he was hurt."

She nodded. "He wandered for a long time trying to find his way back. He must have gone deeper into the woods instead." She closed her eyes again. "I think he found a stream at some point and thought if he followed that it would be good."

"You learn that in Scouts," he put in, "that if

you follow a stream it will usually lead you out, keep you from going around in circles. It also gives you something to drink if you get really thirsty."

She put her hand in his, continuing on. "About dark he found a trail. He got excited, thought maybe it would take him back. But he soon realized he was in a different place." She paused. "He kept following the trail and the stream, because he didn't know what else to do. Then he stepped in a hole—or something—and fell."

Zola winced as if she felt the pain. "That's when he hurt his foot. He hobbled on in the dark, scared at all the night sounds, until he came to a place he thought would be safe to stay."

She looked at him with dark eyes. "This is the part I can't see well. It's by the creek but there seems to be a wide place by the trail. I see two creeks and two trails nearby. The trail he was walking on was steep, going downhill."

Zola stopped, shrugging. "That's all I have."

He frowned at her. "That could be anywhere, Zola. Half the trails in the Smokies follow streams and there are hundreds of places where trails intersect."

She gave him a stubborn look. "Well, that's where he is, Spencer. It can't be too far from here or we wouldn't have been given the knowledge to find him."

Spencer stood up, restless now. "There's no 'we'

in this, Zola. You're the one who's been given this to see."

"Let's both pray," she said, giving him an imploring look. "Maybe we'll get some more. We need to find him."

Watching her drop her head and seeing her lips start to move, Spencer felt convinced enough to offer up his own silent prayers, too. He prayed she would see enough that if it were possible for them to find this child, that he would know where he was more clearly.

"Do you see anything more?" he asked at last.

She shook her head.

"Tell me anything else you saw before." He propped a foot on the boulder where she sat. "Anything, no matter how insignificant it seems."

She closed her eyes in focus. "The trail the boy came down before he got to the place I saw had some rough creek crossings. He felt scared getting across. There was a sort of broken-down bridge at one point but he was afraid to try to walk on it."

Spencer tried hard to think if he'd ever been on a trail that looked like this. He shook his head in frustration. "Did you see anything else, Zola? About where he is now. Anything odd or unusual."

She wrinkled her nose. "There is some sort of sign about being careful about bears."

Spencer's head snapped up. "I think I know

where he might be." He felt adrenalin rush through his system. "There's a campsite farther up on the Little River Trail. It's about a mile and a half to two miles from here. The rangers have posted a warning sign there because there's been so much bear activity. There wouldn't be a sign like that at any place except at a recognized campground."

She grabbed his hand to squeeze it as he talked.

He looked up the trail thoughtfully. "It would seem more likely that he wandered out along the Appalachian Trail or down Sugarland Mountain Trail below the Mount Collins shelter where he started out. It wouldn't seem logical he would have found his way over the ridges and down to the back end of the Little River Trail. Not many people hike the trail to its upper end because of all the rough stream crossings." He searched his memory. "I think there is an old rotted-out bridge toward the end of the trail, too. I walked up there hoping to photograph hawks one day."

Spencer turned to look at Zola's now-hopeful face. "I've only hiked that way once, Zola. My memory might not be right. I haven't received a vision or anything. It just seems likely from what you are telling me."

"I think what you're getting is right," she said, jumping off the rock to take his hand. "Let's hurry. He needs help and he's frightened."

Spencer led the way, and they began to follow

the trail as it climbed higher into the Smokies. He noticed scaly sycamore trees along the way and wished, for a moment, he had time to stop and take a few photographs. It was a beautiful area. The river tumbled along to the right of the trail, and the sound of the cascades often filled the air.

After a mile, they came to a trail intersection. Zola gave Spencer a questioning look then. It gave Spencer an odd pleasure to tell her they needed to continue on straight. He estimated the campsite he knew about was probably a half mile farther up the trail.

"Do you know this child's name?" he asked, curious about the depth of her gifts.

"Eddie," she said with certainty. "It's Eddie."

He shook his head in amazement at her as they walked on.

They crossed a bridge over another stream—pouring in from the left—and then rock-hopped over several other sections of the Little River as it split out. Spencer pointed to their right as the campsite came into view.

Zola took Spencer's hand in a tight grip as they scanned the area. They saw no sign of a child.

"Eddie!" Spencer called in a loud voice.

A small shape hobbled out from behind a group of trees, holding to a stick with one hand and to the tree trunk with the other. "Here!" he called, waving a hand. "Over here!"

Relief surged through Spencer at sight of the boy.

After a happy moment of rescue, and some tears the boy tried hard to brush away, Spencer settled Eddie down on a fallen log so they could examine his foot.

"There are no breaks I can discern," Spencer said, after running his hands over Eddie's ankle and foot. "My guess is that you've got a severe strain, maybe even a torn piece of ligament."

He dug in his backpack to locate an Ace bandage and began to wrap Eddie's ankle in a figure-eight design.

"Nice work." Zola watched. "How did you learn to do that?"

"I was an Eagle Scout. Scouts learn a lot of things they might need to know in an emergency."

Eddie hung his head. "I was dumb and tried to take a shortcut over a hill back to the shelter. I thought I'd seen Garrett go that way. He was my buddy and we were supposed to stay together, but I must have gotten confused. I didn't realize I was lost for a while and then I didn't know what to do. I called out a lot and thought someone would hear me, and answer, but no one did. I turned around and tried to go back the way I came, but I must have screwed up or something. The woods got really dense and thick."

He winced as Spencer finished his bandage. "I walked for a long time and then about twilight I found a stream. I remembered in my Scout book that if you get lost you should find a stream and follow it."

Spencer smiled at Zola. He'd told her that.

"I came to this trail later and I got real excited then, thinking it would lead back to our shelter, but it didn't. Uphill led me to a campsite and the end of the trail, so I started back down the trail then, hoping I would find someone. I was really glad to get out of the woods and all that underbrush and stuff." He brushed at scratches on his arms and face.

Spencer started cleaning up the scratches with water and a clean cloth. He handed Zola a tube of ointment to spread over them.

"I was doing all right, I guess, for a kid, until it got dark. Then I couldn't see and it was really creepy and scary." He made a face.

"I kept going but then I tripped and fell in this hole or something. Man, my ankle hurt when I tried to walk. I managed to get down the trail a little more using a stick and I found this camp-site area."

His voice broke. "I knew I couldn't go on." He pointed. "I slept over there under that rock overhang. And I put leaves all over me to stay warm."

"That was smart," Spencer commented.

Eddie grinned. "I saw it on this TV show once." Less cocky now, he added, "I thought maybe wild stuff wouldn't find me hidden under the leaves, either."

"Seeing the bear sign probably didn't give you a lot of comfort."

Eddie's eyes widened. "I didn't see that until this morning. I was real glad I didn't see it last night."

Spencer laughed, in spite of himself. "Are you hungry, Eddie? Zola and I brought lunch. You can eat a little with us and then I'm going to piggyback you out of here." He looked at Zola. "Do you think you could carry my pack and camera tripod if I carry Eddie?"

"Sure." She smiled at him.

"I'm really glad you came," Eddie said. "How'd you know my name and where to find me?"

"Weren't you praying?" Zola laid a hand over his.

Eddie dropped his eyes. "Yeah. Big time."

"Well, God heard and He sent us."

Eddie looked amazed. "No kidding? How'd He do that?"

"I saw a picture of you in my mind, and Spencer helped me know where the picture was from the times he's hiked in the mountains around here taking photographs."

"Cool." Eddie looked from Zola to Spencer with an awed expression. "Did God tell you my name, too?"

"He did. He was really concerned about you."

"Wow. I'm going to tell my granddad that. He's our minister as well as my granddad. He always told me God answers prayer and to never forget to pray. He was, like, really right, wasn't he?"

Zola smiled. "Yes, he was really right." She handed him a half sandwich. "Here, eat this. There are some chips and sugar cookies, too."

Eddie gobbled down lunch, and Spencer, after eating some of his own, took photos of Eddie before they started back down the mountain.

It was a three-and-a-half-mile hike down from the campsite, but, fortunately, they ran into some other hikers at the Huskey Gap Trail intersection. The two men took turns piggybacking Eddie down to the trailhead. One of the men carried a cell phone with him, and as soon as they got in range of the campground, he was able to call in to let the ranger station know Eddie had been found.

"What's your last name?" one of the men asked.

"DeLozier," he said. "Eddie DeLozier. I'm with Scout Troop 284 out of Knoxville, and our leader's name is Mr. Warren." He bit his lip. "It's not Mr. Warren's fault I got lost. You tell them that."

Spencer smiled at Zola over this comment.

Shortly before they got to the end of the trail, Zola laid a hand on Eddie's cheek. "I'm real glad you're all right, Eddie. But I'd appreciate it if you only told the rangers Spencer and I found you when hiking up the Little River Trail taking photographs."

She smiled at him. "Of course, you can tell your granddad and your family about God hearing your prayers, but I think it might be good if you didn't tell the rangers and the people from the press all of that. I'm sure there will be photographers and reporters from the newspapers when we get to the end of the trail—all glad to report to the media that you're okay. Everyone has been worried, you know."

The child nodded wisely. "Newspapers sometimes make God-stuff sound dumb. I've heard my granddad and my dad say that. My dad told me it's because God-stuff isn't very factual. He says newspapers like factual stuff."

"That's it, Eddie." She leaned over to give him a kiss on the cheek.

The man carrying Eddie laughed then. "When all those media people get to heaven, they're sure going to get a surprise about what's really factual, aren't they, lady?"

"Yes, they are," Zola said, laughing with him. "They certainly are."

Despite Eddie's efforts at cover-up, Spencer and Zola still ended up in the newspaper for finding and rescuing Eddie. It made a good story, after all. Even the two men hikers ended up pictured in the newspaper for their part in helping to bring Eddie down the trail safely.

A little over a week later, Spencer received a

note in the mail from Eddie. He called Zola to tell her about it that evening.

She laughed that warm, musical laugh of hers. "What did he say, Spencer? Read it to me."

"He said: 'Dear Miss Zola and Mr. Spencer . . . Thanks for coming to find me when I was lost. I was scared and really glad you came. I'm glad you listened to God to know where I was. That was way cool. . . . Thanks for fixing my ankle, too. It wasn't broke, but I have a wrap for the sprain until it gets better. My scratches are all healed up, and I've only had one bad nightmare about a bear getting me. . . . My Granddad and my parents are going to bring me to see you when I get better. I hope that's okay. . . . Your friend forever, Eddie.' "

"Ahhh." She sighed audibly. "Isn't that the best? Thanks for calling to read that to me before I fell asleep. If you were here, I'd give you a big kiss, Spencer. That sweet letter made my day."

"You hold that kiss in thought until tomorrow. I'll collect it when you come help me get ready for our houseful of friends coming for dinner."

She laughed. "Oh, I'd almost forgotten tomorrow night is when you're having the potluck at your place."

"Yeah, and you promised to come early to help me before everyone arrives."

He heard her yawn. "Your place is beautiful, Spencer. I don't know what you're worried about. And it's only friends that are coming—David and

Rachel Lee, Aston and Carole, Clark and Stacy, and me." She giggled. "You know, I still can't figure out how Rachel Lee orchestrated getting Clark and Stacy together. She says they've actually had a date and really got along."

"I think Clark is a little smitten."

Spencer walked out onto the porch to check on Zeke, who was nosing around the bushes nearby. "Clark says Stacy likes *Star Trek* and *Star Wars* and that she has a cool collection of X-Men comics. He's enchanted."

Zola's laugh floated over the line once more. A warm happiness welled up in Spencer whenever he heard her laugh.

"Eddie sent a picture," Spencer told her, changing the subject.

"He did?" Her voice rose in excitement.

"Don't get too excited. It's one of those school photos, but it's kind of cute. I have a better one that I took."

"But it's sweet he sent one, isn't it?"

"Yeah."

Her voice changed then, sounding suddenly tense. "Go get Zeke, Spencer. He's nosing around under a tree where some yellow jackets have started building a nest. I don't want him to get stung. Or you, either."

Spencer whistled for the shepherd while she was still talking. The dog reluctantly pulled away from the tree trunk, where he'd been nosing in the underbrush, to respond to his master's call. Spencer could see a few yellow jackets flitting around even in the light from the porch.

Zola was still talking. "After you put the dog up, Spencer, you go pump that hole full of wasp poison when it grows good and dark—and after those yellow jackets settle down for the night. Put a plastic tarp over the nest, too, and then cover it with gravel and dirt to smother those wasps. It's not a very big nest, yet, so it won't be too dangerous to deal with it."

She paused. "You wait until the jackets settle down though, Spencer. Zeke stirred them up digging at their nest."

Spencer didn't even ask anymore how Zola knew these things without being here or even seeing the insects starting to stir.

"Promise you'll be careful around those yellow jackets, you hear? They're nasty when they get riled up." He heard her sigh audibly. "You'll need to call me a little later and let me know you're all right after you deal with them. Will you do that? Otherwise, I'll have trouble getting to sleep."

"I'll call you," he said, letting Zeke back into the house and heading for the kitchen to look for a can of wasp poison.

"It's under the kitchen sink," she said, before clicking off the line.

Spencer rolled his eyes before hanging up his

own phone. "That woman was watching out for you, Zeke," he told the dog. "But, mercy, her knowing things like she does gives me the creeps sometimes."

He wondered again if Zola was the sort of woman a man could be comfortable living with for a lifetime.

Chapter 13

Zola finished sprinkling the last of the coconut on her layer cake and checked the sausage-cheese balls in the oven. She was bringing dessert and appetizers to the potluck dinner at Spencer's tonight.

She looked at the list stuck on the refrigerator with a magnet. Spencer had ordered a baked ham and was providing the drinks. Rachel Lee and David were bringing fresh green beans and a potato salad, Stacy chocolate brownies for a second dessert item, and Clark nacho dip and tortilla chips. Aston was cooking a baked beans dish and Carole bringing spiced, cooked apples. They certainly wouldn't have any lack of food.

She heard a tap on the door and wiped her hands on a cloth before heading to answer it.

To her surprise, it was Perry Ammons from the church.

"Hi, Zola," he said. "I was visiting Maude Gardner down the road and got an impulse to stop by. I hope it's okay."

"It's fine, Perry." Zola opened the door to let him in. "Come on back to the kitchen. I'm getting ready to take something out of the oven. I can fix you a glass of iced tea and we can visit while I keep an eye on what I'm cooking."

"Mmmm, smells good." He sniffed the air appreciatively as he followed her back to the kitchen.

"It's the sausage-cheese balls that smell so good. I'll give you a few when they come out of the oven." She gestured to a chair at the kitchen table. Then she took two glasses out of the cabinet to fill with cold tea already prepared in the refrigerator.

Perry took a long sip of his iced tea after Zola set it down beside him. "I hear I may have you to thank that I was asked to take the interim position as pastor at Highland."

Zola sat down at the table across from him. "Not really. I only planted a little seed idea with Reverend Madison one day. I'm sure he'd have asked you regardless of that. You're a good minister, Perry."

"That's *Reverend* Ammons to you now, Zola." He grinned at her boyishly.

She laughed. Zola had known Perry since they were kids. They'd gone to the same high school together.

Perry toyed with a set of palm tree salt and pepper shakers on the kitchen table. "Actually, Vernon Madison told me he probably *wouldn't* have thought to ask me to fill in when he moved if you hadn't suggested it. He said he assumed I'd be too busy with the Creekside Wedding Chapel to carry a pastoral load."

218

"And are you?" Zola asked candidly.

He smiled. "I might have been, except a retired minister, Henry Wheaton, moved in near Tracie and I a few months ago. Henry was already filling in for us at Creekside when we needed someone to do ceremonies. He's handling most everything now that I'm at the church full-time. It's working out great."

Zola remembered something Spencer asked her earlier. "What denomination are you ordained through, Perry? I don't think you ever said."

"When I got converted back in high school and felt led to go into the ministry, the first person I told was the pastor at Highland Presbyterian then, Reverend Downey."

Zola couldn't help interrupting. "I loved Reverend Downey. He was such a good, kind man."

"Well, I'd never gone to any church except for the times I visited with Tanner Cross at Highland, so Reverend Downey was the only minister I knew. He helped me get my scholarship to college, and, of course, all his ties were with the Cumberland Presbyterian College. So I went there."

She smiled. "So you *do* have the right degree!"

He looked puzzled. "Is there a wrong degree, Zola?"

"No, I mean you have the right degree—and the appropriate training—to take the position full-time at Highland if you're asked."

"Ahhh. And are you seeing I should do that?" He grinned at Zola again.

"Well, sure." She got up to check the sausage balls and seeing they were ready pulled them out of the oven and set the second tray inside to bake. "You'd be perfect."

"Thanks for your confidence, Zola. But I still need to give a lot of prayer and thought to that, to see if I think it's what God wants me to do. That's important to me."

"I know that." She handed him several sausage balls on a napkin. "It's because I know how close your heart is to the Lord that I thought you'd be a good choice for Highland, Perry."

His eyes caught hers in question. "And was it *your* idea or God's idea that I come in as interim, Zola?"

Zola sat down across from him again. "Originally, it was God's idea. It came to me when I was getting the word that Reverend Madison was moving. But when I thought about it later, I realized I agreed with the Lord wholeheartedly that you would be a good choice." She grinned at Perry and wrinkled her nose in fun.

Perry shook his head. "You carry an interesting gift, Zola. But I worry about how freely you use it sometimes—without thinking of the potential consequences. Like with this Aldo Toomey thing. You and Faith might have been hurt if he'd thrown a real bomb into the store. Also, I'm concerned about this talk that Ben Lee believes you're going to find his daughter's killer. This kind of thing could be dangerous for you, Zola."

She sat watching him. "Are you saying you think I shouldn't give people the words God asks me to give them?"

Perry reached across the table to put a hand on hers. "I think you know I'm not saying that, Zola. But I wanted you to know if you ever want to run your visions by someone else before you share them I'd be happy to be that person for you."

Zola squirmed in her chair. "It doesn't work that way, Perry. The knowledge rises up at the moment it's supposed to be given. It isn't the sort of thing one can ponder and think about for a time before sharing. It's a 'right now' kind of thing."

"Give me an example," he said, popping a sausage-cheese ball into his mouth.

She dropped her eyes—thinking—and then looked across at Perry. "Remember when that little boy was missing in the mountains a week or so ago?"

He nodded.

"I was in the mountains with Spencer Jackson on an early morning photo shoot when I saw that child, Perry. I could see where he sat, I could see what he looked like, and I could feel his pain and fear. I saw that he was praying for help and I knew Spencer and I were the ones to be used to rescue him."

She shook her head. "How could I have sat on that, Perry, and waited for a confirmation from someone before I acted? The child could have died. I was responsible to act then."

Zola watched him consider this.

"I see. Is it always urgent in that way?"

"Maybe not always as serious as that, but I always feel very strongly I am supposed to share what the Spirit is giving me right then. Not later. It's like an act of obedience to do it when the word is given to me."

Perry ate another sausage ball and drank some tea, thinking on this. "Your gift is like a mixture of word of wisdom and word of knowledge— both spoken about in Corinthians. It's not common to many."

He looked thoughtful. "I know from growing up with you that your gift has always set you apart. Made you different. That must be hard some-times, Zola."

Zola smiled at Perry. "I came to terms with being different a long time ago, Perry, when only a small girl. I was fortunate my family was accepting of my gift; it would have been hard for me if that hadn't been so."

Zola reached a hand across to take Perry's. "Thanks for wanting to help me, even for worrying about me. That's kind of you."

She stood up to take the last of the sausage-cheese balls out of the oven.

Perry cleared his throat. "I'm a longtime friend . . . but I'm also your pastor now, Zola. I want you to know I'm available to you if you ever need me for anything."

"Thanks," she said, turning off the oven and sitting down again.

Perry sat quietly for a few minutes, and Zola could tell he had something else on his mind.

"You've been seeing Spencer Jackson," he said at last, stating it as a fact, not a question. "How is he handling this aspect of you?"

"It's not easy for him," Zola said candidly.

"I'll bet." He bit into his last sausage ball.

She laughed then. "I think he does better with the big things, like my seeing the lost child, than he does with the small, everyday things I sometimes see."

Kind eyes looked at hers. "Do you want me to talk to him about this?"

"No. We're not to that place yet, and, besides, Spencer has a whole set of peculiar issues I have to deal with, too." She wrinkled her nose. "He has a bunch of trauma from his past he hasn't gotten resolved yet. Our problems are not all one-sided."

Perry stood up to leave. "Well, I know better than to put my oar in too heavily with a dating couple. I'll just pray the Lord will have His best will in your developing relationship."

She grinned at him. "Sounds like a good plan to me."

He laughed. "I like you, Zola. You remember that, and if you ever need me as friend—or a pastor—you know where I am."

"Thanks again, Perry." Zola reached out a hand to take his in a handshake. "I really appreciate that."

She stood on the front porch and waved as Perry drove away.

Back in the kitchen, as she cleaned up, Zola found her thoughts drifting to Spencer. She wished sometimes she *could* "see" things to help in her day-to-day relationship with him, but it usually didn't work that way.

"You know, I could use a little help here in unlocking the dark places in Spencer Jackson, Lord," she prayed out loud. "I'd really like to be able to help him but he sure keeps himself locked up tight."

Not getting any ready answer, Zola began to put all the sausage balls into a storage container. She had work to do.

The day passed by quickly, and Zola was soon caught up helping Spencer at Raven's Den get ready for his guests to arrive. And then later, after dinner, enjoying herself thoroughly with a group of close friends.

By eight o'clock, they all sat around together in Spencer's big living room, finishing up the last of their dessert and drinking after-dinner coffee. The paddle fan overhead hummed softly to accompany their conversation, and the sound of night frogs drifted in from outside.

Aston propped his long legs on a footstool. "I guess you've all heard the latest update on Aldo Toomey." A big grin split his face.

Stacy looked up in surprise. "Isn't that the guy who threw the bomb into Zola's store?"

Aston nodded.

"So fill us in," David encouraged.

"Well, you know he got off with only probation since Zola wouldn't press charges and because it was his first offense." He took a sip of his coffee.

"Plus he got his old job back," Zola added. "He came by to tell me that. He'd turned in his notice, but the Beardsleys let him stay on."

Rachel Lee leaned forward. "Ray told me the company came and repossessed his Corvette, though."

"Well, I'm not surprised at that," Zola said.

Aston grinned. "But that's not all."

Spencer kicked at him with his foot playfully. "Spit it out, Aston. What do you know?"

Aston laughed. "It seems Madame Renee went out of town on a little vacation. While she was gone, someone painted 'fraud' in bright red paint across her rooftop, very visible to anyone who drove down the highway and passed her business.

They also painted 'crook' on her concrete driveway. The graffiti stayed there for almost two weeks until she came back and threw a fit. She went down to the police station sputtering for them to find the culprit who did it."

He laughed again. "Of course, Madame Renee and everyone else who heard the story had their own ideas about who did the mischief, but there was no proof. And Aldo Toomey acted as innocent as a rose when questioned."

Zola giggled, in spite of herself—as did the rest of the group.

Rachel Lee put a hand over her mouth. "We shouldn't laugh about this, but I do admit I'd love to have seen Madame Renee's face when she got home. She has caused Zola so much trouble ever since she moved here."

"She isn't from here originally?" Spencer asked.

"No, from New Jersey." Rachel Lee made a face. "And I wish she'd go back there. She's caused a lot of problems for Daddy's parishioners and for other ministers around the area."

Carole changed the subject. "Aston and I brought a Catch Phrase game to play tonight—girls against the boys. It's fun. You give hints so everyone can guess the words that come up. We played it with my sister Clarissa and her friends, and Aston liked it so much he went out and bought the game."

"Yeah, and since I paid good money for it, we're definitely going to play it, no arguments!" Aston brought the game out, and soon they were all laughing and passing the electronic device among themselves as rapidly as possible.

By ten o'clock, everyone had said their good-byes, loaded up their dishes and leftovers, and started home. Zola helped Spencer clean up in the kitchen, and then the two went out on the porch to sit and watch the stars in the night sky. A wisp of a moon peeked through the dark trees, looking like a shimmering cradle.

"Everyone had a good time." She pushed the porch rocker into a soft rhythm with her feet. "And everyone loved your house."

He stayed quiet for much longer than Zola expected.

"Anything wrong?" she asked.

"No. I was simply thinking how good it can be to spend an evening with friends that you like. To enjoy an easy, comfortable dinner. To laugh and play games without getting overly competitive or without putting someone else down. To feel good when the evening is over."

Zola knew he was comparing this evening with some past time that had been unpleasant and tense for him. She considered what to say.

"As a girl," she said at last, "I spent most of my time with adults. I was a late child, with my only brother, Wayland, ten years older than me. So by the time I turned six, he was sixteen. Wayland seldom wanted to play games with a sister so much younger. And Daddy and Mother stayed busy with their lives on the island and Daddy's practice."

She paused. "I was different, too, from most of the other island children—my father American and an educated man, my mother from a royal family. We weren't wealthy by American standards, but we had more than most of the islanders. Our house was a two-storied white one, built on the side of a hill with a red tile roof and open porches all around. A twining road wound up to it from the coast road, and from the front porch we could see down the hillsides and out to the ocean. It was beautiful. Any of my young island friends who came to visit felt somewhat awed. Most of them lived in one-story huts with thatched roofs or in plain board houses. I was always the rich girl to them and the different one—part Tahitian and part American."

Zola sighed. "By the time I turned four, my gift had surfaced. That made me even odder to the other children."

"Was your brother unkind to you?" Spencer asked unexpectedly. "Did he like you?"

It seemed an odd question, but Zola decided not to comment on that. "I always knew Wayland loved me. He teased me, of course, like older brothers do, but I was sure of his affection.

Wayland always looked more like my mother's people, like the Kasiors. That helped him. He seemed to fit in better on the island; he had many friends."

"How did his friends treat you?"

She laughed. "They mostly ignored me, as older boys are likely to do with a friend's younger sister. I think my life was relatively typical of what could have been expected being a missionary doctor's daughter."

"I see."

Zola had no idea what that comment meant.

She continued. "Wayland married an island girl he'd known since childhood named Samira. He always loved the clinic where my father worked, so he went away to school and came back to be a doctor on the island." She giggled. "A funny thing is that Wayland took many veterinary classes on the side so he could also doctor the animals on Mooréa. There is no vet there but him. It always ate at him growing up that the animals had no one to help them."

She saw a wisp of a smile touch Spencer's face in the light from the house. She was glad to see it.

"And so there might be a dog or a parrot waiting in the reception room right along with the human patients?"

"Sometimes." She giggled again. "The clinic was once a planter's house, donated by the owner when he died with no family. It seemed even more comical to see a goat being led up the sweep of white steps and across the wide colonial porch into the reception room."

Zola heard him laugh. It was a good sound.

"I like to hear you laugh," she told him.

He leaned over to catch her hand in his. "You make me laugh, Zola." He got up and leaned over her rocker, putting both hands on the rails. Then he bent down to kiss her. "You make me happy, too."

"I'm glad." She kissed him on the nose playfully.

He sat back down in the rocker beside her, pushing his chair into a rhythm to match hers. A comfortable silence fell between them.

"Spencer, tell me about your family." She hoped he would answer, that he would talk.

He didn't answer—simply fell silent.

Zola pressed. "You have an older brother, too." She kept her tone casual. "How much older is he than you?"

She thought for a moment Spencer wasn't going to reply again, but then he did. "Bowden is four years older than me. He and my parents wanted a girl the second time to complete the family. My mother came from Savannah originally, and she planned to name me Savannah, had I been a girl. I was told Bowden threw a fit to send me back after I came home from the hospital because I wasn't Savannah. He kept saying they brought home the wrong baby. My grandfather used to love to tell that story over and over."

Zola waited patiently, rocking.

"I suppose, from the beginning, my brother didn't like me much."

Zola bit her tongue on the words she wanted to say, that Bowden was only four, that little children say all kinds of silly things then.

"My mother had Rita when I turned four." He ran his hands through his hair. "It didn't seem right to name her Savannah by then. Besides, it was one of the nicknames Bowden called me when he was in a taunting mood."

Zola felt a small chill run up her spine.

"Families can be difficult, can't they?" She tried to interject a carefree tone.

"Yes, and families can be dysfunctional in some ways. Mine was. My Grandfather Stettler ruled our family. My father followed in the ways he was expected to, worked in the family photography business. Fortunately, Grandfather Stettler liked my mother, Marion. She was a Chatsworth, from a fine, old Southern Savannah family. She had graciousness and charm, and she knew how to behave and to do what she was expected to do."

He paused. "Grandfather Stettler quickly learned the skills my mother had and he liked her earlier dream of wanting to open a catering business in Savannah. Her dream became a catering business added on to the Jackson photography business in Richmond instead. My mother was talented; she made the family richer with her skills. Rita is much like my mother, but less serious and intense. She was the only one in the family who ever seemed to laugh in a way that wasn't stilted, controlled, or malicious."

Spencer sighed heavily. "Bowden turned out exactly like my Grandfather Stettler, and Grandfather doted on him from the get-go. Bowden was the favorite and could never do anything wrong. If he got in trouble for anything, Grandfather forgave it and brushed his behavior aside. This gave Bowden the opportunity to perfect being a bully, and he was never deterred in it."

Zola knew without asking that Spencer had often been the target of his bullying. She winced and fought not to comfort and hug him. She knew it a hard thing for a child to grow up with quiet, subtle abuse—of any kind.

She worked for a light tone. "So, you had a creepy older brother and a somewhat fun younger sister. It could be worse, I guess."

Spencer looked across at her with a scowl.

A long space of silence fell between them, and then he looked at his watch. "I guess I'd better take you home. It's getting late. I need to get out early for a photo shoot."

Zola knew somehow she'd said the wrong thing somewhere, causing Spencer to clam up again.

She went into the kitchen to get her dishes. "It was good of you to host everyone here." She smiled at him. "And it's started a pattern. Aston says he's going to host the next get-together down at his place with Carole to help him."

Zola gave him a playful punch. "Plus, planning this event helped to get Clark and Stacy together. I really think they like each other. It's kind of sweet, both of them being a little odd but getting along so well."

Spencer tensed with some random thought he was having, his face growing broody and dark.

Great, Zola thought. *What a happy ending to the day. Spencer falling into one of his foul moods.*

They drove home to Zola's, almost in silence, and Zola found herself glad to say good-night and leave Spencer to his own gloom at last. It was depressing to be around him when he was like this. And she didn't know what to do to help him.

Chapter 14

Spencer knew Zola was unhappy with him when he took her home. She thought he ought to be able to act cheerful by will—like she did. Well, sorry, but that wasn't how he was made.

Zola tried to help him see his home life hadn't been so bad, like Aston often did. But, then, Aston and Zola hadn't lived through his childhood. They hadn't watched Bowden get everything he wanted. They hadn't watched Bowden never get punished for the cruel things he did and said to others—or the cruel things said and done to him.

Bowden's favorite line, when chastised for taunting Spencer, was, "Oh, I was only teasing. Spencer knows that." But it was more than that. Bowden had a cruel streak, and Spencer, too often, got the brunt of it.

In a surprising twist, Bowden never acted cruel to Rita. He often called her Rita-Savannah. He acted loving to her and encouraged her talents. It was probably the reason Rita never really understood how Spencer felt when Bowden got in one of his moods to bully and tease. She was never his target.

Bowden most often targeted Spencer outside the house, too, with no family witnesses. This might be in the neighborhood, at school, or in the yard.

Perhaps this was why Spencer learned at a young age to retreat, to make himself scarce, to avoid Bowden whenever he could.

Spencer stalked through the fields this morning, thinking these thoughts while he took his photographs. He was taking pictures of rabbits, chipmunks, and random insects today— creatures that made their homes in wild fields, overgrown with weeds and vegetation. He wore boots and jeans to protect his legs from the brambles. His mood was dark, but his pictures didn't suffer for it. He'd caught a fantastic shot of a rabbit, standing poised and bright-eyed, his ears high in the air.

Spencer had come here today because he knew rabbit burrows lay hidden in the high field grass. He'd even gotten lucky enough to snap a shot of baby bunnies still coiled up asleep in their nest.

After snapping a last close-up of a delicate green praying mantis that almost completely blended in with the green plant he clung to, Spencer closed up his camera to start home. The sun stood straight overhead now, the day heating up to be a scorcher. It was unseasonably hot for late April, and Spencer's shirt was already plastered to his back with sweat.

He'd been shooting in an open field not far from Zola's place on Jonas Creek Road. He skirted near her house now as he started his walk back up the mountain to Raven's Den.

Spencer considered stopping, but he hesitated. He didn't know what to do with his feelings for Zola. He stayed torn and divided about whether to pursue her more intently or back away.

His thoughts drifted to her again as he approached the waterfall that spilled down the mountain. He remembered the day when Zola kissed him on the rocks in front of the falls with such warm abandon.

As he drew closer to the pool below the stream, he felt a prickling up his spine. He knew that feeling now. It meant Zola was somewhere nearby.

He heard her before he saw her. She was singing, some kind of happy lyrical melody. He stopped out of sight behind a huge tulip poplar tree to listen, captivated with the sound. Spencer peeked around the tree carefully to see where she was and spotted her swimming in the pool below the falls. She'd told him she liked to swim here on warm days. Spencer smiled. Hot as he was from the photo shoot out in the fields, he envied her the feel of the cool water.

Zola found her footing and stood up then, reaching her arms joyously over her head. Spencer caught his breath. She was naked, swimming without a stitch of clothes on.

He stood concealed, enjoying her beauty, unashamedly as a man, but he watched her in fascination as a photographer, too. It made an unbelievably beautiful portrait. She was smiling, singing, and swirling her hands through the water in graceful patterns in time to her own music. Without thinking about it, Spencer's hand went to his camera. He raised it to shoot, and then he stopped himself. It would be invading her privacy to photograph her this way without her permission. It wouldn't be ethical.

Zola climbed out of the water then, causing Spencer to almost swallow his tongue. Water sluiced over her lush curves and there was nothing hidden from his eyes. She picked her way gracefully over to a rock and grabbed up a silky pareu she'd left folded there. With deft fingers she tied it around herself into a quick dress and then sat on the rock and shook her hair out.

Now Spencer let his fingers snap some candid shots: of Zola shaking out her hair, of Zola leaning back on her arms to look up joyously at the sky, of Zola singing once again and illustrating her song with gestures. It was delightful to watch her and delightful to photograph her. She was a woman so at peace with herself. So happy with the world. So easily able to take delight in simple pleasures. He envied that.

She turned suddenly and saw him.

"How long have you been there?" A butterfly drifted past her shoulder as she asked her question. She held out a hand, and it settled on her outstretched fingers.

Spencer zoomed in for another shot or two.

"Not long," he answered as he walked closer to the water.

Zola stretched her legs out in the sun and threaded her fingers through her wet hair. She looked at him for a few moments thoughtfully and then smiled. "It looks like you could use a swim yourself."

He looked down at his sweat-dampened shirt.

"Probably could," he said.

"You can swim in your boxers. I've seen native men in Mooréa in less than that many times. I don't shock easily."

She sent him another warm smile. "And I won't take any pictures of you."

He felt himself frown. "I wasn't taking them like a voyeur. I was taking them like an artist, catching a beautiful scene that called for remembrance."

Her dark eyes met his. "When did you start shooting?"

"After you dressed," he answered honestly. "It wouldn't have been right to take them before. But I wanted to."

"Well, then." She smoothed her hands through her wet hair. "It's not every day a woman is admired by a man only as a subject for photography."

He eyed her speculatively. "You don't really want me to respond to that, Zolakieran."

She dropped her eyes. "No, I guess not. And I didn't mean to bait you with my words."

Zola scooted forward on the big rock to dangle her feet in the water. "This is one of my favorite places in the world, Spencer. I always feel a sense of joy when I am here, a sense of cleansing."

Spencer walked over to a flat rock by a tree and unloaded his camera equipment. Then he took off his vest and stripped off his sweat-damp shirt. Seeming to pick up on Zola's ease with herself, Spencer pulled off his socks and boots and then dropped his jeans. He waded out into the deep, green pool in only his plaid boxers and then dived into the depths of the water.

The water felt cold but refreshing. He swam across the pool and then rolled over on his back to savor the feel of the rippling currents around him.

Pulling himself to his feet in a shallow spot, he playfully skimmed a handful of water Zola's way. "Aren't you going to come back in?"

She smiled at him. "I don't think I'll tempt fate quite that closely, Spencer Jackson. You're very handsome there in the sun with the water sliding down your body."

"I know the feeling," he said, grinning back at her.

She splashed water at him. "I expect you do."

Spencer swam a little longer, feeling the tension of the day ease out of him in the process, and then he pulled himself up onto the big boulder to sit beside Zola in the sun.

"You're getting me damp again," she complained.

"You'll dry." He gave her a teasing look and shook his wet hair so the droplets sprinkled on her.

To his surprise, she leaned over to kiss him. It was another of those sweet, spontaneous kisses, and she laughed afterward as she cupped his face in her hands.

"You're a handsome man, Spencer Gordon Jackson." Her eyes roved over him in admiration.

He found her lips again and kissed her back. Pulling away, he smoothed back her hair and then leaned in to kiss her forehead. "And you are a very beautiful woman, Zolakieran Sidella Eley Devon."

She laughed a warm, husky laugh. "You're the only person who ever remembers my whole name."

He laughed back with her, propping his arms on the rock behind him to look up at the sky as he'd seen her do. "I've snapped this day into my memory—made a photograph of it in my mind."

"I love you when you're like this, Spencer." She lay back on the rock in the sun, and Spencer dropped back to lie beside her.

The sun shone bright overhead, and the rock felt sun-warmed and hot underneath them.

"I've always been happiest when out of doors," he told her.

They lay quietly for a few minutes, enjoying the pleasure of the day.

Spencer realized he hadn't known enough moments like this in his lifetime. He wished he had.

As his thoughts darkened, he felt a hand steal over to take his.

"Talk about it," Zola said. "Give the pain to the sun and the sky. Let them take it up and away."

He looked toward her. "It's not that easy."

"It can be," she said. "Just close your eyes and try it. Say, sun and sky, I give you this pain today. Take it and carry it away."

Spencer thought about it. A child's game. A playful act.

Without much conscious thought, he repeated, "Sun and sky, take away the pain that's left behind from all the times my brother hurt me."

Zola muttered some words he didn't understand and laid a soft hand on his midriff. "And let the pain be gone forever from Spencer Jackson. Take what fragments you can today, sun and sky, and let them never return."

Spencer felt a little silly and yet much lighter. "Your turn," he said.

She lifted her arms skyward. "Sun and sky, take away the old hurt that sometimes comes to haunt me of losing my mother so young."

Zola laid her hand on her own midriff then.

"And let it be gone forever," she repeated. "Take what fragments you can today, sun and sky, and let them never return."

It almost seemed to Spencer that he felt the pieces of her hurt rising up toward the blue sky. He seemed to feel Zola's relief, and he heard her sigh softly.

The game drew him in then. "Sun and sky, take away all my old hurts from the times my parents weren't there for me as they should have been. Let me forgive them. Let me forget the disappointment. Let me walk away from the past. Let me be free."

Again Zola laid her hand on his midriff and muttered words he couldn't understand. "Let it be gone forever," she said with passion. "Take what fragments you can today, sun and sky, and let them never return."

She lifted her hands skyward then. "Oh, Great Lord above. We commit our hurts and pains of the past to You today. We give them to You and to the sun and sky. We cast the cares of them up to You and release them. Forgive us for not giving them to You before."

Spencer felt an odd lightness of being as she spoke.

She sat up then and reached down beside the big boulder where they sat to grab a handful of small, smooth pebbles.

"Here," she said, handing him half of them. "Throw them off one by one into the water as you remember the sins or sorrows you want to be free of. It's another symbolic way to lighten your load.

It's in the Bible, you know, as a part of one of the old festivals."

Seeing her so intensely involved in the process, Spencer humored her and began to toss the pebbles into the swirling waters one by one.

She scowled at him. "You have to believe you're truly throwing them away, Spencer," she admonished.

He focused his attention then and began to name the sorrows he never wanted to relive, or think of again, with each rock. Zola was right about it bringing a cleansing feeling.

They sat together companionably on the rock afterward, each thinking their own thoughts.

"You're good for me," he said at last with open candor. "I've tried to fight my feelings for you, for reasons hard to explain, but I want you to know I carry strong feelings for you, Zola Devon."

"And I for you," she said, dropping her eyes. "I have tried to fight my feelings for you many times as well."

He stroked her cheek with the back of his hand.

"Do you think I'm normal?" he asked impulsively.

She laughed a throaty laugh. "No. I think you are gifted, and that is better. Who would want to be normal when you could be gifted?"

Spencer shook his head. "You sound like David."

Zola shrugged. "David is quite wise sometimes." She hugged her knees as she turned her eyes to his quizzically. "Why would you want to just be normal, Spencer?"

He thought about it. "I guess because I was always made fun of for being different in so many ways." He looked away.

Zola giggled. "Maya would call all of those people who made fun of you for being who you are *bootoos*—foolish and dumb people."

Spencer smiled at her. "And do you like me just the way I am, Zola?"

She looked him up and down thoughtfully. "I like what I see on the outside very much, Spencer Jackson. And, today, I like what I see on the inside rather well, too. When you free yourself to be natural like you have today, I like you very much. The creative artist in you, the thinker, and the playful man who can revel in the joys of nature —that man I like very much indeed."

Her words touched him and freed up a painful spot in his soul.

He skimmed a rock out over the water. "Sometimes I go out on a photo shoot before dawn and crouch for an hour or more in a blind or behind a row of thick shrubs to catch a shot of water birds as they first fly out into the day. Or to capture with my camera the first rays of light dancing across the water of the lake." He reached over to take Zola's hand. "You make me feel similar joys to those moments, Zola. You've brought light into my life. And beauty and grace. I thank you for that."

He lifted her hand to his lips and kissed it.

With a smile, she melted into his arms then, wrapping her arms around his body and seeking his mouth with her own. It was another of those ecstatic moments—holding Zola and kissing her in the warmth of the sun—with the waterfall thundering behind them. Spencer felt himself oddly content simply to kiss and hold her, to revel in the moment—even when they were touching skin to skin, he bare-chested and dressed only in his boxers and Zola wrapped only in her thin pareu dress, with her body intimate against his.

They pulled up on their knees on the rock, so they could hold each other more tightly and move more closely together in warm intimacy. It was a heady moment.

Spencer recognized, too, when the moment of joy began to turn heated and he pulled away. Zola laughed and tried to pull him back close again, but he shook his head, sliding off the rock to start toward the pile of clothes he'd left on the bank.

He remembered, as their passion sizzled, the caution of Zola's grandfather and of how he'd warned of the natural and spontaneous warmth Zola was capable of, because of her heritage. It might have been possible to take her further today in the midst of this ecstasy, but it would have been wrong.

Spencer pulled on his jeans and slipped his now-dry T-shirt back over his head. Then he sat down to pull on his socks and boots.

Zola grinned at him from the rock. "I don't know if I want to hug you anymore now that you've put back on that old sweaty shirt." She made a face.

"Good," he said, smiling at her. "I need protection from the spell you've been winding around me, island girl."

"Was I?" She looked pleased.

"Very much so."

Zola climbed down off the rock to look for her own pile of clothes. Finding her shorts, she turned her back to slip them on under her pareu. Then she slipped on her tennis shoes.

He smiled at her. "Do you work tomorrow?"

"Yes," she answered.

"What about the next day?"

"I'm off then." She smiled back at him.

"Then we'll go somewhere special that day if you're free."

"I can be free." She cocked her head at him teasingly.

He laughed. "Then I'll pick you up after breakfast and take you up to one of the balds with me on the top of the mountain. I want to get some photos there, and you'll like the views. How does that sound?"

"It sounds wonderful."

Spencer turned to start up the mountain, not trusting himself to spend more time with Zola while she was in this mood.

"You're much lighter, Spencer," she called.

He turned back at that remark, giving her a questioning look.

"Surely you can feel it." She gestured around her head, drawing a circle with her hand. "There's not so much heaviness hanging around you anymore. Don't you feel the change?"

Spencer felt reluctant to admit it, but he realized it was true.

"This has been a good day, Zola," he said instead.

She smiled at him. "Yes, it has."

As Spencer hiked the rest of the way up to Raven's Den, he wondered if the games he'd played with Zola had really helped him remove some of the sorrows of the past he'd carried for so long. Just now, in the haze from being with Zola in so much intimacy, he wasn't sure if he felt lighter from the rush of feelings of being with her or lighter from being freed from some of his darkness. Perhaps he would be able to tell more tomorrow. For now, though, he could definitely say, once again, that it had been a fine day. He knew for a certainty, also, that he'd dream tonight of the water nymph he'd seen rising out of the pool below the waterfall. Despite the artistry of the moment, the man watching the scene hadn't been blind.

Chapter 15

Zola walked down the mountain realizing that she and Spencer Jackson had turned a corner in their relationship. He'd opened up with her at last, shared some of the pain of his past. And he'd shared some of the feelings he had about her.

Oh, he hadn't said he loved her yet. But, perhaps, it wasn't time for that. She wasn't sure if she felt ready to say those words herself. Still, the words had lurked unspoken under the surface for both of them.

Turning the corner from the trail toward her house, Zola saw a familiar figure sitting on the front porch. It shouldn't have surprised Zola to see Nana Etta sitting on the porch waiting for her, and yet it did.

As Zola drew near the porch she saw that her grandmother was crocheting a colorful pot holder while she waited. Always busy hands, her grandmother.

"I have a serious man in my life." Zola told her, coming up on the porch.

"Yes, I saw that. That's why I walked over."

Zola leaned over to kiss her grandmother.

"Not many people know you carry a gift of the sight, Nana."

"Only a little now and again for practical

purposes." She looked at Zola's wet pareu. "You been swimming naked with that man?"

"No." She opened the front door and reached in to get the shirt she'd left hanging over the chair by the door. Her back to her grandmother, she slipped off the damp pareu and pulled on the T-shirt over her shorts.

"He'd been on a photo shoot and came back up the trail to find me at the falls." Zola spread the wet pareu over a chair in the sun to dry out. "Nothing happened but some heart confessions and some of what your friend, Judy, calls 'a little sweethearting.' "

"Hmmmph," Nana said.

Zola sat down in the big rocker on the front porch and started to rock. She wished she could simply savor her thoughts of the day right now instead of facing a cross-examination with her grandmother.

Nana picked up the pot holder to work on it again. "I've seen the boy's a Christian but his walk with God isn't as close as yours."

"Whose is, Nana?" Zola knew she sounded querulous.

"Well, there's a point in that," her grandmother admitted. "You did deliverance on that boy today." She gave Zola a pointed look. "You reckon he understood it?"

"No." She smiled. "But I know he is lighter now. I saw some of his past hurts and pains lift off."

"How'd you do that without him resisting?"

Zola grinned. "Played a little game with him like my mother used to play with me. We gave things up to the sun and the sky. I sort of slipped in the principal part of it—and to the Lord—as we went along. After all, Nana, God is in everything. He's in the sun and the sky."

"I suppose, but it's borderline heathenish and you know it." The older woman glowered at her. "However, I know the Lord wants that boy to get free from some of that past hanging over him."

"Have you been given anything specific about that, Nana?" Zola looked at her questioningly.

"A bit. Not much." She picked at her crochet work. "He experienced a lot of painful things in his early life. It could take time to get past it all. And it might shoot up to haunt the both of you now and then as you go along. You up for that?"

"If he can take on my peculiarities, I guess I can take on his." She giggled. "He has the hardest time with the little things I see sometimes."

She told her grandmother about seeing the yellow jackets and telling him where the poison to kill them sat under the kitchen sink.

Nana chuckled. "I can remember some tales of my own when you saw things of that nature when only a mite—after you first came to live with us. It took a bit of getting used to."

"You see things, too, Nana."

She shook her head. "Not in the same way, girl,

and it's seldom I can recall ever being asked by the good Lord to share them with others. I simply get some knowings now and again."

"Are you troubled about my relationship with Spencer?"

"Some," she admitted. "But Vern and I like him. We neither one have an objection to you taking up with him—unless he gives us a reason to change our minds."

Zola sighed. It relieved her to know her grandparents thought well of Spencer. If they hadn't, it would have worried her.

Nana pinned her with a disapproving frown. "Right now, I'm more concerned over this business with Aldo Toomey and Madame Renee, and with all the rumors I've been hearing about Ben Lee saying you're going to solve the mystery of his missing daughter." She shook a finger at Zola. "I don't like you being involved in danger."

"Oh, Nana, you know Aldo Toomey is basically harmless."

"Yes. But Renee Dupres walks on the dark side. I don't like her mind and words dwelling on you, Zola. She draws ill with her talk and with her words."

"I'll start praying more over that, Nana."

"And so you should. Never underestimate the enemy, Zola." She turned serious eyes toward her. "Keep your armor on strong. And keep your prayer life up."

Zola nodded.

Her grandmother stood up. "You go have yourself a little talk with Benwen Lee, too. You set him straight on a few things. With some prayer, you'll know how to talk to him. This blabbering of his needs to stop, Zola. It's not helping the understanding of what you are."

"Yes, ma'am." Zola knew her grandmother was right. She'd let the gossip Ben generated go on too long already.

Firm eyes caught hers. "I'll be expecting to hear tomorrow of exactly how that conversation went with him."

This was the way her grandmother always dealt with her, laying out a clear expectation so Zola wouldn't procrastinate on the things she ought to do. Her grandmother knew she sometimes avoided dealing with difficult issues, hoping they would resolve themselves without her having to take action.

She sighed. "Should I go talk to Renee, too?"

Nana snorted. "There's nothing in her that would want to listen to you, even if you used all the reasoning in the world. What you can do for her is simply pray for her to have enlightenment. To walk out of the dark and into the light. Then she might be able to hear some truth and know it. For now, you just keep your distance from her."

Zola knew the truth in her words. Every conversation she'd ever engaged in with Renee had been fruitless.

"You want me to drive you home?" Zola asked.

"No." She snapped out the word with annoyance as she started down the porch steps. "The day I need to be driven, instead of walking a short distance over my own farmland, I'll let you know."

Zola hid a smile behind her hand.

Nana paused to tuck her crochet work into her apron pocket. "Why don't you come over to dinner with us tonight if you're through with your daydreaming by then? I'm having chicken-and-dumplings and I made a blackberry cobbler from those berries I put up last summer."

"I'll do that." Zola waved at her.

She looked back at Zola with a frown. "And you put yourself some underwear on under those clothes. It's not decent to go around without underclothes on."

Zola rolled her eyes again as her grandmother started down the path toward her place.

As it turned out, Zola did find a little time to dream that afternoon before she went to dinner with her grandparents. She did a little more dreaming at work the next day, sandwiched between waiting on customers. It was nice to be on the edge of falling in love, she thought, nice to have someone to dream about and think about, sweet to feel someone invading her thoughts.

Spencer had called last night, and as she settled in to bed after a long day, he called again. "I'm calling at ten o'clock again," he said, "because I've learned it's about the time you go to bed."

"Is that right?" she asked, smiling.

"Yeah. I like talking to you right before you go to sleep." His voice sounded husky. "I think ten is going to start being my special time to call you every night."

She yawned. "Maybe you can tell me bedtime stories or sing me some lullabies."

"And maybe I can whisper sweet nothings to you." His voice grew softer.

Zola snuggled into her pillow. "I might like that."

He chuckled. "Yeah, but then I might have trouble falling asleep afterward. Perhaps I should talk about less personal things, like telling you those yellow jackets are totally gone. You know, I appreciate you keeping Zeke from getting his doggy nose stung that evening."

"Zeke's a great dog. When did you get him?"

Their conversation went on like this, becoming more and more relaxed and comfortable. Zola was remembering these warm moments as she followed Spencer along a single-file trail the next morning to one of the grassy meadows on top of the Smoky Mountains.

He wore his photographer's vest, with a camera draped around his neck. He also wore a back-pack, which carried water and part of their lunch, and he carried his tripod over his shoulder. Zola admired his broad shoulders from the back.

She had a small backpack on, too, with the rest of their lunch inside it. Under her arm, she carried an old quilt rolled up with string.

"I thought for sure when you talked about going to a grassy bald we'd hike to Andrews Bald or Gregory Bald."

"Everyone goes there," he said. He turned to grin at her over his shoulder. "Besides, have you ever hiked down to Andrews Bald?"

They'd parked in the parking lot at the end of Clingmans Dome Road at the top of the mountain, and Zola knew the trail to the bald sloped south from the parking lot down Forney Ridge.

She searched her remembrance. "It seems I remember there are some nice views from off Andrews Bald."

"Yeah, and that's all." He laughed. "The trail down to the bald is boring to me and sometimes the open field on the bald is full of gnats and bugs so thick you could choke. The grass on the bald grows really high, too. It's a disappointing place to me. I know other trails that lead to grassy meadows and fine mountain views I like much better."

"And so where does this trail lead?" They'd headed northwest out of the parking lot and climbed up a rocky ridge to intersect a piece of the Appalachian Trail heading out from Clingmans Dome.

Spencer led the way farther along the narrow ridgetop trail. He pointed ahead. "This trail leads to Mount Buckley. You can see it up ahead. It's only a short walk to it now."

The trail opened out on the left to expose a grassy meadow on the top of the mountain slope. The views over the mountaintops here were stunning. Zola paused to take it in.

Spencer turned back to her with a smile. "After we walk to the point at Mount Buckley, where I want to take some photos, we'll come back here, spread out our quilt and enjoy our picnic. You can look your fill then, Zola. This is a great place."

"Yes, it is." She looked behind her. "And not far from the parking lot. I wonder why more people don't walk out here to enjoy the views."

It was a weekday, and there weren't many tourists in the area, but none had taken this trail. They'd all headed up the paved trail leading to the Clingmans Dome Tower or started down Forney Ridge Trail to the bald.

"People are lemmings." Spencer adjusted the tripod on his other shoulder. "They go to the places where they see other people go or that they've heard other people talk about the most."

Zola smiled to herself. It was good to hear Spencer acknowledge that he liked to walk to a different drummer.

The trail began to climb more steeply toward the top of Mount Buckley.

"How tall is Mount Buckley?" she asked.

"It's 6,580 feet, Zola. We're high up in the heavens today. Mount Buckley is the fourth tallest mountaintop in the Smokies. Clingmans Dome behind us is the tallest at 6,643 feet. You can see 100 miles from the tower on a clear day."

"It looks clear today—and not foggy like it is sometimes." Zola gazed out over the rippling mountain ranges with pleasure. "Did you know it would be this nice today?"

"I've been watching the weather." He admitted this honestly. "I wanted to come on a day when I could get some good mountain range photos. They always sell well in the store."

"Everybody loves pictures of the rolling mountains with the hazy colors growing fainter and fainter in the distance." She sighed, looking out at the view.

"Well, I'll give you a picture to frame if you can find a place to put it in your house."

"I'll find a place," she told him. "You just plan on getting some good shots."

He laughed. "I intend to."

The summit of Mount Buckley was a rocky point with trees on the top. Rocky outcrops and grassy patches spread to either side of the point. Zola sat down on a rock to rest and enjoy the views while Spencer took photos.

She closed her eyes, reveling in the peace and quiet of the day. She could hear a woodpecker ratcheting away on a tree down in the valley. The sounds of insects droned softly on the air. She heard the high-pitched notes of a warbler singing—probably having just returned to the upper reaches of the mountains now that late April had arrived. In the quiet, she heard the flutelike sound of a veery, too. This bird usually serenaded only during the early morning and at sunset.

"You're late in the morning to be singing, little friend, but I'm glad you are so I could hear you." Zola's grandmother had taught her to know most all the bird songs when she was small. Those things one learns as a child stay strong in the remembrance.

"What are you smiling about?" Spencer asked, coming over to drop a kiss on her forehead.

The gesture touched her heart. "If you listen carefully, you'll hear the veery singing. I think she's down that ridge in a tree. I can't see her."

Spencer stood very still, listening, until the flutelike song came again. He scanned the trees for the bird. Catching the direction, he put up his camera with its long zoom attached and searched the area.

Zola saw him smile as he clicked off a few shots. "Did you actually see her?"

"I think so. Is she a little brown thing that looks like a jenny wren?" He showed her the digital shots he'd taken.

"Oh, yes—that's her." She smiled in pleasure.

"It's rare to capture a picture of that little songster. Nana will want to see this photo for sure."

"I'll frame it for her, and you can give it to her for a gift."

She reached up to put her hand around his neck and pull him down so she could kiss him. "I love to spend time with you," she told him.

"And I you." He kissed her back.

Later, after Spencer had taken all his morning photographs, they sat lazily on the quilt they'd spread in the grassy meadow looking out over the blue mountain ranges. They'd eaten sandwiches and now munched green, seedless grapes while they enjoyed the views.

"Look." Spencer pointed out over the ridges. "You can see a bit of Fontana Lake there between the mountains."

Zola saw the reflection of the water where he pointed. "I see it," she said. "It's incredible we can see that far from here."

He lay back with his hands behind his head and closed his eyes.

While he rested, Zola got up and explored the meadow on top of the mountain. She picked a few random wildflowers, though she knew she was really supposed to leave them undisturbed. But there were so many flowers here. And they hadn't seen another soul all day on the mountaintop.

She came back to the quilt with a small handful of treats, squatting on her knees to look at them.

"What have you got?" Spencer pulled up to look at her find.

"One or two wild iris." She held out a single flower to him for a closer look. "Did you know there are about four varieties of these in the park? This purplish variety is called blue-eyed grass. Their yellow centers attract the bees. There are a whole sweep of them down to the right."

She pointed and then held up another flower with a grin. "And of course my favorites are the buttercups—these happy yellow flowers."

As he pulled to his knees beside her, she playfully tucked a buttercup into a buttonhole in his shirt.

Smiling with pleasure, he tucked another into her hair behind her ear.

Zola touched his lips with her fingers. She loved seeing him smile like this. "You know, Ralph Waldo Emerson said the 'earth laughs in flowers.' They make me want to laugh, too. They are such joyous creations."

She tucked a flower into the pocket of Spencer's shirt, letting her fingers trace a circle around his heart.

His eyes darkened. "You drive me crazy with desire at times like this, Zolakieran. You are so alive and beautiful."

He wrapped his arms around her and leaned in to kiss her. Zola threaded her hands into his hair and kissed him back with joy.

It was a beautiful moment as they stood on their knees on the old quilt, wrapped in each other's arms—with the floral meadow and the stunning views of the Smoky Mountains all around them.

She heard Spencer sigh as his mouth drifted from her mouth, across her cheek and into her hair above her ear. "You know I'm falling in love with you," he whispered huskily.

Zola's heart sang. "And I with you, Spencer Jackson." She found his lips again and they fell onto the blanket in a tangled embrace.

Spencer lay on top of her, and the feeling of his body spread over hers in the warm sun was wonderful. They kissed and murmured sweet things to each other, reveling in the moment of discovering their awakening love and their response to each other.

Zola bit Spencer playfully on the shoulder and blew softly in his ear. She felt an odd change in his body then, a stiffening. Something was passing through his mind. He was slipping away from her.

Frustrated with it, she searched for his lips again. He kissed her in a different way this time— more intensely—and his breathing escalated. He slipped his tongue between her teeth and took their kiss much deeper, his hands roving more freely over her body now.

Were things getting out of hand? Zola wondered as she responded to him but felt oddly detached in the process.

Spencer's mouth fell to her neck and then drifted down toward her breasts. She wore only a sleeveless spaghetti-strap top, leaving much of her upper body exposed to the sunshine. Spencer's lips roved over her skin. But nothing felt right.

Suddenly she heard it, the voice in his head. He was saying another woman's name in his mind, thinking of someone else while kissing her. Reliving some past moment of passion.

"Geneva. Geneva," she heard him say in his thoughts.

Shocked, Zola let the picture come sharply into focus now. And she knew. He was thinking of his former lover. Even worse, he was thinking of the woman who was his brother's wife.

Zola felt revolted. She pushed Spencer off her, slapping at him to make him stop kissing her. Angry now.

She pulled herself up from the quilt, shoving him farther away from her. Not even wanting him to touch her.

His eyes opened to look at her in confusion.

"How dare you!" She wrapped herself in her own arms protectively. "You're lying here with me, kissing me, telling me you think you're falling in love with me, and you're thinking of your brother's wife!"

She reached out to slap at him as he tried to take her in his arms again.

"Don't you even *dare* to think about putting

your hands on me, Spencer Jackson—not now or ever again."

He sighed deeply and ran his fingers through his hair. "I wasn't thinking about her before, Zola. And I meant what I said. But something you did . . . something that happened with us . . . brought some memories back for a minute. It doesn't mean anything."

She glared at him. "It doesn't mean anything that you're saying another woman's name in your mind, thinking of another woman's kisses, remembering another woman's passion and love when you're with me? You must think I'm crazy to accept that."

He ran a hand around his neck nervously. "I'm sorry, Zola. I sometimes have these flashbacks. Things come into my mind from the past. I can't help it."

She crossed her arms more tightly against herself. "I can accept a lot of your problems with the past, Spencer. Even those things you haven't felt led to share with me yet. But I'll *not* accept another woman's memory slipping into our lovemaking. That's past the limit for me."

She shivered. "Especially when it's your own brother's wife you're lusting after and thinking about. That's disgusting. Did you have an affair with her after your brother married her? Is that part of the guilt and pain you carry around, that you betrayed him with his own wife?"

His face distorted in anger now, and he clenched his fists tightly, frightening Zola for a moment. "We were engaged." He bit out the words. "Geneva and I were engaged. And Bowden stole her away while I was at college. Married her and took her away from me. Just like he took so many other things away from me. It was just one more thing he stole. He enjoyed it, too. He called to tell me about it with gloating, pretending he was trying to break it to me kindly. Telling me she'd never really loved me, that I should be glad I found that out before I married her."

Zola studied his angry face. "And *did* she love you, this Geneva?"

"Yes!" His fists clenched and unclenched at his side. "She told me she did. She showed me she did."

Zola began to gather up her things. "People often say things they don't mean, Spencer. And they often display passion when their heart isn't really in it." She gave him a significant look. "Take today, for instance."

She watched his eyes move to where she'd begun to load up her backpack. "We need to talk about this, Zola. It's not what you think."

"No. It's *worse* than I thought." She pushed him off the quilt so she could roll it up. "It's not only the hurts from your family and the hurts from your brother's bullying you're suffering from, it's the hurt of losing someone you loved. And you're *not* over it yet."

"Zola, you're making more of this than it is. . . ."

Tears sprang to her eyes now. "I won't be second best, Spencer Jackson. And I won't share your heart with an old love who still lives in your memory in that large a way."

She brushed back her tears. "She was very beautiful, wasn't she? Very accomplished. Very poised. The kind of woman men's eyes turned to whenever she walked into a room."

He sat silent, scowling.

She caught his eyes with hers. "And I am everything that is different from her, aren't I? That's what I've felt so many times—you comparing me with her. Measuring me against her." Her voice broke in a sob. "I always came up short, too, didn't I?"

Spencer reached out a hand toward her. "It wasn't like that, Zola."

"Wasn't it?" she challenged.

He ran his hands through his hair again, obviously searching for the right words to say. But not finding any.

"I want to go home, Spencer. I'd walk so I wouldn't have to ride with you, but it's too far." She stood up.

As Spencer packed his gear, he tried saying words to smooth over the moment. But none of them felt right or true to Zola.

On the way down the mountain, he tried once more. "I wish you could understand, Zola. It was a hard time for me when Geneva and Bowden married. And my parents and Rita didn't seem to see any problem with them getting together, blotting me out of the picture." His hands tensed on the steering wheel. "It happened like it always did. Whatever Bowden wanted, Bowden got, and Mother and Dad just acted like it was all right. They didn't even seem to realize how I felt. Or care."

She looked at him. "How many years ago was this, Spencer?"

"Twelve," he admitted sullenly.

"You've pouted over this for twelve years? Felt sorry for yourself and felt abused for twelve years?" She spat the words out angrily at him. "What an incredible waste!"

"You don't understand!" The words burst out of him angrily. "It wasn't right!"

"Oh, get over it, Spencer. Half of life isn't right. But you have to focus on the part that is. And enjoy the part that is. Otherwise, you'll be a very miserable person." She pulled away from him to lean against the car door, wanting to put as much distance as possible between them.

He made no reply, but she saw his hands grip the steering wheel again and heard him breathing heavily with his emotions.

They rode in silence all the way down the

mountain. Finally, Zola spoke again. "They share children by now, don't they? They have children and I'll bet you've never even seen them."

He snapped his reply. "Why should I want to? Why should I want to see their boys?" His voice sounded tight and pained.

"Oh, Spencer, because they're your nephews. They're your family." She turned to him with sorrow in her heart. "And they're children, only little boys. Like Eddie who we found in the mountains. None of this is their fault and yet you've made them pay for it by withholding your love from them all these years. By not letting them get to know their Uncle Spencer."

He took a curve in the road too sharply, obviously upset.

"It's easy to talk about it reasonably, Zola, but it's not easy to live it. Some things are that way. You can't understand them without being in them." He turned anguished eyes toward hers.

Her voice grew soft then. "What I understand is that you're the one who's made yourself suffer all these years for what happened. You're the one who stopped the clock. Everyone else went on. That's sad, Spencer."

"I don't want your pity, Zola." His voice sounded harsh.

"No?" she asked. "But everyone feels sorry for those who can't let go of the past, Spencer."

When they pulled up to her house, Spencer said

quietly, "I wish you'd try harder to understand, Zola. That was a bad time for me. It comes back on me sometimes, that and other times. But I meant what I said about my feelings for you. And I'm sorry you saw into my thoughts. It's one of the hardest things about being in a relationship with you—that you see a person's secret thoughts. It's not really fair, Zola."

She looked over at him before she climbed out of the car. "No, I guess it's not really fair. But I'm truly grateful I was given the sight to see the truth about things today. It hurts enough as it is to learn the truth. I would have hated to learn it when my heart was even more deeply involved."

He sighed. "Listen. I'll call you tonight. We'll talk some more."

"No, Spencer, don't call. And we won't talk some more tonight—or tomorrow night—or anytime soon."

She shut the car door after getting out and then paused, looking back at him through the open window. "I wish you the best in finding your way out of this bad journey you've kept yourself living in, Spencer Jackson. I told you once, and I'll tell you again, you *can* step out of this if you want to. But I don't want to be with you until you make a positive step in that direction."

"Zola, please . . ." He started to say something else, but Zola stopped him.

"No, Spencer. There's nothing else to say right now." And she walked away.

Chapter 16

The next weeks of Spencer's life were as bad as any he'd ever known. His secrets were out, his past exposed—and his relationship with Zola seemed to be over. He tried again and again to see her, to talk to her, to explain his past life more clearly so she would understand. But Zola wouldn't even talk to him. She avoided him whenever possible. And she wouldn't go out with him anymore.

Behind his house the yellow jackets had tried to come back to their old nest. But it wasn't the same for them now. Their old nesting place was spoiled. They couldn't find any contentment in what they'd felt comfortable in before. Spencer knew the feeling. He almost felt sorry for them as they circled the old place they'd once known as home.

He sat on the porch with his dog, watching them. "I know how they feel, Zeke. Their world is out of balance. Mine is too."

Spencer scratched the dog's back affectionately. "You remember I told you I was afraid Zola would be trouble for us. That she'd change us. She sure did. I'm left with a whole new sweep of agonizing memories to haunt me now. And I feel like I've lost my grip on myself. Nothing feels the same and nothing feels right anymore. It's a miserable time, dog."

Zeke whined softly in sympathy.

Spencer struggled to analyze his feelings—never anything he'd been very good at. He searched his memory for one of the last times he'd felt really good and known a peaceful day before this blowup with Zola happened. His mind drifted back over the weeks and to the day at the falls.

"Let's go down to the falls," he said suddenly, remembering the peace he'd known there many times.

It was a hot day already. He and the big shepherd were ready for a dip in the cool mountain stream by the time they hiked down to the waterfall. The long plume of Buckner Branch fell off the cliffs twenty feet into the deep pool below it, the sounds of the cascading water filling the air. Spencer stripped off his clothes down to his boxers, dove in, and swam lazily in the cold current. Later, he climbed out to warm up on a large boulder.

He sighed as a wash of memories hit him. It was the same rock where he and Zola lay together that day and played her silly game about the sun and the sky.

What had she said? Give up your pains and sorrows to the sun and the sky and then say you never want them to return again?

In desperation, Spencer wondered if it would

help to try it today. He closed his eyes. "God, I don't know how to do this stuff like Zola does. I don't have special gifts. I don't see things like Zola does. But I'd like to let the past go if there's a way. I sure wish You'd help me with that. I'd like to let go of all the torment of my past. But I don't know how."

Spencer confessed the hard times of his past and tried to engage in the game Zola had taught him. He seemed to feel better in some ways for the effort—or perhaps from the confession—but the hurt and ache of losing Zola was so strong he could feel little relief.

After drying off, he and the dog made their way back up to Raven's Den. On the back porch, Spencer found Aston, sitting in one of his rocking chairs with his feet propped on the porch railing.

"How long have you been here?" Spencer asked.

"Not long."

Spencer threw his towel over the back of a chair and plopped down into the rocker beside Aston's.

"Zeke and I went for a swim down at the falls."

Aston cocked an eyebrow his way. "Did it help?"

Spencer shook his head. "No. Not much."

"Man, you've got to get this thing worked out. Your work is falling off. Clients have been calling. Wanting commissioned work. Wanting to talk to you, and you've avoided getting back to them. You have some deadlines you haven't met for projects going on." He stopped to look at Spencer. "And you look bad, man."

Spencer sighed and closed his eyes. "I thought it was hard losing Geneva but this is worse, Aston. There's no anger this time, but the pain and regret are terrible."

"Have you tried talking to her—"

Spencer interrupted him. "Yes. A hundred times at least, Aston. She won't answer her phone—or if I show up in person she is coolly polite."

He ran his hand through his hair in exasperation. "I've apologized and told her I'm sorry for everything, but it doesn't help. She keeps telling me she can't be with me until I make a positive change in the right direction, but no matter what I do, it isn't what she wants to see. I've tried flowers, gifts, candy—special things I thought might get to her heart—but nothing works. She won't forgive me. I don't know what else to do, Aston. I simply don't know what else to do."

Aston reached over to pat him sympathetically on the arm. "Have you eaten at all today, friend?"

Spencer tried to remember. "I think something earlier—a breakfast bar or something with coffee."

Aston stood up. "Come on in the house. I'll fix us a big breakfast for lunch. It's one thing you know I can cook well."

"Okay. You're on." Spencer stood up, glad to have some company to take his mind off his troubles.

In the kitchen, Spencer slumped down on a barstool at the counter while his friend started getting breakfast together.

Aston turned toward him, skillet in hand, to survey the piles of mail and circulars spilling over the counter.

"Spencer, have you even looked through all this mail?" He frowned. "There might be something important in here."

"Yeah, sure." Spencer searched through a pile until he found a large cream envelope. "Like this invitation to come home for my parents' anniversary. That's really important." His voice was sarcastic as he waved the envelope at Aston before tossing it in the trash.

Aston fished it out of the trash can and opened it. After looking over it carefully, he said, "This is your answer, Spencer, the way to get Zola back."

Scowling, Spencer threaded a hand through his unkempt hair. "What are you talking about?"

Animated now, Aston sat down on the stool beside Spencer's. "Zola told you she needs to see evidence that you're making a positive effort to change. This is it." He looked down at the invitation again. "Your parents' anniversary is this weekend. Go tell Zola you think you're ready to start the process of healing, and to start letting go of the past and its problems, by going to this anniversary event. And tell her you want her to go with you."

Spencer was stunned. "Are you crazy? The last thing I want to do is to take Zola around my family!"

"You're wrong. If she gets around them, she'll understand more. And if you ask her to go with you there, she'll know she means something to you. So will your family. Plus, Zola will give you support in facing all of them. She's good to have around when there are problems to face. You know that."

Spencer actually considered it for a few minutes. "Do you think it might really work?"

Aston got up to return to his cooking. "I do, Spencer. I really do. And I've told you for a long time I think facing your family will help you get over your past and what happened."

He turned to look at Spencer between turning strips of bacon in the skillet. "It's been twelve years, Spencer. You've changed. They've changed. You won't see things the same now. You're a man now who's come into his own, not an unsure young boy. They won't treat you the same, and if they try to treat you badly—you won't allow it now."

"Do you think so?" Spencer knew his voice sounded doubtful.

Aston shook a finger at him. "I know so. And I

like the idea of your family seeing you with Zola. Meeting Zola. Realizing you can have someone fine and good like Zola in your life."

Spencer blew out a sarcastic laugh. "I doubt my family would see the merit in Zola Devon."

Aston turned to scowl at him. "You underestimate the power of Zola, Spencer. She has goodness. That is always seen. And it is powerful."

Fiddling with the papers on the table, Spencer thought about it. "I wouldn't want them to hurt her, Aston. I've done enough of that."

"I think Zolakieran Devon can take care of herself, Spencer. And I think she'll size things up there pretty quickly."

Aston took the bacon out of the skillet, wiped it out with a paper towel, and broke eggs into it. He popped a couple of pieces of bread into the toaster as well. "Get some plates down and pour us both some juice while you're thinking on this, Spencer. I've almost got our breakfast ready."

They sat down at the counter to eat a few minutes later.

"Do you really think this might work?" Spencer asked again.

Aston nodded between bites. "I do. I had what my people would call 'a witness' to come up here today, Spencer. I didn't know why I came but I think I do now. I think this trip is what is really going to change things for you—and between you and Zola Devon."

When Spencer grew silent, Aston turned his dark eyes to his. "You do really love this woman, don't you? If you don't, then you'd best let all this go and suffer on through getting over her. I don't want you hurting that girl more unless your intentions are serious."

Spencer shook his head. "She'd figure it out if my intentions weren't serious anyway, Aston. It won't be easy living with a woman who can know you like Zola can. I won't be able to have any secrets."

Aston laughed. "That might be good for you, with as many secrets as you've harbored. They've eaten you up for much of your life. Maybe she'll purge all the dark out of you. Make an open, happy man out of you."

Finishing the last bite of his eggs, Spencer looked over at his friend. "You might be surprised to know how much I'd like that to happen, Aston."

"Well, that sounds like progress to me." Aston got up and slapped Spencer on the back.

Spencer saw Aston look at the kitchen clock as he carried their dishes to the sink to rinse and stuff them into the dishwasher. "Why don't you go down and talk to Zola right now?"

Spencer studied the cream invitation lying on the table with a frown. Surely there must be another way to get Zola back without facing his family.

He slumped on the stool. "How do you know she's at home?"

Aston snatched up the invitation Spencer was eying and frowned. "I thought you said you really wanted to see change happen?"

"You're as bad as Zola." His voice was grumpy, knowing Aston sensed his reservations.

Aston picked up the announcement to smooth out the wrinkles in it. "Zola is home babysitting Ava today for Rachel Lee. I have it on good authority from Faith Rayburn at Zola's store. So you have *no* excuse to procrastinate doing this now, Spencer."

He began to sort through the mail on the table, stacking circulars in one pile, correspondence in another, bills in yet another. Always an organized, methodical man.

Spencer smiled. "All right. I'll try it. I have nothing to lose, I guess."

Aston looked him up and down then. "Well, go get a bath and a shave before you go, man. You look like the devil."

"No, that's the guy that's been after me," Spencer mumbled as he headed down the hall toward his bedroom.

Less than an hour later, clean, shaved, and dressed in good navy slacks and a light blue shirt—that Aston said set off his tan—Spencer pulled up in Zola's driveway. She was outside playing with Ava on a big quilt under the tree.

"Big man," said Ava, pointing and smiling at him in recognition.

Spencer grinned and saw Zola smile in spite of herself.

"What are you doing here, Spencer?" she asked. It was a question coolly put, and her smile slipped away now.

"I have an invitation for you." He handed her the cream envelope.

"Listen, I think we've talked about this often enough, Spencer. . . ."

"Just read it," he said.

She sighed and opened the envelope.

Looking up after reading the invitation, she gave Spencer a questioning look. "I don't understand."

"I'd like to go—to try to deal with things and to hopefully move on. And I'd like you to go with me." He caught her eyes with his own. "I'd like you to meet my family, such as they are. Maybe check out my nephews with me."

She studied him with a long searching glance. Then she looked back down at the envelope.

"Your parents' anniversary is this weekend, Spencer."

He nodded. "I know. I've called and booked two tentative flight reservations for Friday. We'll get a rental car when we get there. And we can fly back late Sunday. There's a nice hotel not far from where my parents live, near the park I talked to you about."

Spencer saw her expression soften and felt a glimmer of hope. "I'll take you to see all my old childhood haunts, and we'll see if my tree house is still there. I doubt it, but we could check it out."

She stood up and walked closer to him. "You really mean this, don't you? You want to move on?"

He resisted putting a hand out to touch her. "I want to move on, Zola. I don't know if this will help, but I'm willing to try it and see. Aston thinks it may help. He's a big believer in facing the past to chase off old bitterness that hounds you."

Zola studied him with those serious, soft brown eyes of hers. "I think this might be a good thing for you, Spencer. And, yes, I'll go with you."

His heart lurched, and a sigh of relief slipped out of him.

She moved nearer to him and reached up to touch his face. "I've missed you, Spencer." Her voice was soft.

He reached his hands out to touch her now, to wrap his arms around her and draw her up against his chest. It was heaven to feel her warmth against him again, to smell the apple fragrance of her drifting from her hair.

Spencer yearned to tell Zola he loved her again, but he held the words back, not wanting to press his luck right now. He felt so grateful she was opening her heart back up to him at all.

He felt a tugging on his pants leg. "Ava hug, too!"

They looked down to see Ava holding her chubby arms up, smiling.

Spencer reached down to grab up the small girl to hug between them. His heart felt warm and big enough to readily share its joy right now.

When he heard Zola's rich, throaty laughter float out on the warm air, his joy felt complete.

Chapter 17

Spencer showed up to drive Zola to the airport on Friday after lunch. It had been a busy week getting ready to leave on short notice, and neither had seen each other, although they talked on the phone frequently.

Zola studied Spencer as she opened the door to him. He'd cut his hair. That was the first thing she noticed. And he was dressed to the teeth in preppy clothes and held a suit coat casually slung over one shoulder. As he passed by her, Zola could smell some divine earthy scent drifting off him. This was a surprise, too, as Spencer seldom wore cologne.

"Wow." She raised her eyebrows suggestively, giving him another head-to-toe look.

He smiled, his eyes roving over her with appreciation, too, noticing the tailored gray pant suit she wore with a soft, pink blouse and simple jewelry. Zola knew it was a different look from her usual bright clothes and hoop earrings. When she'd talked with Spencer about the weekend, he mentioned that his family were very traditional. Zola decided she didn't want to make a statement by standing out.

Spencer leaned over to kiss her cheek. "You look nice, too, Zola. *Very* nice."

He draped his jacket on the bamboo coatrack by the front door. Zola could see when he turned his back that there was no ponytail tied behind his neck anymore. He'd truly made a transition in this area of his appearance.

She studied the new haircut—neat and tailored. He'd obviously been to the barber earlier in the week since he sported a tan now where his long hair had been tied back with a leather string on his neck before.

"You've cut all your hair off," she said. She frowned at him, not sure she felt happy about this change. "Did you think you had to change your identity that much for your family, Spencer? In order to be accepted?"

He turned and gave her a challenging look. "Actually, Zola, who I am is not in how I dress or wear my hair."

She felt a smile quirk the corners of her mouth. "Well spoken, Spencer."

He grinned. "I'm working on it, Zola."

Watching him, she noticed that he seemed more at ease with himself today, which surprised Zola when she thought of what they were soon to face.

"My bags are here and ready to go." She pointed to her suitcase and carry-on by a side chair and then looked at her watch. He'd come early.

"I know I'm early," he said, seeming to read her thoughts. "I stopped by to see your grandmother and grandfather before I came over."

"You did?" That was a surprise.

His hand moved to rub his neck again as if missing the length of hair that had been there before. "Yes, I did. I wanted to assure your grandparents I wasn't going to be taking advantage of you on this trip to Richmond."

She could feel a blush begin to creep up her cheeks.

A frown touched his face. "I told them my mother had insisted we stay at the house this weekend rather than at a hotel. Your grandparents seemed pleased about that. It wasn't what I preferred, of course, but I decided if I was going to dive in, I might as well jump in at the deep end."

"I see." She grinned.

He shuffled, uncomfortable now—hesitating before saying something else.

Zola watched him, wondering what else was on his mind.

He rubbed his neck again. "I talked to your grandparents about another matter while I was there." His hazel eyes caught Zola's, serious and intense now. "I told them I was going to ask you to marry me and I wanted to get their blessing."

Zola's knees felt weak, and she reached out to grab the back of the couch to anchor herself. She had not expected this. And certainly not today.

A warm look crossed Spencer's face, and he

reached over to trace the back of his hand down her cheek. "I love you, Zola Devon." His voice held a husky note. "I told you that before and I really did mean it."

He reached for the coat he'd hung on the bamboo rack. "I'd like my family to meet you as my fiancée." He dug a faded jewelry case from his coat pocket and handed it to her.

"This was my Grandmother Chatsworth's mother's ring. Passed down through several generations. It's old, but my grandmother said she hoped I'd give it to my future wife one day. I hope you'll like it." His eyes moved toward the faded blue case. "If not, we can choose something else."

Still feeling stunned, Zola opened the box to see an oval ruby circled by small, sparkling diamonds. The stones were set in a warm gold ring that was burnished with age. The ring was softly beautiful and seemed to speak of the enduring loves and years it represented.

The cherished, old ring called to Zola, but she hesitated.

Her eyes found Spencer's. "Are you only asking me to marry you as protection with your family—and with Geneva—when we go up to Richmond?"

Spencer winced as if she'd hit him. "If I were weak enough to want protection—and, granted, I probably am—I still wouldn't be foolish enough to ask a woman to commit her entire future and life to me simply to insulate myself from a few potentially unpleasant scenes."

Zola felt a guilty flush rise up her neck. "I'm sorry, Spencer. I guess I spoke without thinking."

He leaned one shoulder against the wall. "I know you don't admire how I've handled things with my family, Zola. But it has been a truly happy event in my life to have discovered you."

She dropped her eyes, her emotions a scramble.

Spencer stepped away from the wall and took both her hands in his. "You are the first bright, happy thing that has come into my world in many years, Zola. You warm my heart, my life, my blood."

His eyes captured hers. "You can look deep right now, Zola. You won't see another woman in my thoughts. I want to spend my life with you, share my days with you, have children with you, and grow old with you."

The words sounded sweet, but Zola wondered if another time, given the sight to see, she would see *only* herself in Spencer's thoughts as she seemed to now.

His watchful eyes never moved from hers. She knew he was waiting for her answer.

"All right," she said at last. "We'll take the first step and see how things go."

She heard him release a pent-up sigh of relief before he leaned forward to kiss her with eager warmth. Then he pulled away to take the ring from its box and slip it on her finger.

His voice grew husky again. "This is a sweet moment, Zola. I wish I had a photo of this."

She held out her hand to admire the ring. "Just make a photo memory in your heart, Spencer."

"I will." He smiled at her.

Zola noticed the ring fit surprisingly well, which was unexpected.

"I had it sized," Spencer said, seeming to read her thoughts. "Maya Thomas at your store told me the right size." He grinned then. "She said I'd better not be a *bootoo* anymore, and that I'd better take good care of you and cherish you."

Zola raised an eyebrow. "Did she, now?"

"She did," he replied. "She also told me some good stories about you—like about how you were led to find her after her husband died and then asked her to come work at the store. She said you helped her and her girls to find a house to rent when the resort her husband worked for tossed her out."

Zola frowned. "The resort gave them free housing because Nigel Thomas managed their sales department, but practically the day after his funeral they kicked Maya and the girls out. They had a new manager coming in, they told her, who needed the apartment. They also took away her job at the resort gift shop. It was appalling how she got treated. Out with the old, in with the new—that's how they acted."

Zola felt her anger flare remembering it. "They had to move into a single motel room together. And Maya was having a hard time getting another job with her mixed nationality."

"So I heard." Spencer reached over to stroke her cheek with the back of his hand again. "It was good of you."

"Not really. The Lord connected us. I was opening the store and needed her, and she needed me. She's a wonderful store manager. It was a blessing I found her."

"The more I learn of you, the more I love you." He leaned over to kiss her again.

A frisson of passion surfaced, and Spencer moved in closer, pulling Zola into his warmth, running his hands up under her hair and then down over her back, drawing her closer to him.

He pulled away reluctantly to look at his watch. "I hate to shorten this moment, my future Mrs. Jackson, but we have a plane to catch."

Zola pondered the sound of that title over the next hours as they checked into the airport, boarded, and took off for Richmond, Virginia. Flying shortened a seven-hour drive to a forty-five minute flight.

It was Spencer's father who met the plane—coming forward with a face wreathed in smiles as they came into the terminal. He was about

Spencer's build, with a kindly face. His hair, once dark, was now threaded with gray, receding on both sides of his forehead. He had the same hazel eyes Spencer did.

He shook his son's hand firmly in welcome and then leaned in to give him an awkward hug. Spencer's return hug looked equally self-conscious, but Zola saw a glimmer of a tear in the corner of his eye.

She stood back quietly to watch them welcome each other. It had been twelve years since Spencer had been home to Richmond, but Zola knew he'd seen his parents several times over the years when they visited in Savannah. Still, since he'd moved to Gatlinburg, they hadn't seen each other at all.

Zola watched the look of love in Spencer's father's eyes and felt her spirit lighten. Regardless of what had happened, this man still held deep love for his son. She found that very promising.

Introductions made, they collected their bags and located Gordon Jackson's spotless luxury car in the airport parking lot. The international airport lay east of Richmond, and their route to the Jackson home took them south and then east of the city. On the way down the freeway, Spencer's father opened up to talk congenially about sights along the way, telling them about changes in the city since Spencer had last been home. Zola could see he was making an effort to be sociable to put them both at ease. It was kind of him.

Zola watched Spencer lean forward eagerly from the backseat as the car turned onto rural lanes nearer to his family homeplace.

Spencer had tucked Zola into the front seat beside his father, letting her be the one to respond with politeness to his father's comments. Yet, despite himself, Spencer joined in the discussion now, pointing out familiar spots to Zola along the way. Zola could feel the eager excitement in him build as they drove up the quiet lane to the country residence belonging to the Jackson family.

The house, a sprawling one of angles, gables, and porches set behind a charming white picket fence, was cloaked in a mix of stone, shakes, and white lap siding with a dark gray roof. The home sat on a sloped green lawn, neatly landscaped, with a background of hardwood trees and an arch of ivy growing over the front porch entrance.

It seemed hard to imagine, from appearance only, that this had been anything but a happy home.

"It's beautiful," Zola said.

Spencer's father smiled at her while Spencer sent her a telling sideways glance. He wasn't as comfortable as he was portraying.

A smiling lady came out the door as they drove up. She tripped down the sidewalk, her eyes eagerly focusing on Spencer as he stepped out of the car. Obviously Spencer's mother, she reached out to hug him. Zola noticed her embrace was given with fondness but careful restraint.

She held him at arm's length then. "You look very good, son. Welcome home."

Zola wondered if Spencer's parents noticed the change in his expression at that last word—or saw him wince. He looked up at the house with wary eyes now, a feigned smile still pasted on his face.

Spencer's father took Zola's arm and introduced her. "Marion, this is Spencer's friend, Zola Devon. Zola, I'm sure you've realized this is my wife and Spencer's mother, Marion Jackson."

Zola shook her hand politely, noticing she had warm brown hair like Spencer's but that in other ways Spencer looked more like his father. Mrs. Jackson wore her hair pinned up in a neat bun and had small pearl posts in her ears. Her clothes were obviously expensive and fashionable, a silky cream shirt tucked into tailored tan slacks with matching sling-back shoes and a tasteful belt.

Spencer slipped his arm into Zola's, drawing her closer to him. "Zola is my fiancée now." He held out her hand, adorned with the ruby ring.

"Oh, it's Grandmother's ring." Marion studied it with a wistful expression. "Mother told me she gave it to you some years ago. I'd almost forgotten."

She smiled at Zola. "I can remember my

grandmother—Spencer's great-grandmother—Amelia Chatsworth wearing that ring." A memory touched her face wistfully. "She was always very much in love with my grandfather Randal Gaynor Chatsworth. That ring carries much affection."

Zola, surprised, looked at her more closely then. "I could feel that," she said. "Thank you for sharing that with me."

Marion seemed embarrassed at her lapse into fancy, and quickly recovered herself. "We must get you both up to your rooms so you can get settled," she said. "Spencer, I've put you in your old room, although, of course, it's been remodeled since you left. And I've put Zola in Rita's old room. It's tastefully decorated now with some nice antiques I found at auction, and I think she will find it restful."

Spencer leaned closer to Zola to say softly, "Rita's choices of décor in her bedroom always set Mother's teeth on edge. I'm sure Mother was thrilled to redecorate the minute Rita moved out."

"I heard that," his mother said. "Your sister is gifted, but she had appalling taste in her teenage years. That room was always a virtual kaleidoscope of colors and it seemed that she repainted the walls in some new, vibrant shade every year."

The room, after they'd climbed the stairs to find it, was tastefully decorated in sandalwood, tan, and cream with subdued botanical prints on the walls.

"I hope you'll be comfortable here, Zola," Marion Jackson said.

"I'm sure I'll feel right at home." Zola smiled at her.

She saw Spencer smirk as he put her suitcases on a low table. Zola knew he was remembering the bright colors and eclectic furnishings in her old farmhouse in Tennessee.

A short time later, after freshening up, Zola added a neat little vest to her traveling outfit, to replace the gray coat jacket, for dinner. She left the vest unbuttoned, her one informality. It didn't seem likely from Marion's or Gordon's dress that she could expect casual dress, or jeans, for dinner.

As they went downstairs, Zola noticed that Spencer still wore his dark slacks and pin-striped shirt. She quickly saw that Friday night dinner was served in a fine formal dining room complete with shining crystal and silver-edged china.

Furthermore, a cook or housekeeper soon scurried in and out of the dining room bringing in a tureen of soup and salads as a first course. Zola sighed. It was undoubtedly going to be one of those fussy, formal dinners. She hated those.

She leaned in to whisper to Spencer before they walked into the dining room. "Is this the norm here for evening dinner at your home?"

"Yep." He swept a hand around. "Just a quiet, typical little dinner at the Jackson home."

Spencer's mouth tightened. "I warned you it would be different from anything you're used to. But you can expect it to get worse when all the family arrives—unless things have changed a lot."

They hadn't. And the evening did get worse.

The family that night included Spencer's parents, Grandfather Stettler Jackson and his current wife Charlene, Spencer's sister Rita and her date Bryan Hall, and Spencer's brother Bowden and his two boys, Trevor, nine, and Austin, seven. The only missing family member was Bowden's wife, Geneva.

The boys seemed very curious about Spencer and pleased with the small gifts Zola and Spencer brought them. They were still young enough to be thrilled with bags of plastic dinosaurs and two colorful kites.

They spilled the dinosaurs out on the floor with enthusiasm until their father made them put them on the sideboard until dinner was over.

"Geneva had a charity function tonight," Bowden announced as they all sat down to eat. "She regretted it, but she'll look forward to seeing everyone tomorrow night at the anniversary party."

Zola had been curious to see Geneva in person, but she felt glad, in a sense, to postpone the meeting. There was enough tension to deal with at the dinner table.

"Well, how did you meet Spencer-Savannah?" Bowden asked her, leaning his elbows on the table to study her as he asked the question—and shooting a challenging look at Spencer.

Zola felt Spencer tense at the question and saw him scowl at Bowden. She and Spencer had been seated across from each other where she could see his expressions clearly. He'd become tense and uncomfortable as soon as everyone settled down to eat.

Smiling at Bowden, and ignoring his obvious roving assessment of her, Zola answered him. "Spencer's gallery is near my store, Nature's Corner, in the mall in Gatlinburg." She had no intention of telling him anything more personal.

Spencer's grandfather jumped in. "Is that one of those new-age stores that sells kinky aromatics, incense, and wind chimes?"

It was a rude question, as Bowden's had been. But Stettler Jackson asked it with a charming smile as though he had every right to ask anything he wanted of anyone.

Zola studied him. He was dressed in a neat suit, his hair white above a tanned, age-blotched face. His eyes shone sharp and bright, but Zola could sense an edge of cruelty underlying his smiling expression. He'd made it clear from the moment they sat down to dinner that he was in charge of this family, as he was obviously used to being in charge of many other aspects of his life.

He even cut his own wife down to size the first time she tried to be welcoming and congenial to Spencer. Zola noticed she backed off dutifully. The boys, too, ate without making any conversation, evidently trained that dinnertime was a time for adult conversation only.

"My store is not a new-age store, Mr. Jackson, but I do sell wind chimes as one of my products. I find people are very fond of them and that they sell well."

"Tinkling bunches of nonsense dangling from people's porches and in their houses, jangling about every time you bump into them. Never could stand the things myself." He grinned as if entertained with his own observations. "Do you and Spencer make any money with those tourist-town stores?"

Truly, he was insufferable, Zola thought.

"Honestly, Grandfather," Rita interrupted. "You know Spencer has become quite successful. Quit picking at him and Zola."

"Just asking a good business question, girl." He shook his fork at her. "Besides, it's typical you would care so little about profits. You've always been happy if you could just piddle in the kitchen and play house decorating cakes."

Zola saw a flicker of annoyance cross Rita's face before she grinned and responded, "My play-housing with cakes just won me the Virginia Culinary Award for the year, Grandfather."

Stettler continued to wave his fork in the air. "Yes, and it gave our business a little helpful recognition when your picture got in the paper."

"I'm pleased my work could help the business." Rita grinned, obviously almost tickled with the whole conversation. She turned raised eyebrows of amusement to her dinner partner, Bryan Hall. He grinned back at her, as though they had some sort of conspiracy going together.

Zola liked them. Rita had dark short hair, brown like all the other Jacksons, but cut in a jaunty style that reached just below her chin. She wore a silky purple blouse and black skirt, and was dressed nicely for dinner, but the blouse was less formal and she wore a cute scarf tied carelessly at her neck. Her earrings, which looked like little silver fishes, dangled down from her ears to flash in the light from the chandelier. Through all the introductions and the early getting-acquainted comments over dinner, Rita had seemed to be the only one in the group, besides Bryan Hall, unaffected by the atmosphere at the table.

She looked at Zola now. "Bryan is the anchor newscaster for WXV2 television here in Richmond," she said. "We met when Mother and I catered his sister's wedding."

Bryan smiled a newscaster's smile at Zola. "My parents spent more money on that wedding than I spent on my last car."

"Hush, now, Bryan." Marion playfully shook a finger at him. "That's how Rita and I make our money—catering weddings and events."

"The money we made off the photography didn't hurt either." Bowden lifted his wine glass toward Bryan in a toasting gesture.

He turned a gaze to Spencer. "You'd have done well to hitch your star to the Jackson business, Two Spence. You might have done better for yourself by staying with the family than launching out on your own."

"There, there, Bowden." His mother offered a smile toward Spencer. "Let's not criticize Spencer for his life choices. We're all so glad to have him here with us. And to have Zola here, too."

Zola heard Spencer's grandfather mutter to his wife. "Spencer owns a poky little gallery in a resort town, when he could have worked with the Jackson Studio. Never will understand it. Boy never had a lick of common sense."

It was a nasty, awful thing to say, but everyone simply let it ride—and no one contested it.

Zola opened her mouth to protest but saw Spencer give her a cautionary shake of his head.

Interestingly, it was Bryan Hall who came to the rescue. "I was in DC this last fall, Spencer, when you had an exhibit there and when a series of your photographs were selected for that Brighton Award. That was a fine ceremony, and I enjoyed your acceptance speech, telling about where you shot all the pictures." He looked around the table. "Spencer has a very fine name around the country as a nature photographer. And he has five best-selling photography books out. Rita has them at her apartment and they're spectacular."

He seemed genuinely surprised that the family wasn't more aware of their own family member's success.

Everyone seemed suddenly interested in their food.

Bowden broke the silence by starting a new line of conversation. "Guess who I saw the other day, Spencer? That little Conner girl. You know, the one who had a crush on you in high school? Awkward little girl with dark curly hair. Bit of Mexican blood, if I remember. She asked about you. You always were the one to attract the unorthodox sorts of girls to you."

Bowden glanced Zola's way as he dropped this last comment.

It was such an obviously offensive cut that Zola could hardly believe he'd uttered it over the dinner table. The slur toward her, as partly Tahitian, was unmistakable, and the insult toward Spencer blatant.

Once again, no one said a word. No one seemed to notice, and no one offered sanction. What a family! Zola could begin to see why Spencer hated growing up with this bunch.

She caught a somewhat apologetic glance coming her way from Rita, who shook her head slightly and rolled her eyes—as if saying to Zola, "typical comment from Bowden; just let it ride."

Stettler Jackson seemed delighted at the turn of the conversation. "The girl I remember most is that little pigtailed tomboy, Anna Kabotsky. Girl took after her mother and didn't have much in the way of looks at all. Followed around after Spencer and that Peter Bradley he played with all the time. You know, that boy didn't go into the law like his father—got into the forestry service instead, a big disappointment to his family. Could have gone far. And that girl, Anna, never married. Of course, I can see why."

"Grandfather," Rita put in. "Anna Kabotsky became a medical doctor. She's a well-known children's physician now."

He scowled at her. "Well, a woman has to find something to do when no one will marry her."

Zola began to feel ill.

These were beautiful people on the outside. Obviously successful and obviously well educated. But they were hard and critical and unloving on the inside. How sad for Spencer to have grown up constantly faced with this. No wonder he'd escaped and not come back more often.

She looked at Spencer's older brother, Bowden Jackson, across the table—an incredibly handsome man. Of all the family members, he'd been blessed with the most stunning looks, and he oozed charm and charisma. He was obviously successful in his own right, and, yet, he felt this need to put others down, to humiliate them with these clever, cutting remarks. It seemed a shame.

Zola looked over to see Spencer watching her. She saw a sad look cross his face. Perhaps he'd hoped his family would have changed over the years, but obviously that was not the case.

Spencer's grandfather focused his attention on Zola and Spencer. "You two sleeping together? That seems to be what all the young folks do these days."

It was another tasteless thing to say, especially with two young boys at the table. They looked up now with wide eyes.

Zola saw a steely look pass over Spencer's face. "That's enough, Grandfather. Zola is my fiancée, and she comes from a fine and good family. I'll not have you saying derogatory things about her here around our table."

"It's hardly *your* table when you haven't shown your face here in twelve years," Stettler Jackson snapped back. "It figures you'd finally wander back when you found a girl you wanted to show off. Although there's hardly a comparison between her and your previous fiancée."

Even Spencer's mother gasped over that one. "I think that comment moved over the edge of good taste," she said, giving her father-in-law a pointed look.

Zola noticed that Bowden seemed delighted with the turn of events.

Spencer stood up. "I believe I've lost my appetite suddenly."

He looked at Zola. "Zola, if you're finished, perhaps we could take a walk. You haven't had a chance to see the lake behind the house yet. There's a nice path down to it."

Zola stood up gladly.

As they left the room, she heard Stettler Jackson murmur, "That boy never could stand up to a good fight. Always wimped out when faced with a sporty confrontation. Found an excuse to run. He obviously hasn't changed a bit."

Rita piped up. "And you've obviously shown him a few good reasons not to come home again for a long time, Grandfather. Honestly! You and Bowden always have picked on him."

At least someone spoke the truth.

Chapter 18

Spencer tucked his arm through Zola's as they strolled down the winding pathway toward the lake.

"I'm sorry, Zola. My family was rude to you."

Zola snorted. "That's an understatement." She hugged Spencer's arm against her. "I'm sorry for you, Spencer. I know you'd hoped things would be different after all these years."

He blew out a sigh.

"Were they always like this when you were growing up?"

"Yes, I guess they were." He kicked at a pinecone in the path. "It was always worse, of course, when my grandfather joined us. Friday night was always his traditional night to come. On Sundays we went to his house after attending church in Richmond." His tone grew sarcastic. "I can remember those as truly hideous times, too."

"Tell me what you observed tonight, Spencer. Put it into words. You're older now. You've been away a long time. You should have a different perspective."

Spencer looked down to see Zola's serious brown eyes watching him, waiting for his answer. *Oh, well—why not,* he thought.

"I see that nothing is different, Zola. My

grandfather is still a pompous ass. He is still rude to everyone and says whatever he wants to, without any sanction. His new wife, Charlene, is another bimbo. She tinkled with laughter over his comments, as if they were humorous. She looked vacuous and seemed unintelligent."

He snapped off a dry tree branch in irritation. "Charlene is only one of a string of that sort of women my Grandfather has squired around, and often married, since his first wife, Sylvia, died young. I never knew her; she died giving birth to a second son after my father. The baby died, too, and that left my father as the only child in the Jackson family. None of the women Grandfather dated, or later married, bore him any more children."

It was darker now as they turned a corner away from the light of the house, but a full moon lit their way. "I did notice tonight how different my father is when my grandfather isn't around. Dad seemed almost kind and thoughtful when we arrived earlier."

"I noticed that, too," Zola said. "He was genuinely glad to see you, Spencer."

Spencer's pent-up anger burst out then. "So why does he just sit there when his father goes on like that at the dinner table—and is rude to his guests? Why does he put up with it when Grandfather says things that are boorish and out of line?" Spencer scowled. "He does the same thing when Bowden acts that way, too. Just overlooks it. Lets it ride. It is rare for him, or my mother, to ever come to the rescue of guests or family members that are attacked. I never could understand that, Zola. It always seemed wrong."

Her voice grew quiet. "I noticed that when your Grandfather is crossed that he retaliates with an angry attack, never an apology. Maybe that's why."

Spencer laughed softly. "Yeah, you learn quickly that with Grandfather Stettler, and with Bowden, it's better to take it and keep your mouth shut than to retaliate. It nets you more abuse to defend yourself or to counter either of them."

"Maybe that's your answer." Zola squeezed his arm. "Your father grew up with that—trained from an early age to keep his mouth shut. Kind of like your nephews do."

"Yeah, that was sad to see, wasn't it? Two boys so young already closed off like that. Maybe they both get attacked, too, if they dare to speak up or draw attention to themselves."

Zola leaned her head against his shoulder. "They're cute boys. I wonder if we could have them down to the mountains sometime, Spencer. Give them a taste of another kind of family life."

He smiled down at her. "Like your family?" He leaned down to kiss her head. "You're kind to be worried about those boys."

"You should know how they feel." She paused, thinking. "Spencer, what other family helped to teach you that your own immediate family was . . ." She searched for the right word.

"Dysfunctional?" He finished her sentence with a chuckle. "Well, my friend Peter Bradley's family was healthy to spend time with, despite what Grandfather said. They weren't really surprised that Peter decided to go into forestry to become a park ranger versus studying law. I don't think they were disappointed in Peter, either, like Grandfather suggests."

She smiled up at him. "I'd like to meet Peter some time."

Spencer found her hand. "He'll come for our wedding. He owes me; I went to his." He laughed. "And we'll go out to Wyoming to see him sometime. He and his wife are in Yellowstone National Park now."

They reached the quiet lake, and Spencer led Zola to a bench on the patio beside it. The moon made a soft, flickering reflection on the dark water. Spencer had always liked it here.

"You know, your sister Rita seemed to handle things well at dinner." Zola brought the conversation back to the meal they'd just left. "There seemed to be a sort of joke going between her and her date. Did you notice that?"

"I did." Spencer nodded. "Rita always seemed to be able to see the humor in the situation with our family, to brush things off better than I ever could."

"You're a serious person who takes things to heart," she said.

"Is that good or bad?" He frowned.

She smiled up at him. "It's simply who you are. Sensitive, artistic, a person who feels things deeply. People respond to the same situations differently because of who they are. Some people can laugh things off and some people can't."

He thought about that. He liked the way Zola put problematic understandings about people into simple words. Introspection had never been his strong suit.

Zola tossed a small pebble out into the lake. The ripples spread out in rings in the moonlight. "Your mother just sort of plays the gracious hostess part, doesn't she, Spencer? In fact, neither she nor your father seemed to participate much in the dinner conversation at all. Did they talk more when you were growing up?"

"Come to think of it, I guess they didn't. Both of them were always rather quiet and reserved people."

"Introverts."

"I suppose. They always opened up more when you were with them singularly. In groups, they sort of faded softly into the woodwork."

"They're not fighters, either."

"No. I guess not." He scowled. "I wonder if it's been hard for them, always being under Grandfather's watch. Having to deal with him."

Zola jumped in. "You mean having him insult their friends, be rude to their guests, dominate their social gatherings, and seldom offer a nice word about anyone?"

He squeezed her hand. "You make me feel almost sorry for them."

"Perhaps you should." She patted his arm. "You were able to escape. They never could."

"Do you think they wanted to?" It was a new thought to him.

Zola's face tilted up to his in the moonlight. "Maybe you should ask them."

He laughed. "I'm not sure I'm that brave."

"Hmmm. Well, I get a sense there is a whole other suppressed person underneath the persona of both your mother and your father. Have you ever seen that other part of either of them?"

"I don't know. I'll have to think about it."

And he did, through the night and into the next day.

Breakfast was quieter. When Spencer came down the stairs toward the kitchen, he paused in the hallway to listen to his mother and father talking with warmth and affection with each other. They even laughed several times.

He wondered at that. Then he realized he, Bowden, and Rita were gone from home now. His parents had settled back into the pattern they'd known before their children came, the way they were when they were young and first fell in love.

Spencer walked into the kitchen and saw both of them look up and smile. He felt love radiating from them—and it surprised his heart. He was glad when Zola tripped in behind him to cover the moment.

Now he and Zola were trekking down old trails through the Pocahontas State Park—trails he'd walked a million times as a boy—all filled with memories from his childhood.

It was a warm June day, and they both wore shorts, T-shirts, and well-worn canvas shoes. Spencer also wore an old, battered backpack he'd found on a nail in the back of the garage.

"I feel happy memories coming off you," Zola said.

He took her hand companionably. "Yes. Being here makes me remember I did know many happy times growing up. It wasn't all bad being a part of my family. As Aston said, no one beat me, I was well provided for, my parents weren't alcoholics or drug addicts. I was never locked in a closet."

She sighed. "Aston knew some of those sorrows, didn't he?"

"Yes, and yet he survived and overcame them." Spencer shook his head. "I should probably feel ashamed that I allowed the small problems in my upbringing to bother me so. When Aston used to share his childhood stories with me, I felt guilty for my emotional baggage."

"It isn't easy to shake off hurts from childhood."

Spencer looked around with pleasure. "I always felt happy here, though—tromping through the woods and fields, playing by the streams and lakes in this park. Climbing trees and exploring. Pretending in boyish games and believing impossible dreams."

Zola squeezed his hand. "Well, try to remember the good more often than the bad when you go back home. The good is as easy to pull up into your remembrance as the bad is—if you work at it."

"Is that what you do?" The thought seemed to surprise him.

She beamed a smile at him. "Of course. Attitude is a choice, Spencer. You can choose to be happy, to focus on what is positive, good, and true. Or you can choose to be unhappy, to focus on only the negative."

Zola stopped walking. "Try this." She turned to look at him. "Frown consciously and think of some really negative, unhappy things."

He cooperated indulgently.

"It starts making you feel all down in the dumps, doesn't it? Depressed and heavy?"

He had to admit it did.

She grinned at him. "Now try this. Smile big and think of some really positive, happy times."

He began to grin back at her as he made the transition.

"You began to feel the heaviness lift, didn't you?" She cocked her head to one side. "You see how much control you have over your own attitudes and moods? Much of it is simply choice."

"It's like that Scripture." He searched his memory. "Whatsoever things are true, honest, just, pure . . ."

"And lovely," she finished. "Yes. Think on those things. And the God of peace will be with you."

He reached over to gently smooth her hair. "You know, I told Zeke I had a sense you would change us if we stayed around you long enough."

She laughed. "Well, I don't think I've changed your dog very much, Spencer, but if I've brought you a little more love and peace, I'm not sorry for that."

He stopped and cupped her face, leaning over to kiss her. "Neither am I, Zola. Neither am I. And I'm grateful for the changes."

They walked on, holding hands.

"Look!" he said suddenly, pointing ahead. "There's my old tree house over there in that big maple tree." He veered off the path to scramble through the brush toward the base of the tall tree.

Then he grinned back at Zola. "I didn't think it would still be here."

She picked her way down the side path, following him. "That tree house looks surprisingly well kept, Spencer. I think someone has kept it up or fixed it up recently. I see a fresh board or two among the old ones."

They stood at the base of the large maple, looking up at the tree house high above them.

"Let's climb up," Spencer said impulsively. He put his feet on the first board and began to scale the tree on the nailed-on boards.

He wondered if Zola would be plucky enough to climb the old tree on the rickety boards. The tree house rode high in the branches of the old maple. But Zola surprised him and shinnied right up behind him.

Spencer showed her around the loft house and then sat on the board floor with her, their backs leaning against the tree trunk. He told her boyhood stories and funny tales then. They were good memories, and he felt glad he had them to share with her.

"I'd liked to have known you as a boy." She crossed her ankles in front of her. "I think we might have been friends—you and I."

"I don't know, Zola." He laughed and pointed to a female gender symbol scratched into the tree trunk with a big *X* painted across it. "This was a 'no girls' tree house. No girls allowed—and no exceptions. Peter Bradley and I made a pact about it."

"I see." She looked disappointed.

He scooted over closer to her, pulling her into his arms. "Little boys don't know a lot of things they should in their youth." He kissed her slowly and with pleasure. "Life is definitely better with girls in it."

She giggled and kissed him back.

Spencer felt glad for this happy interlude before the family gathering tonight. He knew he'd have to deal with his grandfather and brother again at the anniversary party. And he'd have to face Geneva. Spencer really didn't know what to expect with that. It troubled him, too, to know Zola would be there to watch it all. If he still held feelings for Geneva, it would be hard to hide them from Zola. The whole idea of the evening ahead made him antsy and nervous. He hoped he hadn't botched things up royally with Zola by bringing her to Richmond with him.

Chapter 19

The anniversary party for Spencer's parents was held in the historic section of downtown Richmond in a fine old establishment called The Colony Club. It was elegant, tasteful, and upscale—and beautifully decorated. Over two hundred guests were expected. Gordon and Marion Jackson had been residents, and business owners, in the Richmond area for a very long time, and many friends and business associates turned out to wish them the very best on this special occasion.

Zola may have spent most of her life in the rural regions of Tennessee, but she had royal Tahitian blood. She'd been to many formal events in the islands and knew how to dress and act appropriately in high society.

She saw Spencer's eyes rove over her appreciatively once again as they started into the main ballroom of the club. The twinkling lights of the chandeliers winked off the sequins on her dress.

"You look very beautiful, Zolakieran Devon."

She smiled. "So you've told me, Spencer Jackson, but of course I'm pleased to hear you say it again. And you look very handsome yourself."

It was a formal night, and Spencer and most

of the other men attending wore tux coats. The women wore long, shimmering dresses. Zola's was white-sequined on the top with a black-sequined skirt below, flowing from a high waistband. She'd tamed her cascade of curls back with jeweled combs and wore black pearls from the islands in her ears and in a drop pearl necklace. This dress was one she'd worn before to a happy occasion with her family . . . and wearing it again gave her confidence. She knew she looked stunning in it.

Spencer led Zola through the crowd to where his parents stood greeting their guests at a small alcove near the row of banquet tables. The banquet tables were loaded with food, lavishly displayed, and a beautiful tiered cake stood to one side.

Zola leaned toward Spencer. "Did Rita create the cake?"

"Yes." Spencer looked toward it and smiled. "She's fantastic, isn't she?"

Zola nodded. The cake was a masterpiece with sugared ribbons that looked like real satin looped around the cake layers, and with incredible, delicate flower creations spilling over the top and sides.

Spencer and Zola joined the circle of family and friends around Spencer's parents. They lingered there at Gordon and Marion's request, along with Rita and her date, Bryan Hall, to greet their parents' friends and to be introduced to friends and associates they hadn't met yet.

Zola managed to lean in to compliment Rita in a lull between greeters. "I love the cake, Rita. It is absolutely unbelievable."

Rita smiled. "Maybe I'll create your wedding cake if you'll invite me down. I like you, Zola, and I'd enjoy the chance to get to know you away from the bosom of our happy family." Her voice took on a humorous tone toward the end of her words, and she lifted her eyebrows meaningfully at Zola and wiggled them.

Zola suppressed a grin.

Rita leaned closer to her. "Honey, with this family, you need to learn to laugh. It's the only way to keep your sanity." She pointed toward the doorway. "For example, here come Bowden and Geneva now. They always come late to every event so they can make a grand entrance. Grandfather and his current woman of the moment won't be far behind."

Zola looked through the crowd to see Bowden and Geneva poised at the ballroom doorway. Bowden, like Spencer, was dressed in a tux—a handsome man, even more handsome in crisp, formal dress. Geneva, as Zola had envisioned, was incredibly beautiful.

They moved through the crowd like a Hollywood couple, drawing attention with their confidence and beauty. They were a striking couple, and they stopped to greet friends along the way with artful diplomacy.

As they moved closer, Zola could see that Geneva wore a sleek, form-fitting red dress. It dipped low in the front and was made of a sheer, silky material that glided over all her curves revealingly. Her blond hair glinted in the light of the chandeliers, as did the diamonds at her ears and a multitude of sparkling bracelets on her arms.

Zola looked over to see Spencer following her progress across the room with his eyes. She sighed. She didn't like the look she saw.

Geneva dutifully greeted Marion and Gordon, Rita and Bryan, and then came to stand in front of Spencer. "Well, well," she said in a throaty voice. "Look who we have here."

She took his hands, wrapped them behind her, and walked right into the embrace she'd created, kissing him full on the mouth. "It has been a long time," she drawled, pulling back slightly to study him, while keeping his hands captured in hers behind her back.

Bowden stood by, watching with indulgent pleasure.

Geneva backed away then, sure of the effect she'd had on Spencer. She'd caught him off guard with the kiss and rattled his reserve. Zola could hear him breathing more deeply than normal. Oh, boy.

Bowden tucked an arm into Geneva's. "I don't believe you've met Spencer's little fiancée, Zola Devon. She owns a nature shop, or something, near Spencer's gallery down in that little tourist town in the mountains."

It was a typical subtle put-down from Bowden.

Geneva held out a hand languidly toward Zola. "My, what lovely golden skin, Zola. Most of us need to spend hours in the tanning bed to get that look. How nice that it comes natural for you. Are you Hawaiian or Asian?"

Zola avoided the outstretched hand. "My father is a missionary doctor in Mooréa in the South Pacific Islands. He married my mother there."

"He married a little native. How sweet."

Zola smiled at her. "Actually, he married one of the Kasior daughters of the Pomare dynasty."

Bryan, the newscaster, jumped on that fact. "I know about that family. They're not reigning now but they're still recognized." He looked thoughtful. "That makes you—in a sense—a royal princess by relation, doesn't it?"

"I guess." Zola shrugged. She saw Geneva stiffen, a hard look coming into her eyes.

"Bowden," she said smoothly, linking her arm through his. "I see the Arnsworths coming in. We need to go speak to them. You will excuse us, won't you?" She passed a cool look over them all dismissively as she and Bowden started moving away.

Then she looked back over her shoulder. "I'll want the sixth dance, Spencer. It was always traditional for us to share the sixth dance together, if you'll remember."

Spencer made no response.

Rita patted Zola on the back as the couple walked away. "Well done, princess. You rattled the cage of the queen." She leaned over to hug Bryan. "And you, Bryan Hall, just went up a notch in my estimation. Very well done indeed!"

He laughed. "Glad I could be of service. Hey. It looks like people are starting to go to the buffet. Does that mean we can, too?"

"Lead on!" she said, taking his arm and starting toward the line already forming.

Zola turned to see Spencer's eyes still following Geneva across the room. Swell. He looked mesmerized.

Spencer seemed to sense her watching him and turned his eyes back toward her. He looked suddenly puzzled as his attention refocused. "Are you really a princess?"

"Only by bloodline, Spencer. The Pomare dynasty is not in power anymore in the islands."

He scowled. "You never told me about that."

She took his arm as they started toward the buffet line, too. "The subject never came up, that's all. I'll tell you all about it later, if you want."

He seemed satisfied. Or maybe it was only that he was distracted. Geneva, with her golden girl looks and sexy red dress, certainly seemed to be a distinct distraction.

They loaded their plates with food from the buffet and nibbled on it as they visited around the room. Many people remembered Spencer and wanted to say hello to him. With pleasure, Zola saw that Spencer's professional reputation was better known, and more celebrated, with his Richmond friends than among his family.

A heavyset buxom woman in a jeweled dress laid a hand on Spencer's arm. "I have several of your lovely photographs in our entry hall, Spencer." She smiled at her husband beside her, a genial-faced balding man with an equally heavy girth. "Robert and I do so enjoy telling everyone they were taken by one of our neighbors. And that you used to come climb in our trees as a boy."

Spencer answered distractedly, and Zola looked to see his eyes following Geneva around the room. Her tinkling laugh trilled out—carrying across the ballroom from her social group.

When the dancing began, Zola and Spencer waited politely until Spencer's parents started the first waltz number to a round of applause, and then moved out onto the floor. Her steps soon easily matched his.

"You dance very well, Spencer."

"All of us were sent to ballroom dancing classes." He wrinkled his nose with distaste. "I hated them, but I learned what I needed to learn."

He spun her easily around in a turn.

"You dance well, too, Zola."

She looked up to now see his eyes clearly focused on her. They were warm with affection and admiration.

She smiled at him. "We both clean up nicely when we need to."

Spencer chuckled. "That we do."

He pulled her into a closer embrace as they circled the ballroom. It felt nice to be the center of Spencer's attention again.

Zola danced with a number of different partners after that. Spencer's father danced a waltz with her, and Bryan Hall made her laugh through an old fifties number. Spencer, too, was caught up in obligatory dances with family and old friends.

Several times Zola caught sight of Geneva. Her red dress was hard to miss. Zola noticed Spencer wasn't the only one she acted overly intimate with as a married woman. She flirted with many of the men at the gathering.

Zola's eyes wandered to Bowden on several of these occasions, only to find him involved in flirtations of his own—schmoozing, networking, dancing with many women. Seemingly unconcerned about Geneva. When they came together, there seemed to be something plastic and contrived in their relationship.

The sixth dance, that Geneva insisted belonged to her and Spencer, was a sultry slow number.

Zola wondered with annoyance if Geneva contrived that in some way. While dancing with a talkative dentist, reminiscing about a trip to the Smokies, Zola kept an eye on the couple. Geneva had wound both arms around Spencer's neck and plastered herself closely against him. Zola could see her talking and laughing intimately with him, and she didn't like the enraptured look on Spencer's face.

"How long have you lived in Tennessee, Miss Devon?"

The question brought Zola's attention back to her partner. He was a nice man, and Zola answered his question and soon got into a discussion with him about favorite places in Gatlinburg.

When the dance ended, she looked around for Spencer but saw no sign of him. Wishing for a break from the noise and heat of the ballroom, Zola let herself out a side door into a corridor that led to a lovely courtyard.

She could hear the sound of a fountain and murmured conversation. Zola stopped short behind a pillar and a screen of greenery when she recognized Geneva's and Spencer's voices.

Through the edge of the potted ficus trees, she could see Geneva standing by the fountain, with her hands running up Spencer's chest.

"Oh, come on, Spencer. Don't tell me you haven't thought of me and wondered what it would be like to be with me again." She reached up a hand to trace a red-nailed finger down his cheek. "I've certainly thought about you. And I like the handsome, more confident man you've become."

Her talk was intimate, and her actions not ones a married woman should engage in.

Zola felt guilty for watching and listening, but she wanted to see how Spencer would react. It was important to her.

Just now, he was quiet, watching Geneva intently.

"Do you still think I'm a beautiful woman, Spencer?" She hunched her shoulders forward, revealing more of her bosom with the move.

Zola rolled her eyes. It was such an obvious ploy.

She heard Spencer draw in a breath. Great.

Geneva swayed toward him, offering her lips up to him.

But Spencer stepped back. "You're a married woman now, Geneva."

She let her hands rove up his chest again. "So? Surely you've seen that Bowden and I both give each other liberty."

Spencer scowled. "That may be," he said. "But I am an engaged man, Geneva. There is someone else in my life now."

"That cute little island girl?" Geneva laughed dismissively. "Oh, really, Spencer. Surely that girl is not someone you're going to actually marry. She's hardly your type."

"Isn't she?" Spencer's voice sounded hard. "And who is my type?"

Geneva practically cooed. "Well, we were always very good together."

Spencer stepped back. "Maybe once, but you've changed, Geneva. Or maybe I'm the one who's changed. I don't remember you being so brittle and insensitive before about the feelings of others, or so self-serving."

Offended, Geneva stepped back, her eyes flashing with anger at the insult. "You were never very perceptive about people, Spencer—always very naïve and unrealistic. It used to worry me." Her voice sounded annoyed.

Zola saw her study her nails one at a time, trying to regain her composure.

"Did you ever really love me, Geneva?" Zola saw Spencer watching her carefully as he asked this. "I always wondered how you could go to Bowden so easily . . . not even call me yourself to tell me it was over between us. It wasn't the honorable way to act."

Geneva rolled her eyes and shook her head. "Honorable is hardly a word I would use to describe me, Spencer. That's a word more suited to you." Her tone dripped with sarcasm. "For me, better words are clever, smart, or ambitious. While you were young and dreamy, and not sure who you were or what you wanted twelve years ago, I knew exactly what I wanted. And I began to see early on that it was more advantageous for me to marry Bowden than you."

She stepped away from Spencer, her eyes hard now. "There was always a sexual chemistry between Bowden and I. And Bowden liked competing against you to win me." She smiled at some secret thought. "I admit it was one reason I led you on, to keep that competition going with him. I was always playing both of you, almost from the first."

Zola saw Spencer's eyes widen, heard his quick intake of breath.

Geneva shrugged, pushing her row of bracelets up her arm. "Quite frankly, Spencer, I kept you in my pocket—not sure Bowden would ever come up to scratch." She smiled again, tapping his chest with a long nail. "You see, I wanted to get into the Jackson family and their network. I knew my floral business would flourish there—and I wanted in. Jackson's was the most prestigious photography studio in Richmond, the family name good, and your mother and your little sister had brought so much to it with their catering skills . . . expanded it. Made it even better. I knew it was the perfect spot for my floral business to fit in. My mother's small business was nothing compared to what I knew we could have if we merged with the Jackson Studio."

She walked over to prop her foot on a wrought-iron bench, leaning over to adjust a vivid red high-heeled sandal, and exposing a long length of her leg in the process. "I could never understand why you wanted to go off and study away from Jackson's. The business just reeked of prestige and money. Your Grandfather Stettler married into the Winthrops—and then inherited that gorgeous old Winthrop mansion downtown for the business. That was a shrewd move on his part. I always heard that little Sylvia Winthrop, who Stettler first married, was a bit of a drip. But your grandfather was ambitious, too."

Geneva paced thoughtfully. "The Winthrops were soft, sweet, good people. I see some of that in your father, and I saw it in you. It worried me. But Bowden. He's just like his grandfather, and more like me, too. We're interested in going somewhere. We're interested in money."

She brushed back her short blond hair. "That's everything, you know, Spencer, having money and prestige. Look around you tonight. This is the way I wanted to live. I wasn't certain you wanted to go in the same direction. Oh, I could probably have persuaded you. But it was easier linking up with Bowden. We're so much alike."

She walked over to run a hand freely down Spencer's chest again. "Bowden gives me a free rein in most all areas—and I do him. You might not have felt comfortable about that."

Zola saw Spencer tense.

Geneva didn't seem to notice. "It was always in my favor that your grandfather liked me, too. Good ole Stettler." She laughed. "He knew I'd be good for the business and the family. I think he worried, too, that you might not come up to snuff. You know, he caught Bowden and me together one time on a sofa in the office, while you and I were still engaged—and the old guy seemed delighted."

She moved up closer to Spencer again. "You didn't have to stay away so long just because I married Bowden. We could have continued to have fun, too, if we were discreet. We can now."

She dropped her hand down Spencer's chest to his belt and tucked her fingers inside it. "I could meet you somewhere later."

"I doubt that will happen, Geneva, but you hold that thought in your mind if you like." He patted her on the bottom and then turned and walked back toward the ballroom.

Geneva stood there for a moment watching him, and then she pivoted and followed another pathway to a side door further down the courtyard.

Zola stood quietly behind the pillar, still stunned at what she'd heard.

She heard someone clear a throat behind her and jerked around, expecting it to be Spencer. Expecting to be caught eavesdropping. To her surprise, it was Spencer's father.

He gave her a soft look. "Maybe now, you'll see why Spencer's mother and I felt a little relieved when Geneva decided on Bowden instead of Spencer. I think she'd have broken Spencer . . . or at least hurt him. She never really loved him, you know, and Spencer needed that in a woman."

"Why didn't you tell him?"

Gordon Jackson shrugged. "He wouldn't have believed me. Especially with Bowden being involved." A sad look came into his eyes.

Zola studied him, seeing more than she should have about Gordon Jackson in that moment. "How can you stand being in this family, Mr. Jackson? Living out this part allotted to you?"

Unsurprised at her questions, he answered, "I was the only son. There was no one to run Jackson Studio except for me. In many ways, I love it. I love photography, and I like capturing the happiness of people at significant events in their lives. I'm not very good at the business end, but my father is. Bowden is, too. Their skills in that area free me to do what I love most—take pictures."

He propped a foot on a low brick wall beside the greenery. "I thought once I might like to photograph wildlife or be a biology teacher. But it was foolish for me to walk away from the studio I also loved. Sometimes I wonder if Spencer might have come back to work in the business if all this with Geneva hadn't happened. If he might have found happiness here, too."

Zola thought about this. "No . . . I think he had another destiny, Mr. Jackson, and found that destiny. I've heard him talk about it, about how much nature photography called to him and how much he loves the life he's chosen. I've watched him work, too. He's wonderful at what he does, Mr. Jackson. Do you know that?"

"Of course." He seemed surprised at her question—and almost annoyed. "We have all his books in our home. His mother and I have a scrapbook of his accomplishments we've kept. Some of his photography hangs in my study and Marion has some in her sitting room. We are proud of him, Zola. We just hated for him to go so far away. You'll understand one day when you have children of your own."

Zola looked toward the door Geneva used to slip back into the ballroom. "Doesn't it trouble you to have Geneva for a daughter-in-law for your son Bowden?"

He shrugged. "She and Bowden are a good match. I'm not sure how deep their love is, but they respect each other. They're both gifted, social, and ambitious. They make a good pair and they are very good for the Jackson Studio."

Zola made no comment to that. Being good for the business was such an important factor to all the Jacksons. Except to Spencer. Zola's heart felt a wrench of pain for all she'd heard Geneva tell him tonight. It had to have hurt.

Her eyes traveled to the door Spencer had walked through. She wondered where he was and what he was doing.

"I think I'd better go back in now." Zola put a hand on the older man's arm. "It would be nice if you shared with Spencer some of the thoughts you shared with me tonight, Mr. Jackson. Spencer never understood why you and his mother seemed so callous about his breakup with Geneva."

He nodded. "I'll try to do that before he leaves. Perhaps it is the right time to talk about it with him now."

Zola bit her tongue. Or perhaps it was twelve years past time, she thought with a flash of anger. Obviously, all of them knew Geneva had been unfaithful to Spencer long before he even left home. And they all knew Geneva's affection for Spencer had been feigned. They should have at least tried to warn him.

She felt like slamming the glass door behind her simply thinking about it.

Inside the ballroom, she found Spencer searching for her, carrying her light wrap and purse. "I think I'd like to leave now, Zola. I've said our good-byes."

Zola nodded and tucked her arm in his, wishing she had the right words to say to comfort him.

Chapter 20

Spencer let himself into the house after a morning of shooting photographs near an overgrown, abandoned farm. He liked the photos he'd taken of ivy and morning glories, sprawling with abandon over an old shed, and of the fine shot he'd snagged of a big hornet's nest hanging from a tree by the barn. He even liked the countless photos of rats he'd taken by an abandoned farmhouse. Spencer hid in a blind, out of sight, and watched the rats work their way in and out of the maze of burrows they'd built under the porch, endlessly gnawing and eating, their little jaws working feverishly.

Noticing Zeke wagging his tail like a flag in welcome, Spencer squatted down to give the dog some quality attention. "You'd have liked to chase all those rats around I found today, Zeke."

Spencer scratched the dog behind the ears in his favorite spot.

Noticing Zeke's big incisors made him recall an odd fact about rats. "You know, Zeke, I read if rats don't keep chewing on things to wear down their teeth, their incisors will grow right through their skulls. They'll even gnaw cement or brick. I've watched them do it."

The shepherd pricked up his ears intelligently

as if he understood every word. Putting a leash on the dog, Spencer took him out for a walk. He'd been gone all morning, and he knew Zeke was ready for some exercise.

When he came back, he found Aston sitting on the porch.

"I haven't seen much of you lately," Aston said.

"I've been working." Spencer clipped off the leash, telling Zeke that he could prowl around the porch within sight. The dog knew his parameters.

Spencer sat down in a rocker beside Aston's and propped his feet on the rail.

"You've been brooding." Aston gave him a candid look. "I thought that trip to Richmond would do you some good, help you get past old problems and anger. Set you free to move on."

Spencer scowled. "Well, it opened a whole new panorama of facts I learned my family hid from me. They let me spend years pining over a woman not worth mourning over."

"So are you going to continue pining?" Aston took a long drink from the canned cola he'd brought with him.

Spencer bristled defensively. "It's not that easy, Aston. It takes a while to get things worked out."

Aston drank his cola, waiting for Spencer to add more.

"My family all knew, Aston, and they didn't tell me," Spencer blurted out, clenching his fists. "My father talked to me about it before I left. He

331

said he and my mother knew, even before I left for college, that Geneva was playing both Bowden and I on a string, sleeping with Bowden behind my back while we were engaged. My grandfather caught them once and he didn't even tell me. In fact, Geneva said he seemed delighted they were involved."

"And?"

"It makes me mad, that's what." Spencer kicked at the rail. "My father said he and my mother hoped my going away would help resolve everything, that I'd get over Geneva while away from her. He told me they were actually relieved when Bowden came to them to announce he and Geneva had decided to marry. They thought Geneva and Bowden better suited and more alike."

Aston stretched his long legs out in front of him, crossing one ankle over the other. "Sounds like they were right, from everything you've told me."

"Maybe, but none of them told me!" Spencer bit out the words, his anger rising just talking about it. "They all knew Geneva was sleeping around on me with Bowden and none of them ever told me."

Spencer got up to pace around the porch. "Even Bowden came to me before I left. Said he felt glad I knew now about he and Geneva. He claimed that's why he tried to tell me all those years ago that it was for the best she broke the engagement to marry him. He knew Geneva had only been using me to get to him. It made me feel like a total fool, Aston—having all of them tell me that stuff."

Aston shook his head. "You need to let this go, Spencer. You should see now that Geneva was not the woman for you, even if your family knew it before you did. You need to realize it's a blessing you didn't marry the woman. She obviously didn't love you. She'd have made your life a misery."

Spencer punched a fist into his hand. "That doesn't make all of this mess any easier to swallow."

"It should." Aston shrugged.

"Well, it doesn't!" Spencer practically hollered. "It makes me even more angry. They let me believe lies for twelve years—and never even tried to tell me the truth."

Aston's brown eyes looked over at Spencer with candor. "You have to take some responsibility in this. You never went home to learn the truth until now. That part is *your* fault, Spencer."

"Well, thanks a lot for the understanding, Aston." Spencer's tone was sarcastic, and he walked over to the porch rail, turning his back on Aston.

Unperturbed, Aston replied, "I'm only trying to help you get things into perspective. Whatever happened in the past is over, Spencer. You can't go back, but you can go forward. And you need to do that. You've been up here brooding on this for two weeks since you got home from Richmond. That's long enough. Clark and I need you down at the gallery to sign some papers and to help us make some joint decisions. I came up here today to get you since you don't seem to be answering your phone calls these days."

"I told you I've been working." Spencer knew his excuse sounded lame. He had been avoiding his friends—and the gallery—since he got back.

Aston stood up. "You wanna ride down with me?"

"No. I need to grab a bite to eat and put my gear away." Spencer looked at his watch. "I'll be down in an hour."

Aston checked the time on his own watch. "I'll expect you."

Spencer remembered his manners as Aston started to leave. "By the way, congratulations again on your wedding plans, man. Carole is a good woman."

Aston and Carole had gotten engaged while Spencer and Zola were in Richmond and planned to marry in only a few weeks.

"Yes, sir, Carole is a good woman." Aston flashed a white smile at Spencer. "You know, I talked her into not waiting until Christmas for the wedding, like she wanted to, promised her I'd take her to the beach at Savannah if we got married sooner. A friend of mine owns a house there we're going to stay in for our honeymoon. I told her July was the only time we could use it."

Spencer scratched his chin. "And is that true?"

Aston grinned. "Not quite. But it's true that those weeks after our wedding date are the only time we can use the beach house this summer."

Spencer laughed.

"There's no reason to wait after you've found the right woman." Aston gave Spencer a pointed look.

Spencer's laugh faded. "I think Zola's and my relationship is our own business."

"Your relationship with Zola is in jeopardy of dwindling away to nothing for your neglect of her." Aston started off the porch. "Maybe you can go over and take her out to dinner when she gets off work today. I know she was in the shop doing inventory when I left, even though it's supposed to be her day off."

Spencer walked over to the porch rail to look out over the mountain. "We've had a couple of fights," he admitted. "And I'm not happy over this mess with Madame Renee that's going on."

"There you are, thinking about yourself again, man." Aston walked back up on the porch to stand beside Spencer. "How do you think all of this is making Zola feel? Do you think she's been thrilled to come home and find that Renee Dupres has been spreading stories all over town that Ben Lee's daughter is alive and well—and being held captive? She claims she saw it in her crystal ball that someone kidnapped Ben's daughter and is keeping her prisoner against her will."

Aston ran a hand impatiently over his head. "So much pressure has come on Police Chief Bill Magee that he's had to reopen the case and start combing the countryside looking for Seng Ryon Chen again. It's a mess."

"I agree with that," Spencer added with annoyance. "And Zola had to go and tell a newspaper reporter she didn't think Renee Dupres was right in her assumptions, that she didn't get a witness Seng Ryon was in the area, or that she had been kidnapped."

Spencer kicked at the porch rail. "So now the paper has the two of them back and forth in the news like rival soothsayers!"

"I agree the press has had a royal field day with this." Aston shook his head. "You can imagine Ben Lee desperately wants to believe Renee Dupres. He wants to believe his daughter might still be alive."

"Well, it's all like a big soap-opera scandal." Spencer crossed his arms in irritation. "It embarrasses me to be a part of it."

Aston raised his eyebrows. "I see."

"No, you *don't* see." Spencer crossed the porch, pacing in irritation. "You're marrying a normal woman—not some weird seer that's always getting herself in the newspaper!"

Aston walked over to put his face into Spencer's. "Listen, man. I love Zola Devon enough to resent a comment like that about her."

"And you think I don't?" Spencer pushed his way out of Aston's face. "I'm worried sick about her, Aston. Worried about all this publicity and about all these people calling her, coming into her store, stopping her on the street to ask her questions. I'm also concerned about Ben Lee literally avoiding Zola now, angry at her for suggesting to him that he shouldn't get his hopes up. I just wish sometimes Zola could keep her mouth shut, Aston. If she thought Seng Ryon Chen wasn't kidnapped or being held captive, she didn't have to say so, did she?"

"Zola's honest. She says what she thinks is right and true." Aston cocked his head. "Would you like her to lie?"

"No." He hit his hand on the back of the rocker. "I only wish she'd be more discreet. She doesn't always have to say everything she knows. Especially in a volatile situation like this!"

"Have you told her that?" Aston asked.

"I have." Spencer lifted his chin. "It's one of the things we fought over."

"And the other thing?"

Spencer considered not answering that, but realized Aston would learn the answer from

Carole, or from one of the women at Zola's shop, if he didn't reply.

He turned to look at Aston. "Zola tends to agree with you that I've been brooding too long over my family. She doesn't understand why I'm not relieved to learn the truth about everything. She doesn't see why I can't simply be happy now and let the past be the past. Zola is of the belief that happiness is something you can turn off and on —like hot or cold water."

"Perhaps she's right." Aston raised an eyebrow.

"And perhaps she's not." Spencer bit out his answer in annoyance.

Aston glanced at his watch again. "I need to get back to the store. And we've used ten more minutes of your hour. So you'd better go clean up and get a bite to eat."

After arriving at the gallery, Spencer walked around the store looking at some of the new photos Aston had chosen to hang. He felt pleased as he studied them. At least the turmoil of his emotions wasn't affecting his work.

"You've been doing good work lately." Aston walked up to stand beside him.

"Yeah. Well, at least something in my life is consistent."

Aston clapped him on the back. "Zola Devon could be consistent in your life if you'd let her."

Spencer purposely didn't answer him.

Aston started toward the back of the store. "I'll

get Clark and we'll talk over our business out here, in case someone comes in the gallery."

An hour later, business aside, Spencer sat on the wall beside the fountain in the Mountain Laurel Village Mall. He was trying to collect his thoughts before he went into Nature's Corner to see Zola. He wondered if Aston was right that he'd been neglecting Zola, if he hadn't been there for her when she needed him.

An exotic dark-haired woman let herself out of Zola's store, slamming the door behind her. Spencer found himself oddly fascinated with her gypsy dress and the way she'd painted her red lipstick around the outside of her lips as well as on them. You didn't see that often. Her hair was dyed as black as coal and wrapped up in some kind of scarf.

She looked up, saw Spencer, and headed toward him, shaking her finger. "I've told her and I'll tell you—I want Zola Devon to stay out of my business!"

Spencer must have looked confused because the woman pulled herself up straight and lifted her chin. "I am Madame Renee Dupres. I have a special inherent gifting for predicting the future and I help people with their lives." She waved her hand in a flourish. "I'm sure you've heard of me. People in this area have come to me for twenty years with their problems."

"I don't believe we've met." Spencer held out a

hand. "I'm Spencer Jackson." He wasn't sure what else to say.

She placed her hands on her hips and leaned over until her face was nearly even with Spencer's. "I know well enough who you are. And you'd be wise to well consider whether you want to continue a relationship with Zola Devon. She's a woman with a confused gift."

Spencer felt an uncomfortable prickle down his spine.

The dark-haired woman smiled at him candidly, sensing his discomfort. "I'm not a woman you should make angry, Spencer Jackson. I will be keeping you in my thoughts. You be warned."

She swept away then before Spencer could form an answer.

He watched her walk away and then got up and went into Zola's store. Maya and Zola were both at the counter, but no customers were in the shop at the moment.

"I just met Renee Dupres."

Maya made a sign with her hand. "Bah! That crazy, *facety* woman! A botheration, half *eediat* and a *samfi*! She came in here pitching a fit and ran all our customers out. Crazy *bootoo*. May *Jah* have mercy on her. She has a dark soul and doesn't know it."

Spencer looked over at Zola to see her watching him carefully. "Renee threatened you, didn't she?" Her voice was soft.

Spencer looked back on the woman's words, trying to recall if she did. "She just seemed angry," he said, not wanting to repeat exactly what the woman said.

Maya shook her finger in the air, obviously still annoyed. "Do you know what that woman's real name is?" She smiled in satisfied knowing. "Mildred Renee Dupler. But she changed it to Renee Dupres to more suit the fortune-telling business. A phony and a *samfi* even in her name."

Spencer grinned. He liked Maya.

"What is a *samfi*?" Spencer asked, enjoying Maya's colorful Jamaican words.

"A *samfi* woman is a con woman," Maya answered, grinning. "And a *facety* woman is a bad-mannered and nasty woman. She is that, too!"

Zola walked from behind the counter to lay a hand on Spencer's arm. He felt an odd sense of calm come over him with the contact. "Nothing of her words will come to you, Spencer. Nothing. You pay her no mind."

He looked at Maya. "What was she throwing a fit about in here?"

Maya put her hands on her hips. "You know that woman has been trying to draw attention to herself by saying poor Ben Lee's daughter has been kidnapped and is being held against her will somewhere. Crazy, *facety* woman! She's gotten people so upset with her nonsense that Bill

Magee has had to send his officers out inquiring and looking for a kidnapper. Pah!"

Spencer leaned against the counter. "How do you know she actually hasn't been kidnapped, Maya?"

Zola dropped her eyes.

"Hmmmph." Maya sent Spencer a pointed look. "I thought you were a smarter man."

Zola looked up then. "Maya, Spencer doesn't have the confidence in my knowing that you have."

"Well, I'm sorry for his foolishness then." She studied Spencer. "Perhaps you are still a *bootoo*."

Spencer bristled. "I'm simply trying to keep an open mind. No one really knows what happened to Seng Ryon Chen. Her disappearance has been under investigation for months and there are no factual answers."

Maya crossed her arms. "And you're more disposed to believe a *facety*, *wutless*, *samfi* woman that you are your own woman who has a good heart?"

"Zola doesn't know what happened to Seng Ryon either, Maya." Spencer felt annoyed over having his loyalties questioned.

Leaning over the counter, Maya said softly, "Zola says she saw for a surety that Seng Ryon has not been kidnapped and is not being held somewhere against her will. That is enough for me, Spencer Jackson. It should be enough for you."

"Did you actually *see* that?" Spencer turned his attention to Zola.

She nodded. "I did."

He considered that. "Okay. But why did you have to tell a reporter that? You didn't have to."

She spread her hands. "The reporter was here when the knowledge came. I was *supposed* to tell him." She took a deep breath. "I didn't know he'd make a circus of it in the paper, pitting my words against Renee's."

Spencer bit his tongue to keep from saying she should have expected that from the news media. However, he didn't want to create more difficulty with Zola today. They'd had enough fights over this.

"I didn't know all of the story," he said, reaching for peace.

"Well, now you do," Maya said, annoyance touching her voice. "This is not an easy time for Zola. Ben Lee came in here today, too. He gave Zola trouble, got angry and raised his voice. Foolish man." Maya made another one of her signs in the air. "When Zola got back from Mooréa, he came in here every week insisting she should get some knowing about what happened to his girl. Now he comes in here insisting she quit saying what she knows! *Eediat* man!"

Zola whispered to Spencer, "That means idiot."

"I figured that one out." Spencer grinned.

A couple came in the door, smiling and chattering, and Spencer could see a group of tourists looking in the window, admiring the rock fountain on display.

"Maya," he said, before things got busy. "Do you think you could handle the store if I take Zola to dinner? We'll bring you back something."

"Nah. You take Zola to dinner and then see she goes home." She waved a hand dismissively. "It isn't even her day to be working. She was here doing some inventory. Besides, she needs to come back into town tomorrow for the shower for Carole. She can come back in the store to finish inventory while Faith is working."

Spencer noticed Zola's face fell at mention of the shower.

Maya leaned over to touch her hand. "Are you sure it will be all right for you to go to a luncheon shower down at the Chen Palace Chinese Restaurant?"

"Of course." Zola smiled at Maya and patted her hand.

Seeing Spencer's confusion, Maya turned to him. "Juan Hee Chen, Seng Ryon's husband, owns the Chen Palace. His daughter, Nina Chen, is one of Carole's friends and she organized the shower—and of course set it at her family's restaurant. This was long before the problem with Madame Renee began. Now I worry, with all that's going on, that it might be a strain for Zola being there with all the Chen family tomorrow."

"It will be fine, Maya. Don't worry. And it's going to be a lovely shower for Carole."

Maya looked wistful then. "Ahhh. It's hard to believe my little girl is getting married." She looked at Spencer and smiled. "But Aston is a good man. They will make a good match."

Spencer nodded in agreement.

"You two go on now." Maya headed over to greet the customers looking around the store. "See you *inna di morrow*, Zolakieran." She waved a hand at Zola in dismissal.

Spencer saw a smile touch Zola's face. "See you tomorrow, too, Maya."

Spencer opened the door for Zola as they headed out of Nature's Corner. "What do you want to eat tonight?"

She grinned at him. "Not Chinese!"

He laughed. "What about barbeque at Bennett's?"

"That sounds good," she said.

Spencer took her arm as they walked across the mall courtyard, glad to be in Zola's company again. He knew he'd been difficult lately, but there'd been a lot to come to terms with after Richmond. He hoped Zola understood.

Chapter 21

Zola enjoyed her dinner at Bennett's with Spencer. He'd made an effort last night to see they had a good time, but she still felt troubled about his doubts of her knowledge related to Seng Ryon.

She sat stirring her coffee idly in her grandmother's kitchen this morning, letting Nana's comfortable conversation drift over her.

"Zola?" Her grandmother's call of her name interrupted her thoughts.

"Yes, ma'am?"

Nana Etta shook her head. "I asked you a question, child, and then turned around to see you lost in woolgathering." She sat down at the table across from Zola. "What's on your mind, girl?"

Zola watched her grandmother begin to efficiently slice strawberries after removing their leaves and stems. Always busy hands. It was comforting and familiar to watch Nana work.

"Spencer is upset over this business with Madame Renee." Zola snatched a freshly sliced berry before she continued. "Perhaps it's childish, Nana, but I hoped he would believe more in my gift. I want that with a husband. It would be hard to live with someone who doubts me and dismisses me in that area."

Nana kept to her task, listening.

Zola wrinkled her nose, thinking. "Furthermore, I've found it hard to understand the broody mood Spencer has fallen back into since we came back from Richmond. You'd think he would feel relieved to learn the truth about everything, be able to put the past more behind him. Be able to move on."

She drummed her fingers on the table. "It also has hurt me that he's shut me out of his feelings and all but avoided my company for nearly two weeks. It bothers me to think I might face times like this frequently if we marry, times when Spencer will shut himself off from me and not be willing to share his thoughts with me."

Her grandmother looked up and caught Zola's eye. "I notice you said *if* we marry, Zola. Seems to me an engaged woman shouldn't be thinking in terms of if."

Zola crossed her arms defensively. "Well, there have been a lot of problems lately, Nana. And it hasn't helped anything to also experience this trouble with Madame Renee and Ben Lee right now. It's upset Spencer."

"It upsets me, too, child. It would upset anyone that cares for you." Nana frowned at her. "I told you before I don't like you getting mixed up with Madame Renee. That woman is dangerous."

"Well, I didn't exactly mean to get involved. That young man from the newspaper came into my store telling me about all Renee's predictions and asking me what I thought and . . ."

Nana interrupted her. "And you had to go and tell him what you thought."

Zola glared at her. "No. I *had* to tell him what I *heard*. There's a difference. I heard very clearly right then that Renee was wrong. That her erroneous conjectures were causing Ben and his family to get up false hopes and causing the police department to be out on a wild-goose chase looking for Seng Ryon."

"Did you see where Seng was or if she was still alive, Zola?"

Zola shook her head. "No. I didn't get that."

"Are you sure you were supposed to speak it when you weren't given the rest of the understanding, child? Even those who hear from God can easily make mistakes sometimes, maybe not so much in what they hear but in whether they should tell it. Even you should realize that telling information to a newspaper reporter is asking for notoriety and instant publicity."

Zola leaned forward to look at her grandmother intently. "It may seem foolish that I told it to a reporter, but I really believe I was supposed to, Nana."

Nana continued slicing berries. "Well, you yourself just admitted that it might *look* foolish to have given such information to a reporter—so perhaps you can imagine how it must look like

348

and feel like to Spencer. After all, the man's not quite used to the ways of the Lord you walk in yet. He's bound to have some difficulty coming to terms with it all."

Zola sighed. "I might have known you would take his side."

"Are there sides in this?" Her grandmother looked up in puzzlement. "I'm simply thinking there are different viewpoints. You can't expect a man—or anyone, for that matter—to feel the surety you do when you get a word from the Lord like you do. After all, it's coming up from your own spirit. Another person won't hear the same thing unless God gives it to them as well."

She slapped at Zola's hand as she reached to get more berries. "Quit eating all the berries, girl—unless you slice some on your own. I'm meaning to make a strawberry pie with these today."

Zola got up to get a knife from the kitchen drawer and rinsed a handful of fresh berries to slice up for herself.

"Have you doubted that I did the right thing, Nana?" She sat back down and began to cap the berries with her knife.

"I'll be honest enough to say I've had my moments of doubt because of all the trouble that's occurred. It's sure stirred up a lot of ruckus and publicity. That's not usually God's way of doing things."

Zola squared her shoulders. "Seems to me like

the Bible has a lot of instances where trouble got stirred up."

"Maybe." Nana continued her work with the berries.

Zola gave up trying to argue. "I admit this has been a really difficult time. Ben Lee came in the store this week, angry and upset. That young newspaper reporter tagged along with him, enjoying every minute. He quoted Ben in the paper hollering, 'Time will show whether you or Renee has the greatest gift.' I hated seeing that in the newspaper, Nana."

Nana reached over to pat her hand. "Will you be all right going to the Chen's restaurant today, Zola, with all that's happened?"

"It might be a little uncomfortable for me, but it would be worse if I didn't go at all. This is Maya's daughter, Carole, who's getting married, Nana. The Thomas family is dear to me. That's more important than whether I experience a little discomfort." She stood up, knowing she needed to head back to the house to get ready for the bridal shower. "Besides, Ben won't be there and Nina would be disappointed if I didn't come."

"Yes, but remember Nina's father, Juan, Seng Ryon's husband, will be there as will Nina's brother Frank, his wife, Zia, and their teenage girls. They all work at the restaurant." Nana took Zola's hand in hers. "Promise me you'll find a way to excuse yourself and leave early if things become difficult, girl. Don't stay on if the situation becomes awkward or if ugliness breaks out."

"I won't, Nana."

Later in the afternoon, as Zola walked out the back entrance of the Chen Palace, she found herself feeling greatly relieved that things hadn't been awkward during the shower. The Chen family, seeming to sense her discomfort, made an effort to be especially cordial to her. The day was Carole's, after all, and everyone wanted to be sure it proved special for her.

She heard Nina Chen's voice behind her. "Zola, wait up."

Zola turned around near her car in the parking lot to wait for Nina.

Nina, a pretty Asian girl with sleek, black hair, came running up to Zola, smiling. "I wanted to tell you I'm so glad you came today, Zola. All of this about Ma Ma has been so distressing. I know you only said what you felt was right when you disputed Madame Renee."

The girl frowned. "We all felt distressed when we learned Wai Dad—that's what we call my grandfather Ben Lee—went to that fortune-teller. It made all this unpleasantness come back for us. I want you to know none of us have confidence in her words. We know she is only a woman seeking attention for herself."

Zola gave Nina a hug. "Thanks for coming to

tell me that, Nina. It means a lot. I've hated all this publicity for your family."

"Well, I will let you get back to your store now—and I will get back to work myself—but I am so glad I caught you to tell you how we feel."

Nina turned and headed toward the back door of the restaurant.

Zola stood watching her for a moment, relieved at their conversation. She saw Nina's father— Seng Ryon's husband, Juan—come out on the back porch to take a smoke as Nina went back inside. Zola waved at Juan, glad to learn the family didn't foster ill will toward her.

She felt an odd tug on her leg then. Looking down in puzzlement, she could suddenly see below the pavement of the parking lot. A face drifted mistily into view. Zola clutched her heart and caught her breath raggedly as a shaft of fear shot up her spine.

"He is the one!" she heard the shadowed figure in the pavement say. Zola could see a shroudy hand point toward Juan in the doorway. "He is the one who murdered me and I want my vengeance! See that I get it. You see I get it."

Zola felt the tug on her leg again, and thought her legs would fold up under her, she was so frightened.

Her gaze lifted to Juan's, and she saw him scowl at her.

"Does he see it, too?" she wondered. "Does he know that I know?"

Zola feigned a smile and forced her wobbly legs to take her to her car. She got in, backed out, and started away. Looking in her car mirror, she saw that Juan had walked down from the porch to watch her car as she drove away. She saw him drop his cigarette to the ground and stub it out in irritation, an angry frown on his face.

"Oh, good heavens," Zola said to herself, trying to calm the escalated beating of her heart. "What if he knows what I saw? Will he follow me? What in the world should I do?"

She couldn't seem to think straight for the fear that raced through her. And her leg still felt cold and clammy where that gruesome hand had touched her.

Chapter 22

Spencer had driven into Knoxville to get photo supplies and returned late in the afternoon to his house at Raven's Den. He was surprised to find several messages on his answering machine, asking him if he knew where Zola was. One was even from Nana Etta, Zola's grandmother.

He let the dog out and took his cell phone to the porch so he could keep an eye on Zeke. Then Spencer called Etta Devon.

"Mrs. Devon, this is Spencer Jackson. I just got home and found your message."

"I'm so glad you're back." Mrs. Devon's voice sounded agitated. "Zola is missing. She went to the bridal shower at the Chen's restaurant at lunchtime, but no one has seen her since. Nina Chen was the last person to see her as Zola left the shower."

"Nina is Ben Lee's granddaughter." Spencer remembered. "Did Nina say anything to upset Zola? Did she threaten her?"

"The girl says not." Spencer heard Mrs. Devon take a deep breath. "She said she went out into the parking lot behind the restaurant to reassure Zola that the family held no hard feelings toward her. She said she and Zola hugged with affection before they parted."

"Do you believe her?" Spencer whistled at Zeke, whose ears had pricked up at sight of a gray squirrel.

"I do," Etta Devon said. "I sense the meeting with Nina is not the problem."

Spencer overlooked that comment. "Where did Zola go when she left Nina?"

"Well, that's just it. No one knows for sure." Mrs. Devon paused, her voice breaking with emotion. "She was supposed to go to the store to work on inventory."

"I heard she and Maya talking about that yesterday." Spencer recalled. "But maybe she decided not to go. After all, Faith was there. Maybe she went shopping or something." He looked at his watch. "It's only about five p.m. now."

"No, she didn't go shopping. My boy Ray and his son Wayne found Zola's car an hour ago, parked down the road from her place in an abandoned barn just across from Caney Creek."

Spencer felt a thread of alarm now. "I was down at that old farm place taking photos yesterday. What would Zola be doing down there? And why would she leave her car there?"

"I don't know that. But I get a bad sense about this." Etta took a deep breath. "We have family out looking everywhere near the old farm but we can't find any sign of Zola. It worries me that Zola would go over there, hide her car, and not call anyone, Spencer. That's not like her. It's not like her to worry people in that way. I'm thinking something bad has happened. That someone threatened her—or frightened her in some way."

"Well, why wouldn't she go to someone she trusted if that happened? Like to you or to Maya?" Spencer scratched his head, trying to make sense of it all.

"I don't know that, son."

They both grew quiet for a moment.

"You give some thought and prayer to where she might have gone, Spencer. You've come to know her well." Nana paused. "Also, keep an eye on Raven's Den and the hut she loves there. She might go there or she might come to you."

Spencer looked down the path from his house leading to the point at Raven's Den. "I'll go look now, Nana. And I'll call you if I find her. Promise you'll call me if you hear anything, too."

"I will." Nana sighed. "I've got a bad feeling, Spencer. I don't possess the gift Zola does, but I know when something's not right. And I get a real sense of evil."

"Have you called the police?"

"Vern did about thirty minutes ago when he, Ray, and Wayne still couldn't find any sign of Zola. Chief Magee says it's too early to send out a search when she's only been gone a few hours and when there's no evidence that anyone threatened her."

"I see." Spencer's mouth tightened.

He hung up from Etta Devon and put Zeke on his leash to walk down to the hut at Raven's Den. He, too, had an uneasy feeling about Zola being missing all afternoon. She would never worry her grandparents like this without cause.

Zola had made enemies lately—Madame Renee, Ben Lee, and before that, Aldo Toomey. Who knew what other people could be on the list? Not everyone felt happy with the insights Zola received. He certainly hadn't been when he first met her.

A sliver of fear threaded up Spencer's spine at yet another thought. There still might be a murderer out there nervous that Zola knew too much. Spencer had long worried about this in relation to the disappearance of Ben Lee's daughter.

Arriving at the hut at Raven's Den, Spencer found no one there. He looked around carefully but couldn't find evidence anyone had been there. He walked back to the house and made return calls to Maya, Faith, Aston, and others who'd left him messages, hoping he might learn some fact to help him search for Zola. But no one knew anything more than Etta Devon told him earlier.

In frustration, Spencer called Ben Lee, asking him if he'd seen Zola.

"Why should I see her?" His voice sounded annoyed. "Has she been looking for me to make more trouble?"

Spencer forced himself to make an evasive answer and hung up. If Ben Lee knew anything, he certainly wasn't revealing it.

His call to Aldo Toomey netted him no leads either. Aldo and some friends had driven up to Bristol for the NASCAR races and had been gone for two days.

Calling Madame Renee proved a waste of time also.

"I have not seen Zola Devon—not in the natural or in my meditations." Her voice took on a smug tone. "But I wouldn't be surprised if tribulation came to her. She is a woman asking for trouble in the way she uses her gifts."

Not trusting himself to answer, Spencer hung up on her. Annoying woman.

You'd think she might show some compassion.

He paced the floor until Zeke whined, picking up on his anxious mood.

Regretting upsetting the shepherd, Spencer decided to take Zeke for a walk. With all that had gone on, he'd forgotten to do that since getting back. Besides, it might help him walk off some of his tension.

He leashed Zeke and started up their familiar path to Shinbone Ridge. At the split in the trail, Spencer paused thoughtfully. The falls were a favorite place of Zola's. Would she go there if troubled? Spencer decided it wouldn't hurt to walk along Buckner Branch to check.

Arriving at the pool below the falls a short time later, Spencer scanned the rocks and the open area around the cascades. There was no sign of her. He turned to go but noticed then that Zeke was pulling on his leash, not wanting to turn back.

Looking down, he saw the dog staring intently across the creek, his ears pricked. "What is it, Zeke?"

The dog whined, his eyes still trained across the creek where a rock wall rose up behind the trees.

Ordinarily, Spencer would have reined in the dog with a rebuke, for not complying in obedience when he'd turned to go back, but this time he paused, his eyes scanning the scene before him. He couldn't see a rabbit or a squirrel, but that didn't mean Zeke couldn't smell or sense one.

Following the odd premonition he felt, Spencer picked up the big dog and carried him in his arms as he jumped across the rocks. Zeke struggled to get down as they reached the bank, and Spencer gave the dog his head to follow the scent he'd picked up.

Zeke wove around through the trees and along the rock wall until he found a deep crevice in the cliffs. There he stopped until Spencer could catch up.

Looking down in surprise, Spencer saw the dog's tail wagging.

He leaned down to look below the crevice into a shallow cave and saw a figure huddled in the dark. It took only a moment for Spencer to realize it was Zola.

Calling her name, Spencer loosed the dog to go to her and then hunched over to work his way back into the cave himself. He found Zola huddled in a blanket in the low, damp cave, her arms wrapped around Zeke.

"What are you doing in here, Zola?" he asked as he pushed the dog away to get closer to her.

Her tear-streaked face looked up at him. "Oh, Spencer, I'm so glad you're here. I've been so frightened!"

She looked past him with big eyes. "No one followed you, did they? There's no one with you?" Her voice sounded strained and anxious.

"It's only Zeke and I." He leaned over to kiss her forehead. "Let's get you out of here, Zola. It's freezing and damp in here. Your skin is cold and you're shaking. Come on." He held out a hand.

"I'm scared." She curled up in the blanket, reluctant to leave.

"That isn't the right answer, no matter what you're scared of." He gathered her up in his arms to hug her, alarmed at how chilled she felt. "Let's go back to the house and talk about this in front of the fire. You need to get warmed up."

Seeing her eyes scan the entrance, he took her hands in his. "There's no one out there, Zola. And there's no one at my house. You'll be safe there."

After a little argument, he persuaded her to follow him out of the cave. He took the dog across the stream and then came back to help Zola across the rocks. He wished he wore a coat to wrap her in, but he knew she'd begin to warm up some as she hiked up the hill to the ridge.

"What's happened, Zola?" He asked as they started up the trail.

She walked beside him, holding onto his arm with one hand and clutching the old quilt around her with the other.

"I saw something bad." Her voice was a mere whisper. "And I don't know whether someone else saw it, too, or not. I think he did and I thought he might come after me. That's why I needed to hide."

"Why didn't you tell someone?"

Her breath caught. "I was afraid someone else might get hurt if I did."

Spencer realized then why she'd hidden her car and headed out on her own.

Zola shivered. "Juan Chen murdered his wife Seng Ryon, Spencer. I saw it."

He blinked in surprise. "How did you see this, Zola?"

She paused, her eyes finding his. "I saw Seng

like a ghost below the pavement in the parking lot behind the Chen Palace Restaurant."

Spencer knew his eyebrows lifted, because she frowned at him. "I know it sounds strange, but I swear, Spencer, it happened." She shivered again. "Ben's daughter, Seng Ryon, reached out a hand and touched my leg. It was awful, Spencer. I've never had any kind of sight like this before. God has never let me experience anything this terrible. I hated it. I didn't want to see those things."

He put his arm around Zola and hugged her close while she spilled out the rest of the story. Spencer knew Zola would never make up anything this bizarre. She ended her story crying raggedly.

His voice grew gentle. "Zola, you remember Ben Lee said for weeks that he prayed God would show you what happened to his daughter." He leaned over to kiss Zola's forehead. "Evidently, God answered Ben's prayer."

"But why in such an eerie, horrible way!" She shuddered.

"I don't know," he said, leading her up the path.

Back at the house, Spencer started a fire while he sent Zola into his bathroom to get a warm shower. He found her a T-shirt and a robe to put on while he dried her wet clothes in the dryer. Her outfit was damp from the cave, and she was still chilled and shaking from the hours she'd spent hiding there.

He called the Devons, Maya, and Aston to let them all know Zola was all right. Without asking Zola, Spencer also made a call to Police Chief Bill Magee, who said he'd drive up immediately to talk to her.

"She's had a bad experience, Bill. Don't make it worse for her when you come. But be prepared to listen."

Zola grew upset when Spencer told her he called Bill.

"He won't believe me, Spencer." She started to cry, the anxiety of the day kicking in. "And what will happen if he actually does? It will tear a whole family apart and I will be responsible! I know all the Chens. They will never forgive me for being the one to reveal this."

"I don't believe that," Spencer said, going to answer the door to let Bill Magee in.

Bill sat on the couch and let Zola tell him the whole story. Admittedly, it was an incredible one, but he listened calmly, never questioning Zola.

Between the telling, Zola sipped on hot cocoa Spencer had heated up for her. Her big eyes still held anxiousness and fear.

Bill Magee scratched his chin. "You say you saw Ben Lee's daughter under the pavement. I assume that means she was buried there." He pulled out his cell phone. "There's an easy way to check that one out. I'll call Dean Murphy at the paving company, see when he put in that new blacktop behind the Chen Palace."

He made the call, talked briefly, and hung up. "Well, we've got enough for me to get the judge to get a paper to dig up that parking lot. Dean said he laid the blacktop the next morning after Seng Ryon went missing."

"What will you tell the judge when you call him?" Zola chewed on her nail anxiously.

Bill smiled. "I'll tell him I got an anonymous tip saying someone thought they saw Juan Chen out digging in the parking lot before they did the paving. And that they thought they saw something fishy going on—but didn't put it together until now what they might have seen."

Zola frowned. "But that's a lie."

Magee laughed and rubbed his chin again. "Well, in this case, Zola, I think a bit of a fib is better to use than the full truth." He patted her knee fondly. "If this blows up into a murder, I'd like to leave you out of it. Plus testimony of seeing a ghost or spirit in the pavement isn't likely to be admitted in court."

After a little more discussion, Bill Magee stood up to leave. "There's nothing for you to be afraid of anymore, Zola."

He looked down at her thoughtfully. "You know, I've been a Christian since just a boy, but I really marvel, Zola, at how God uses His ways to show you things the way He does."

Zola started to respond, but Magee shook his head at her. "Yeah, I know stuff like this is in the Bible, Zola, but somehow folks don't expect it to still be happening today."

Spencer grinned. "I don't think folks expected to see it that much in the Bible days, either, Bill. Things haven't changed that much."

"Well, I reckon that's true. We're all real interested in saying we believe in the supernatural of the Bible until we get confronted with it in the here and now."

Zola held up a hand to Bill. "Thanks for being so kind."

He took her hand and patted it. "You just rest and get over this. I guess it was a bit of a scare for you, seeing what you did."

Spencer walked out to the car with Chief Magee.

"Do you think Juan really murdered his wife, Bill?"

"It will be easy enough to check it out." His voice trailed away. "In this business, I frequently find the perpetrator of a crime is right in the victim's family. Sad to learn it, but it's often true."

"Well, thanks for being so willing to check this out and for not ridiculing Zola." Spencer took Bill's hand in a firm handshake.

"I don't always understand Zola, but I'm fond of her. She's got a good heart, and things she's seen have helped a lot of folks." He frowned. "I don't mind her getting mixed in an investigation like I mind that crazy fortune-teller on the highway putting her oar into things."

"Madame Renee?"

"Miss Mildred Renee Dupler has caused problems in these parts for nigh about twenty years." He shook his head. "It's rare anything she says she sees in her cards or her crystal ball amounts to anything. Most times, it just causes a bunch of trouble for folks. Like that business with Aldo Toomey and now this with Ben Lee. I've had to put staff out looking for a kidnapper due to the publicity generated by Renee's predictions. People are gullible about believing fortune-teller nonsense."

Spencer kept his voice casual. "Do you think Madame Renee will try to cause trouble for Zola if this murder turns out to be legit?"

"Only if she gets wind of it somehow." He got in his car. "I'll keep an eye on it, Spencer, if this comes to anything."

Chapter 23

Zola didn't usually travel to Mooréa in summer, during the height of the tourist season in Gatlinburg, but this time was an exception. She simply had to get away. Pressures coming against her were intense, and she'd lost her peace. And her confident faith.

She sat now on the shady veranda of her father's house, high on a hill above the coast at Temae. Down through the palms and trees around the island house, she could see the sparkling waters of the Pacific Ocean spread out before her. She had taken many calming walks up the beach in these last days, letting the sound of the ocean waves soothe her soul.

Hearing the door open, Zola looked up to see her father coming out to join her, carrying his morning coffee and the newspaper.

He sat down at the table with her. "You're beginning to look more rested, daughter."

Seeing his kindly, familiar face, Zola felt a surge of love.

Stanford Devon crossed an ankle over his knee and began to study the newspaper while sipping his coffee.

His dark hair was graying and receding from his forehead now, and age lines marked his face, but the same peace Zola always remembered still radiated from him. Her mother told her it was this same peace that always so soothed his patients. Stanford Devon had always been a man confident that he was in the will of God for his life. Zola envied him that right now.

He glanced up to catch her eyes studying him. "Ready to talk yet, Zola?"

She smiled at him. "There's not much more to say than what I've told you. I know you've talked to Nana Etta. You know what happened."

His eyes moved to her open Bible, still on the table from her morning devotions. "It was a hard vision you were given."

Zola bit her lip. "Do you think the Lord is going to start giving me this sort of sight on a regular basis, Daddy? Do you think He's changing my gift, escalating the kinds of things I will have to see?"

His eyes moved out over the ocean view in thought.

"I don't know, Zola, but I doubt it." He took another sip of his coffee. "It seems to me this was an unusual situation."

"It was a frightening situation. And I know that fear and faith are opposites." She clenched her hands anxiously. "I didn't act in faith when I saw this murder, Daddy. I panicked. I ran. I felt terrified. I didn't act like a good ambassador for the Lord."

"And that's worrying you, is it?"

She nodded.

His voice dropped kindly. "Have you taken it to the Lord?"

"I've tried. I cast the cares over on Him and then they keep washing back on me like the waves coming in on the beach."

He chuckled. "It's like that sometimes. But keep working at it, Zola. Those cares will stay where they're supposed to eventually and you'll get your peace back."

"That's what I so want, Daddy. I hate being anxious and worried, carrying problems around that I should be able to let go of." She rubbed a hand up her arm restlessly.

"Well, then, maybe this experience will help you have a better understanding of folks experiencing the same difficulties." He gave her an appraising look. "We all have troubling seasons. Those times disturb our lives in every way—in the physical, emotional, and spiritual sense."

"I guess you see that often while doctoring people."

He smiled and looked at his watch. "Speaking of which, I need to get down to the clinic soon."

"I can come to help you later," Zola offered.

"No need." He folded up his newspaper. "Zola, can I ask you a question?"

"Sure." She smiled at him.

"Tell me about this man you've met."

Zola knew she blinked in surprise.

"Your Nana told me you've gotten serious about someone, a photographer in Gatlinburg. She and Vern like him. She says the man is worried about you, upset that you went off without telling him you were leaving." He took off his glasses to clean them while he waited for her answer.

Zola searched for the words she needed. "I care for him, Daddy. I know he cares for me. He's experienced problems, too, that he's been working out. I tried to help him with those. And when I was afraid, it was Spencer who came to find me. I felt his strength then and was glad of it."

She spread her hands. "But how can I ask anyone to share my life when these hard visions might begin to come my way more often? The publicity grew terrible after this, Daddy. The press learned my part in what happened with Ben Lee's daughter. It got written up in the newspaper and then the tabloids came hunting for me and hunting for Madame Renee. They wanted to sensationalize the story of the rival fortune-tellers. It was simply horrible."

Tears started in her eyes, and Zola reached up a hand to wipe them away. "The press began to hound me in the shop and at home. They began to try to interview Spencer and my family."

She shook her head, upset even to discuss it. "Sometimes in the past the local media picked up on some helpful counsel I gave to someone or some way I was given knowledge of something." She searched her memory. "Like with the little boy, Eddie, who got lost in the mountains. But it didn't feel horrible like this. And the publicity passed on quickly."

Her father dug a handkerchief out of his pocket. He was still a man who carried a handkerchief with him every day. And was always ready to offer it.

Zola wiped her eyes with it, feeling comforted with the familiarity of the gesture.

Stanford Devon crossed his leg again, thinking on what Zola had told him. "It seems to me, daughter, that a man who wouldn't stand by his woman in a time of trial like this isn't much of a man. Has your Spencer indicated that he wanted to break it off with you because of what happened?"

"No." She admitted that with honesty. "He was angry and irritated that I got involved in the beginning. That troubled me. I would like Spencer to be one who believes in what I am, in what I hear. But after the murder came out, he said he believed God wanted to reveal it through me. He even said he thought God showed me what happened to Seng because Ben Lee prayed I would see what happened to her."

She folded the handkerchief anxiously in her hands. "But how can I ask anyone to share a life with me if I continue to have ongoing problems like this in it? It's not fair to ask that of anyone, Daddy."

"You said you shared his problems. Were you always patient and understanding about them?"

Zola dropped her eyes. Leave it to her father to nail her with that one.

"No." Her answer was quiet. There was no point in trying to lie. Besides, it would have been wrong.

He smiled. "Then perhaps you need to realize that Spencer is human, too. He won't always be perfectly in tune with you or understand everything you are thinking or feeling. Nor will he always witness clearly with everything you receive from God, unless it is given to him, too. But if he loves you, he will do his best. Just as I'm sure you will do your best to understand him. That's what love is, Zola. Not always being perfect, but caring and trying. And trusting."

He leaned over to take Zola's hand in his. "Perhaps you need to trust your love for Spencer and his love for you more. You need to trust God's love for you more, too, Zola. I don't think the Lord expects you to live alone just because He has given you a little more measure of one of His Gifts than most people walk in regularly. And I doubt He will walk you into a place like this— that is so hard—very often in your life. He doesn't usually ask us to do what we can't handle."

He winked at her. "Plus, another time, I think

you'll fight more to stay in a place of faith and not let fear overtake you."

"Yes, I will." And as Zola spoke these words she knew they were true. It caused a beginning sense of peace to spread over her.

Stanford Devon came over to kiss his daughter's cheek. "You enjoy a good day, daughter. Calm down, pull comfort and wisdom from the Spirit of God within you, and listen to your heart. I think you're ready to do that now."

Zola offered a long prayer after her father left and then made her way down the familiar winding path through the palms to her hut perched high on a knoll above the sea. She'd first seen a meditation hut on the other side of the island when only a girl and later learned the legend and purpose of building one. She built this and later the one at Raven's Den in the mountains after her mother died. Her huts had always been special places to her.

A sense of peace flowed back into Zola as she sat on a rough bench, her arms on the rails of the hut, looking out over the beauty of the ocean. Hearing a noise behind her, she turned to see Spencer standing in the shadows.

Her hand went to her heart in surprise. "Spencer! Whatever are you doing here?"

His mouth quirked in a smile. "And where else would I be? Where you are is where I belong, Zolakieran Devon. Whether it be here in Moaréa or in the mountains of Tennessee or anywhere else."

She felt the tears spill down her face at his words. Spencer slid onto the bench, took her into his arms, and buried her face up against his chest.

"How could you leave me without coming to me, Zola? Please don't ever do that again. I love you. You're my life. I've learned I can't function or be happy without you."

She reached up to touch his face. "I was afraid being involved with me would hurt you, Spencer —cause you more pain and problems. I thought you'd experienced enough of that in your life."

"And you wanted to make that decision for me?" He uttered a sound of despair. "Zola, I have no life without you. Knowing you has brought me back to life. You've changed me, enriched me. Strengthened my faith. Healed my heart. Brought me happiness. Don't you know that?"

The words seemed as sweet to her as the smell of the fragrant frangipani blossoms on the nearby tropical trees.

She traced a finger down his cheek. "It might not always be easy living with me, Spencer."

He caught her fingers in his to kiss them. "It might not always be easy living with me either, Zola. But we'll draw on each other's strengths and help each other with our weaknesses." He looked deeply into her eyes. "And we'll always be honest with each other. That's important to me. We won't keep things from each other. And we won't run away when there's trouble. We'll run to each other."

The beauty and rightness of the words swirled through Zola's being, filling her with gladness.

She threw her arms around Spencer, laughing and kissing him with new joy. "I am so grateful you've come, Spencer!" Her genuine laughter rang out. "However did you find me here?"

He grinned. "I went to the clinic and your father told me where I might find you."

She felt her eyes grow wide. "You met my father?"

"Yes, and I liked him." He looked around him. "I like it here, too. I brought my camera. I think I'll take some pictures while I'm here."

"Is that right?" She gave him a saucy smile.

"Yes, and I thought maybe you'd like to get married here." He ran his hands down her arms possessively. "We could enjoy a little honeymoon before we go back home. We could have one of those island weddings you were always telling me about."

She blinked in surprise. "You mean the ones where the bridegroom rides in on an outrigger canoe to meet the bride on the shore. In native dress and everything?"

His hazel eyes flashed. "You are of Tahitian royalty, after all. It seems like it would be fitting." He grinned mischievously. "And think how great the photographs would be!"

She swatted at him. "Leave it to you to be thinking about photographs!"

His warm eyes darkened and he leaned over to kiss her with passion. "Believe me, Zola Devon, that isn't all I'm thinking of right now."

The anxieties of the past seemed to flow out over the ocean waves at last, without trying to return, and Zola felt her inner peace and calm flow back into her.

"I love you, Spencer Jackson."

"And I love you, Zola Devon."

After some glorious moments of kissing and rejoicing, Spencer pulled back with reluctance.

They both sat quietly then, elbows on the rail of the hut, looking out at the ocean together.

Spencer broke the silence. "I thought you might like to know that Madame Renee has left town."

"To get away for a time, like I did?" Zola knew the media pressure on Renee had grown intense, too.

"No, Renee moved permanently."

"How do you know that?" Zola turned questioning eyes to his.

"Bill Magee told me." Zola heard him chuckle then. "Someone, probably Aldo Toomey, painted 'Fraud' on her driveway and roof again. And the media coverage portrayed her so unpleasantly she decided to relocate. I hear she moved to live near her sister in a tourist town in North Carolina."

Zola frowned. "I feel mean-spirited to admit how glad that makes me."

Spencer took her hand. "Nana Etta said it's an

answer to longtime prayer from many people and she told me to tell you that. She said to remind you many things that seem bad at the time work for the greater good in the end."

"That's true." It was wonderful how often God brought good from bad.

Joy rose up in Zola again, and she leaned over to throw herself impulsively into Spencer's arms once more, kissing him with warm abandon.

He groaned. "We'd better get married soon, Zola."

"Yes." She stood up, smiling. "Let's go talk to Daddy about it right now. And when we get back to the mountains, we'll have a nice reception at the church for all our friends there."

Spencer took her hand as they started up the path toward the house. "I can't wait to see Aston's face when I tell him I managed to get married before he and Carole." He looked down to catch Zola's eyes. "What are the Tahitian words for *I love you,* Zola?"

She smiled at him. "*Ua here vau ia oe.* But I am happy to simply hear the words in English, Spencer—and often."

He squeezed her hand. "I'll do my best to remember to say them often . . . and to show them to you always, Zola."

"I couldn't ask for more," she said, her heart singing with joy.

Discussion Questions

1. Zola Devon has an unusual gift as a seer, often receiving messages or words from God for others. Remembering the first chapter of the book, how would you feel if you were shopping in Nature's Corner and Zola offered one of her messages to you? Stories of individuals with gifts like Zola's abound in biblical and other faith-based stories, but they don't occur as commonly in our world today. Why do you think this is? Do you think it was hard for Zola to be obedient in giving the words she felt God wanted her to share with others?

2. Spencer Jackson first met Zola in her shop, Nature's Corner. What happened at that meeting? They met the second time at the hut at Raven's Den. What happened at this encounter? How were the two meetings different? How did these early interactions highlight some of the differences between Spencer and Zola?

3. What did you think about Spencer's business colleague Leena Evanston? Why was Spencer so drawn to her? Why was he reluctant to contact the police or prosecute her after she

tried to rob him? What would you have done in a similar situation?

4. Spencer has a strained relationship with his brother Bowden. What things in the past happened to foster the problems between the two brothers? Spencer has also not been close to any of his family for years. What caused these breaches? Do you have strained relationships with any of your family members? Why do you think problems with close family members are often the most difficult to resolve?

5. Why is the hut at Raven's Den important to Zola? Why didn't Spencer tear down the hut when he built his home on the mountain? Later in the book, as a reader, you visit Spencer's childhood memory spot and Zola's island hut in Tahiti. Zola tells Spencer: "A person needs a place where they can go to find peace and get collected in their soul." Do you think this is true? Do you have a special place where you go to find peace or did you have one as a child?

6. Zola Devon is both Tahitian and American, and she has spent parts of her life in both places. How does this multicultural background make her unusual? Was she always comfortable with the aspects of herself that

made her different from others? Zola tells Spencer at one point: "The world is not always kind to non-conformists, to those who are different." Do you think that is true? How has Zola found ways to be more comfortable in her own skin and to accept herself as the unique person she is? How has Spencer fought some of these same battles in being different?

7. Animals can often play an important part in our lives. How did Spencer get his dog Zeke? And how are they bonded as owner and pet? How did Zola get her cat Posey? What was Posey's story? Both pets played sweet roles as companions and comforts to their owners. Do you have pets that are meaningful like this in your life?

8. What did you think about Zola's grandparents Nana Etta and Papa Vern? How did they influence Zola's life positively? Are you a part of a big, extended family like the Devons'? What aspects of their family life seemed similar to yours? How did Zola's family contrast with Spencer's in interacting together, sharing in a dinner or family event, and in caring for one another?

9. What kind of photographer is Spencer Jackson? How did he become a photographer, and what brought him to Gatlinburg to open

the Jackson Gallery? Why didn't he choose to work in his family's photography business?

10. Good friends enrich our lives. Rachel and Maya are two of Zola's friends. How did these friendships develop and how is Zola's friendship different with each woman? How did Spencer meet Aston Parker? What factors drew them together? In what ways do Spencer's and Zola's friends help and support them in the story? Which of your friends are especially meaningful in your life? Do you have close bonds with friends of other races or cultures like Zola and Spencer did?

11. Zola and Spencer's relationship hits many snags as it struggles to develop. What problems hinder their relationship? What things about Zola most worry Spencer? What things about Spencer trouble Zola the most? What events occur that bring resolution to these problems and finally bring the couple together at the end?

12. Two serious problems evolve for Zola in this story in relation to her gift as a seer. The first is with Madame Renee, and the second is with the missing daughter of Benwen Lee. What causes difficulties for Zola in both of these situations? How do both come to a head before the book closes and how are they

resolved? What did Zola learn about what happened to Ben's daughter Seng Ryon Chen? How and in what way did learning this knowledge frighten Zola?

13. Why did Aldo Toomey throw a smoke bomb into Zola's store? What things happened in his life that led up to this event? Why didn't Zola press charges? How does Aldo later take revenge on Madame Renee?

14. How does Spencer gain the opportunity to photograph the hoarfrost on the mountain? What new respect does Zola find in watching Spencer work in this situation, and what new appreciation for Zola does Spencer gain from this day? On another photo outing together, Spencer lends a hand to help Zola find a lost child. What happens in this situation? How does finding Eddie bond the couple in a new way?

15. At the waterfall on Buckner Branch, Zola helps Spencer give up and release some of his past hurts and pain. She has him throw pebbles into the water, remembering the sorrows or sins he wants to be free of. What did you think about this scene? How did this time help bring a cleansing and new lightness to Spencer? What criticisms did Zola's grandmother have about it afterward?

16. Spencer and Zola enjoy many happy time outdoors, both loving and delighting in nature. They share a happy day with Spencer photographing frogs, spiders, and scenes around the farm. Another day Spencer takes Zola with him to hike and photograph outdoor vistas on top of the Smoky Mountains near Mount Buckley. What happened to spoil that day and bring Spencer and Zola's relationship to a turning point?

17. When Spencer finally goes home for his parents' anniversary, taking Zola with him, what happens at that family gathering? What did Zola see about Spencer's family on her visit? Did you like Spencer's family? What does Spencer learn and realize about Geneva that he didn't know before? How did this free him and yet make him angry at the same time? What did you think about how Spencer's family kept truths from him?

18. Why does Zola go home to Mooréa unexpectedly near the end of the book? What is troubling her that drives her home? How does her father help her? What causes Spencer to follow Zola to Mooréa and how does the story end?

Center Point Large Print
600 Brooks Road / PO Box 1
Thorndike, ME 04986-0001 USA

(207) 568-3717

US & Canada:
1 800 929-9108
www.centerpointlargeprint.com